OU

THE
NEXT ROUNDUP

**Center Point
Large Print**

The Fortunes of the Black Hills Series:
Beneath a Dakota Cross
Shadow of Legends
The Long Trail Home
Friends and Enemies
Last of the Texas Camp
The Next Roundup

THE NEXT ROUNDUP

———◆◆×◆◆———

STEPHEN BLY

CENTER POINT PUBLISHING
THORNDIKE, MAINE • USA

BOLINDA PUBLISHING
MELBOURNE • AUSTRALIA

This Center Point Large Print edition is published in the year 2004 by arrangement with Broadman & Holman Publishers.

This Bolinda Large Print edition is published in the year 2004 by arrangement with Broadman & Holman Publishers.

The text of this Large Print edition is unabridged. In other aspects, this book may vary from the original edition. Printed in Thailand. Set in 16-point Times New Roman type by Bill Coskrey and Gary Socquet.

US ISBN 1-58547-380-4
BC ISBN 1-74093-220-X

U.S. Library of Congress Cataloging-in-Publication Data.

Bly, Stephen A., 1944-
    The next roundup / Stephen Bly.--Center Point large print ed.
        p. cm.
    ISBN 1-58547-380-4 (lib. bdg. : alk. paper)
        1. Large type books. I. Title.

    PS3552.L93N49 2004
    813'.54--dc22

                                                                2003055713
                    Australian Cataloguing-in-Publication.

Bly, Stephen A., 1944-
The next roundup / Stephen Bly.
174093220X
1. Large print books.
2. Western stories.
I. Title.
813.6
            British Cataloguing-in-Publication is available from the British Library.

For
Julie Kingery
and
all the gang at the Bly book fans discussion site

*"For this cause I bow my knees unto
the Father of our Lord Jesus Christ,
of whom the whole family
in heaven and earth is named."*

Ephesians 3:14–15 (KJV)

The Fortunes of the Black Hills–1900

Henry "Brazos" Fortune–Sarah Ruth Fortune
(d. 1895)   (d. 1872)
children
Todd
Samuel
Robert
Patricia & Veronica (indentical twins, d. 1869)
Dacee June

Todd Fortune (49)–Rebekah (Jacobson) Fortune (45)
children
Hank (19)
Camilla (18)
Nettie (17)
Stuart (16)
Casey (14)

Samuel Fortune (48)–Abigail (O'Neill Gordon) Fortune(45)
children
Amber (Gordon) Fortune Justice (26)
m. Wade Justice, 1897
Garrett (13)

Robert Fortune (46)–Jamie Sue (Milan) Fortune (46)
children
(Little) Frank (24)
Patricia & Veronica (identical twins, 22)

Dacee June (Fortune) Toluca (36)–Carty Toluca (36)
children
Elita (13)
Jehane (12)
Ninete (11)

Author's Notes

An orphan once told me he felt like Lewis and Clark because he was an explorer, a pioneer. He was going down a trail no one had gone before.

Most of us follow some pattern of family tradition. We still do things the way Daddy did them . . . and Grandpa . . . and who knows how far back. The way we vote, the make of car that we drive, even the color we paint the house often reflect a long line of family preferences. But the orphan has no pattern, no direction, no leading. That, of course, can be good . . . or bad. While they have no path to follow, they have no rut to climb out of either.

Frank Fortune is not an orphan.

The Fortunes of Deadwood had dominated the northern Black Hills of South Dakota for twenty-five years. There was a strong tradition of courage, vision, and personal faith in Jesus Christ. Frank had no problem in that way following in the footsteps of his father, Robert, or his grandfather, Brazos.

But for the last quarter of a century, Fortunes had been prospectors, mine owners, businessmen, and community leaders.

Frank wanted to be a cattleman.

He learned the tales of the cattle business on his grandfather's knee. While standing at Brazos Fortune's graveside on the slopes of Mount Moriah Cemetery, Frank pledged that he would build that ranch that his grandfather always wanted.

At nineteen he got a lease on government land that no

one wanted. He bought cows, hired men, worked from sunup to sundown, distanced himself from family events, and ignored his own personal life.

Some say he was lucky to have a herd of fifteen hundred by the age of twenty-four. Some say he was way too lucky and questioned whether the cattle had been purchased or stolen. Frank knew they were the result of incredible focus and hard work, but now it looked as if all might be lost . . . to rustlers, to neighbors, to disease, to the trials of unfenced rangeland at the dawn of the twentieth century.

He needed something to happen.

And it did.

Within a week Frank Fortune found his future. It would be different than he thought. Different from Grandpa Brazos. And yet very much within the Fortune tradition.

It would start with the smile of a pretty lady.

Like the Lord's grace and mercy, some things never change.

Stephen Bly
Broken Arrow Crossing, Idaho
Winter 2002

CHAPTER ONE

RAFTER F RANCH, WESTERN SOUTH DAKOTA, SUNDAY, SEPTEMBER 23, 1900

STIFF DENIM JEANS rubbed Frank Fortune's cold legs like sandpaper. He leaned forward in the saddle, broad shoulders square above the saddle horn. His blue eyes squinted through the prairie sun that broke over Black Bear Butte. With a fingerless leather glove Frank clutched the loop of the four-strand maguey rope and watched the eyes of the big white-faced cow forty feet in front of him.

"Just wait, boy," he whispered to the chestnut gelding. "Wait for her to move away from that stump. Thataboy . . . just wait."

The wide-rumped horse strained at the reins. His ears stood straight up. His neck quivered.

Frank's voice was a low monotone. "If you bolt toward that cow, she'll dive back into the brush, and it will take half a day to push her out. Just wait . . . she's movin' . . . look, she's movin' . . . one more step and I can loop her from here. That's why I carry this sixty-foot rope."

The cow took a step to the right.

Frank stood in the stirrups and circled the loop twice above his head.

A rifle report held low to the ground by the press of a cool Canadian wind echoed over the rolling brown prairie. The initial explosion came from the north. The gunshot forked like a gurgling creek hitting a large granite boulder and circled the cow, the horse, and the roper.

The cow broke to the left.

The horse bolted after it.

The loop circled the dead stump.

And Frank Fortune stared north, but only for a split second.

When he grabbed for the reins, he didn't release the rope. The rope held hard and tight to the stump and yanked Frank out of the saddle.

Everything but his left foot.

His boot hung in the stirrup, his back slammed into the Dakota dirt. The rope burned his fingers as it sliced open the palm of his leather glove and jerked out of his hands.

"Whoa!" he screamed.

His wool vest ripped in the back when it hit the brush. The pain when his left elbow crashed into the rock dripped tears on his dirt-covered cheeks. He tried to kick off his boot as the horse dragged him after the cow but turned on his stomach instead. Dirt and rocks filled his shirt and tore at his chest and scratched parallel red lines across his stomach like fingernails on a chalkboard.

"Stop! Whoa!" he screamed.

Frank's gloves shredded, his hands bled as he tried to keep his head from pounding into the rock and brush.

The cow scampered up Rattlesnake Creek, which in September was no more than a shallow stream running through slimy white clay and granite boulders.

The horse cut to the right and followed the cow. Fortune was now no more than a tin can tied to a dog's tail.

When the horse slowed, Frank reached out his raw hands to grab a sapling, then yanked his foot.

The horse lunged forward.

The boot dropped to the water.

Frank rolled to his back in the two-inch-deep stream and tried to catch his breath. Cold water burned into the cuts on his fingers and back. The pain that throbbed in his elbow numbed his mind.

I won't be able to move for a week. I'll lay here until they come looking for me. Every bone in my body must be broke. When they find me, they'll bury me up on Mt. Moriah with Grandpa and the others of the Texas Camp. Lord, I do believe that dyin' would feel a whole lot better than this.

Upstream the cow stopped running.

The horse quit pursuing.

The cow hiked her tail.

The horse stretched out his legs and leaned forward.

"No!" Frank hollered.

Then he pulled with all his strength. He rolled out of the creek to the bank on the north side of the stream just as the water changed color. He sat up and held his left elbow.

I can't believe this. There is nothin', absolutely nothin' funny about this!

He flopped back down on the dirt and continued to gasp.

How did I ever rope that stump? A gunshot? The gun-shot threw me off. If Howdy is up there shootin' coyotes, I'll skin him alive. This must have been the way Saint

Paul felt when he said, "Come quickly, Lord Jesus." I should have taken that city job with Uncle Sammy.

Another gunshot jerked Frank to his feet. He staggered to the creek, holding his aching ribs and looking at his bleeding hands.

"Thank you, Mrs. Cow, for your timely deposit. I'm not goin' to wash in that. But I guess I have to retrieve my boot."

He grabbed his water-filled boot and his battered hat from the brush, then led the horse up out of the draw to the rise on the rolling prairie. He shook the sticks, dirt, and rock out of his clothing and yanked on the wet boot. The cool breeze through the ripped shirt and vest felt good on his bruised and bleeding back.

The horse glanced down the draw at the cow grazing next to the tiny stream.

"Oh, you pinned her alright, Carlos," Frank muttered. "And now you're feelin' proud." He tucked in the remnants of his shirt. "How am I doin'? Horse, I'm glad you asked. My elbow is killing me, my back is ripped and raw, I have horrible pain in my ribs, and another sharp pain above my right eye. I can barely walk. My mouth and lungs are full of dirt. That cow purtneer plopped in my boot. But other than that, I'm just fine."

He reset the saddle and tightened the cinch. "Look, horse, if I can get on your back, I expect you to ride me straight to the cemetery. If there is an open grave, I'm just goin' to roll into it, and you can kick dirt over me."

With his bloody fingers he shoved his left foot in the stirrup. He clutched the saddle horn with both hands and pulled himself up in the saddle. But the pain stabbed his elbow. His left arm fell limp, and he found himself only halfway up on the horse.

Carlos turned left to spy on him, and when he did took away any momentum Frank had for tossing his right leg over the horse. Still hanging out in the stirrup, he clenched the saddle horn and tried to keep from being tossed to the ground as the big horse spun to the left.

"Quedarse! Carlos, quedarse!"

The horse continued to spin, and Frank felt his grip loosen.

"The cow! Donde esta la vaca?" he hollered.

The gelding stopped spinning and stared down at the creek and grazing cow.

Frank slowly pulled his right leg over the cantle. *This is the last horse I ever buy from Uncle Sammy. Never again. When he says, "Little Frank, he just needs a few miles on him . . ." I'll say . . . "Good, as soon as you ride him to Oklahoma and back, let me take a look."*

His backside burned as he eased down and yanked the .50 caliber Sharps carbine from the scabbard.

"Someone's up there shootin' on Rafter F land. I would have been better off if they had just shot me," he muttered.

A flinch of the knees caused the big horse to trot north up the rise of brown prairie grass. Each step jarred Frank's ribs, elbow, and forehead. He paused at the summit of the prairie roll. To the west daylight crept down the distant mountains, turning the Black Hills green and brown. An erratic column of dust grabbed his gaze. He waited for the galloping rider to approach.

He patted the horse's neck, then gently rubbed his sore

elbow. "It's Howdy Tompkins, Carlos. There isn't anyone else on the ranch who rides like that, except maybe Amber or Aunt Dacee June when they come to visit."

He held his ribs and tried to take a deep breath. *And oh my, I'm glad none of the family is at the ranch today.*

Frank jammed his carbine back in the scabbard and rested one hand on the saddle horn. He yanked a damp red bandanna from his back pocket and rubbed dirt out of the creases next to his eyes.

I'm twenty-four years old. I'm not supposed to have crow's feet yet. And I'm not supposed to hurt this much. And I'm not supposed to rope tree trunks. But then I'm not supposed to have fifteen hundred head of white-face herefords, either, so it goes with the job, I reckon.

Howdy raced the copper dun stallion past Frank and yanked him to a halt thirty feet down the hill. He trotted back to Frank.

"Excuse me," Howdy greeted. "I'm lookin' for handsome Frank Fortune, the boss of the Rafter F. You didn't happen to see him before that railroad train ran over you?"

"I don't want to talk about it," Frank said.

"That's good, 'cause I don't want to know. But I would like to figure out who's shootin' up there. You surmise it's the rustlers?"

Frank pulled off his broad-brimmed felt hat and picked grass and weeds out of his hair. "That's what I intend to find out."

Howdy pointed at his forehead. "Do you aim to just ride up there alone and bleed all over 'em, or would you like some help?"

"It ain't that bad," Frank said.

"I don't reckon so. I seen Howard Garfield after he got hit by that twister down in Oklahoma. He looked a whole lot worse. 'Course, he was dead."

Not until they dropped down into Hidden Gulch did they see another soul on the prairie.

Howdy yanked out his revolver. "Would you look at that? Them Mexicans is butcherin' a Rafter F beef!"

"Put your gun back in the holster, there's a woman up there," Frank cautioned.

"There's two women rustlers. Don't that beat all? What's the world comin' to when a man can't even trust a woman with his bovines?"

An old man with a round black sombrero stood over the downed cow with a hook knife and a hacksaw. He wore a white canvas apron over his ducking trousers and white cotton shirt. The cow had been shot behind the ear.

Two women, one old, one young, squatted near the low, smokeless campfire. The older one pressed out tortillas on a flat granite rock.

All three looked up when Frank and Howdy rode into camp. They stared at Frank, but none of them reached for the Winchester 1886 octagon-barrel rifle propped up against the wheel of the wood-paneled wagon.

Frank lifted his right leg over Carlos's head and slid to the ground. His ankle twisted. He staggered, then handed the reins up to Howdy, who now draped his .44/40 carbine across his lap.

With his right hand resting on the holstered walnut

grip of his Colt Peacemaker, Frank pointed at the dead animal. He noticed his shirt sleeve ripped to his elbow. "You just killed a Rafter F beef."

The old man grinned. "Si."

"You know that cow belongs to me, don't you?"

"Si."

"But you went ahead and shot it anyway?"

"Si."

"And now you are goin' to butcher and eat it?"

"Si."

"It don't bother your conscience to be killing someone else's beef?"

"Si."

"Don't look like he's too bothered," Howdy sang out.

The older woman looked up at the man. "Que dice este hombre?"

The old man shrugged and continued to grin at Frank and Howdy. "Quirre ustedes comida?"

"I think he is inviting us to stay for breakfast and help him eat this steer," Frank grumbled.

"I don't think he understands a word you said." Howdy rode up a little closer. "Hey, old man, did you know your women ain't as purdy as that dead cow?"

"Si," the old man replied.

"See there," Howdy laughed. "He don't know what you're sayin'."

"Neither do you, Howdy, 'cause this youngest one is quite fetchin'." Frank walked over to the dead animal. He pointed to the Rafter F brand on the brown hide. "That's my brand. This steer belongs to me. You under-stand?"

"Si!" The man handed Frank the hook knife.

Frank refused to take the knife. "I'm not going to gut my own steer." He heard the young woman giggle.

She had a wool blanket around her shoulders, and her black hair cascaded down her back. She stared down at the small sage fire.

Frank squatted down next to her. His leg gave out, and he tumbled forward on his hands and knees, almost into the flames.

She covered her mouth with her hand when she giggled this time, then raised her brown eyes up to him.

"Oh . . . my, oh, my . . ." Frank mumbled.

Howdy rode closer. "What is it?"

Frank rocked back on his haunches. "Uh . . . I, eh . . . well . . . ," he stammered. He took a deep breath and pulled off his hat. He ran his fingers through his oily, dirty hair.

"What is it, boss? What happened?"

Lord, this is the most beautiful woman I've seen in my life. "I reckon," Frank puffed as he gulped a series of short breaths, "we'll let them have this beef."

"What are you talkin' about?" Howdy fussed. "You told us we can't let one rustler get away with it or they would all move in."

Frank struggled to his feet and glanced at the woman who let the blanket slide off her shoulders. "But . . . but . . . but . . . ," Frank stammered.

"You ain't makin' no sense at all!"

The young woman stood up beside the old man and smiled, revealing straight white teeth.

"Oh, my . . . maybe you are makin' sense,"

Howdy muttered.

Frank cleared his throat. "How did such a purdy Mexican rose like you get up here on this Dakota prairie?"

"Boss, you're a regular sweet talker when they don't understand a word you say," Howdy said.

The young lady winked at the old woman and kept her hand over her mouth.

Frank Fortune held his felt hat in front of him. "Señorita, hable usted Inglis?"

Her big brown eyes stared down at the fire. "Si."

"You do?" he gasped.

"Si."

"You understood ever' word we said?" Howdy added.

"Si."

Both men stared at each other.

The woman strolled around the fire. The blanket dragged like a royal train behind her black cotton dress. "The man on the horse with the tobacco-stained vest said I looked no better than a dead cow, and you, Mr. Boss, look as if you've been drug behind a carriage from Monterey to El Paso. Yet you called me 'a purdy little Mexican Rose' with a rather condescending tone."

"Shoot, do your mama and daddy speak English too?" Howdy said.

The older woman looked up from pounding out the tortillas, and grinned. "Mama and Pappa? No, solimente survidumbre. Hablemos pococito Inglis, pero señorita hable bueno." Her smile revealed a silver tooth. "Don't you think?"

"What did she say?" Howdy hooted.

"The old man and woman are servants," Frank translated. He turned to the young lady. "Now, I feel like a fool."

"With the way you look, none will notice the foolish part," she said.

"I was dragged by my horse," he admitted.

"That much, we can all tell. There is also a strange smell."

Frank looked down. "Eh, that's my boot."

She strolled around the tiny fire. "At least we are outside, and you did not track it on the carpet."

"Is them two really your servants?" Howdy asked.

"Yes. And they are also my very close friends," the young woman replied.

Frank limped over to the dead animal. "Did you shoot my steer?"

When he spun around, the young lady was laughing. "Yes. And two coyotes that moved in on it."

He glanced down at his ripped shirt and scratched arm. "Why?" *I can't believe I'm visitin' with a beautiful lady, all torn up and bloody.*

"We wanted meat."

"But it didn't belong to you." *I can't believe I'm visitin' with a beautiful lady, no matter what I look like.*

The young woman pulled the blanket around in front of her and began to fold it. "We did secure permission."

"Permission? From who? This is my steer."

"From whom, you mean."

He felt his face flush. "I don't feel like a grammar lesson right at the moment. You shot my steer. You have to pay."

She handed the folded blanket to the old woman. "Of course."

He raised his thick, dark eyebrows. "You are goin' to pay?"

"Yes, of course. I will pay whatever is fair. I'm not a thief, Mr. Frank Fortune."

He glanced up at Howdy and back at the raven-haired lady. "How did you know my name?"

"Your name is on the letter."

"What letter?"

She strolled to the panelled wagon, pulled a brown envelope from under the seat, and handed it to him. She stared at the dried blood on his hands. "I'm sorry I laughed at you. You look hurt. Can I get you some iodine?"

He took the envelope, then mumbled, "I've been hurt worse."

"I fail to see what difference that makes."

"Who's this letter from?" he demanded.

She folded her arms across her chest. "I presume you do read. Or do you need your grinning friend to read it for you?"

"My name's Howdy, ma'am." He tipped his hat.

"Why?" she asked.

"Why, what?"

"Why is your name Howdy?"

"Mama said that's the first word out of her mouth when I was born."

"I like that," the woman replied. "I'm glad she didn't say 'Good heavens!'"

"What's the letter say, Boss?" Howdy asked.

Frank Fortune cleared his throat.

Little Frank, this is a letter of introduction for Señorita Dearyanna Rodriguez and two members of her servant staff. You might remember Señor and Señora Rodriguez from down in Arizona when I was stationed at Ft. Huachuca near the Mexican border. The Rodriguezs are dear personal friends of your mother and mine. You've heard us mention them often. Miss Rodriguez is doing graduate studies in botany at the University of California and wants to study the plants and fauna of the Badlands. She's spent several days here in Deadwood reviewing Professor Edwards's notes and now will be exploring the Rafter F. I told them by all means to take some meat and I would personally pay for it. Treat them like family, son, because they certainly treated me that way on more than one occasion.

By the way, your mother says to remind you that the wedding rehearsal is Friday night, and she expects you to stay with us through the weekend.

Aunt Dacee June insists she's bringing the girls out to the ranch after the wedding, so you might want to straighten up the big house.

Love, Dad

Frank folded the letter and handed it back to Dearyanna.

"I will be happy to pay you for the steer."

"No, it was my mistake. Daddy's right. He has often mentioned your family and his scouting trips

21

in Sonora."

"That is very kind of you. I am sorry I did not check in with you first. We tried to find the headquarters but must have taken a wrong turn."

"That's alright, ma'am," Howdy called out. "A lot of folks can't find it. We had to build a signal fire one time so the crew could find their way home at night."

She burst out laughing. "That is a delightful lie, Señor Howdy."

He grinned from ear to ear. "Thank you, ma'am. I try my best."

The older woman pointed to the tortilla. "You stay por comida?"

Frank kept his gaze on Dearyanna Rodriguez. "No, ma'am . . . we got chores."

"I don't reckon a little breakfast would hurt, Boss."

"I don't believe there's any part of me that isn't already hurt."

"You do have a nasty gash on your forehead," Dearyanna said. "Let me get some iodine and clean it off."

"No . . . eh . . . thank you . . . I wouldn't want you to go to that trouble."

"Nonsense. You read your father's letter. We are to treat each other as family."

Howdy let out a holler. "That's right, Boss. You jist treat Seniorita Rodriguez like she was your own sister."

Frank glared up at Howdy. "We've got to go, ma'am. We have pressing business."

"We do?" Howdy said.

"Did you know we have met once before?" Her waist-length black hair swayed from side to side as she strolled around the fire.

"We have?" Frank replied.

"Once, at the fort in Arizona. My family came up for a visit."

"I don't remember you, but I do remember your parents."

"That is because your sisters locked me in the privy."

"They did?"

"And you rescued me, don't you remember?"

"You are that skinny little . . ."

"Smelly girl? Yes, that is a wonderful childhood memory. I cried all the way back to Mexico."

"I apologize for my sisters' behavior."

"Thank you. They apologized themselves when we were in Deadwood. They are very pretty and excited to be getting married."

"Yes, I've tried to stay away."

"Thank you for your generosity with the steer, Señor Fortune."

"You're welcome, Señorita Rodriguez."

"May I say something . . . strictly as a family friend?"

Frank pulled off his hat and stepped closer. "Yes, ma'am."

She lowered her voice to almost a whisper. "I thought you should know that in addition to your vest and shirt, your denim trousers are ripped in the back as well."

Frank backed toward his horse. "They are?"

She nodded.

"We are definitely not staying for breakfast!"

"Good-bye then. Will we be seeing you again?"

Frank swung into the saddle quick. He felt the cold saddle leather against the back of his thigh.

"Yes, ma'am, you surely will," Howdy grinned.

She looked startled to have Howdy answer. "And how about your boss? Do you let him out on his own often?"

"No, ma'am. We try to look after him."

"Do a better job next time. I do wonder what he looks like without torn clothes, dirt, and blood."

"He ain't much better than this. Trust me," Howdy chided.

Frank shook his head. "Isn't it amazing that I pay the man's salary and he talks about me like this?"

"He don't pay all that much," Howdy hooted. "But I reckon I ought to quit ribbin' him or I'll draw line duty for a month."

"Line duty?"

"There are no fences on this place, as you probably noticed," Frank said. "To the north, there is a property line at the top of a rise. Everything north of Buffalo Gap is railroad land. On this side is Rafter F. We've been havin' some cows disappear up that way. I have a two-man crew takin' shifts and ridin' that line twenty-four hours a day. The boys consider it a lonely assignment."

"Livin' out of a bedroll for weeks at a time is tirin', señorita," Howdy offered.

"Our little wagon gets cramped too."

"We do have room at the big house, if you folks ever get up that way," Frank offered.

"Thank you. We might avail ourselves sometime. But my real purpose is to study the plant life out here. I presume the worst of the Badlands are to the northeast."

"Yes, ma'am." With steady precision, Frank wrapped his red bandanna around his left hand. "Be careful. We have had rustlers out here."

"If I come across some, how will I tell them from your vaqueros?"

"The rustlers will be cleaner," Howdy said.

"Our men ride Rafter F brand horses," Frank explained. "But if you spot rustlers, stay clear. They are a wild gang. Keep yourself safe."

"Thank you, Señor Fortune."

"Frank. Call me Frank."

"Why does your father call you Little Frank?"

"My whole family calls me that. My Grandpa had a very good friend who was called Big River Frank. So when I came along and was named after him, I became Little Frank. Of course, Big River Frank was shot and killed before I was born, but I'm still Little Frank."

"Does it bother you to be called that?" she asked.

"Not by my family. They mean it as a term of affection."

"Even though we are 'like family,' I will not call you Little Frank. But I might call you Francisco."

Howdy laughed. "Yes, ma'am, you do that. I reckon the boys will get a chuckle out of that."

She looked at the thin cowboy. "And you shall be Señor Hola."

"What's that mean?" he asked.

"Howdy."

Howdy leaned across the saddle horn. "Hola Tompkins. I like that."

"Build a signal fire for us in about a week, Señor

25

Hola, and we will find your headquarters."

"Yes, ma'am, I reckon I'll do that."

"You'll need to check with the boss first, to see if he wants company."

"Why?" Howdy grinned. "He's been actin' like a moon-eyed pup since he saw you. It's a dead cinch he'd like you to come around."

"Howdy!" Frank barked.

She grinned. "I believe you just got line duty."

Howdy tipped his hat. "Yes, ma'am, I believe you're right."

Fortune turned Carlos west and kicked the horse's flanks. The big gelding bolted up out of the gulch. Frank felt the wind whip across his sore bare back.

Frank and Howdy rode west toward the distant Black Hills until they reached Lost Springs.

Fortune eased himself out of the saddle. He examined the split in the thigh of his jeans. "Why didn't you tell me my trousers were ripped in the back?"

"I figured with the wind blowin' through, you could figure it out for yourself. Besides," Howdy added, "you told me we were goin' to chase rustlers, and it didn't seem to matter."

Frank dipped his bandanna in the spring water and washed his face. "I didn't appreciate the 'moon-eyed pup' comment."

"Jist tryin' to help." Howdy climbed down off the copper dun and tightened the cinch. "Boss, it's about time you thought about your future. You ain't goin' to want to live in that big house all alone all your life."

"I'm a young man. There's plenty of time."

"You keep up like today, and you ain't got that many more years left."

Frank stood and could feel blood drip down his forehead. "Speakin' of future, it's time you thought about just how many weeks you want to spend up there, ridin' the line."

Howdy squatted down next to his horse and pulled a small leather pouch out of his vest pocket. "Now, a man ain't that testy unless the arrow hit close to the mark."

Frank studied Howdy's freckled grin. "She is a looker, isn't she?"

"A looker?" Howdy pulled a packet of paper from his shirt pocket, tore one off, and began to roll a quirley. "Now there's an understatement. But at least you are lookin'. That does show signs of progress, Boss. The boys say you ain't looked at anything but cows for five years."

"I glanced at Marla Jolene a time or two."

"Not in the past three years."

"I've been busy."

"No man is that busy."

Frank stood and tied the bandanna around his forehead wound. "I reckon I didn't make too much of an impression."

"That ain't true. You done good. Why, some women is attracted to injured dogs and sickly strays."

"You're doin' wonders for my confidence today." Frank put his hat on the back of his head.

Howdy drew a sulphur match across his boot and lit the hand-rolled cigarette that draped off his lip.

"That's my job."

"If it didn't sting so bad, I'd just crawl in the springs and wash all the dirt and rocks off me."

"Why clean up now? You ain't expectin' to meet more women out here, are you?"

"No, but dirt and blood don't exactly sit well on me."

"Don't know why you didn't let that señorita doctor you. I was thinkin' about fallin' off my horse just to get some of her attention myself."

Frank Fortune slowly rubbed his chest. "I think I busted my ribs. They hurt worse than my elbow . . ."

"Not to mention that gouge in your head and numerous cuts, scrapes, and bruises. I can tell you got horse drug, but I surely don't know how it happened."

"I don't want to talk about it."

Howdy Tompkins swung back up in the saddle. "I don't reckon you want to tell me where your ol' McGee is either?"

Fortune yanked the cinch tight on his horse. "I need to retrieve it."

"I ain't goin' to find a bovine draggin' a rope, am I?"

"No."

Howdy stood in the stirrups and stared north. "Are you expectin' a posse?"

Frank Fortune led Carlos over by the copper dun stallion. "What do you see?"

"Enough dust for a dozen riders comin' south off Wildcat Mesa."

"If they are raisin' dust, they aren't rustlers. They aren't that cocky in broad daylight yet. I reckon I'd better go see."

"What do you want me to do?"

"Are the boys still brandin' on Cimmeron Flats?"

"It's early in the mornin'. I reckon if they have 'em rounded up by now, they are."

Frank stuck his foot in the stirrup, grabbed the saddle horn, then paused. "Gather the boys and meet me at Buckskin Pass. I'll stop this bunch there."

"You goin' to need some help?"

"Don't know 'til I see who they are."

"No, I meant, are you goin' to need some help gettin' in the saddle?" Howdy chided.

Frank Fortune lost sight of the horsemen as he rode down into Claybank Gulch. The brush and scrub poplars made riding difficult. His vision was limited to a few feet. He pulled out the single-shot Sharps converted carbine, checked the chamber, then laid it across his lap.

Lord, I'm gettin' way too jumpy. What with rustlers and the railroad buyin' up land and cows dyin', I don't trust anyone ridin' on this ranch anymore. I spent years, day and night, buildin' up this herd. I don't go to town or slack off or waste time or money. But now it feels like it's slowly slippin' away. Ever' cow I lose, I take it personal. It's like I've failed. I know, I know . . . they all say I'm young. Sometimes I wish Grandpa Brazos was here to see the place. Other times I'm glad he isn't.

Frank stopped and stared up at the clear, blue Dakota sky. *Grandpa, I know it isn't your Texas, but it's my Dakota. Sometimes I don't know what to do. What would you do if you were losin' cows and runnin' fifteen hundred head on public land? I know, Grandpa, that's why you gave me this old Sharps of yours. You'd chase 'em all the way to Montana, and those that didn't run, you'd just shoot.*

But this isn't the days of '76, Grandpa. We got laws and lawmen and courts and judges. It's the twentieth century. It's modern times. There's electric lights in most every town of consequence and indoor plumbing. A man can't ride twenty-five miles without crossin' a railroad track. And this is one of the last big ranches without fences. They say back east there is blacktop streets, nick- elodeons with movin' picture shows, and Amber even rode in a self-propelled carriage.

This is my century, Grandpa, and I need to fit in. But to tell you the truth, I like yours a whole lot better. I surely wish I could have worked cattle with you one day in my life.

Frank glanced down at the bloody, shredded gloves.

Not this day, of course. But some other day, you and me ridin' side by side. We rode out to Cheyenne Crossing one time. I'll never forget. Just me and you. We rode up there on the mountain, and you pointed to where Big River Frank took that bullet meant for you and Aunt Dacee June.

At that moment I knew that all I ever wanted to do in life was to be a hero in your eyes like Big River Frank. But you didn't live long enough, Grandpa. Sometimes I reckon maybe you and Grandma are lookin' on.

He trudged through the brush and followed the dry creek bed north. He couldn't see out on the prairie at all. When he broke onto the sandbar, the trail widened. The undergrowth thinned. He glanced up the draw where the trail narrowed again in the cliffs of Buckskin Pass.

I'm assumin' that those riders will continue south. I surmise they will cross the gulch right here. But I don't know why they are here and what they are lookin' for. Maybe Señorita Rodriguez has others in her entourage. I didn't ask. A steer is a lot of meat for three people. When that Russian count came to hunt, he had nearly sixty people with him. But he was royalty.

Frank Fortune caught himself smiling. *She was pretty enough to be a princess, that's for sure. Why, I couldn't hardly catch my breath when she . . .*

The sound of pebbles tumbling down the cliffs of Buckskin Pass caused Frank to sit up. When he did, there was a sharp pain in his ribs. He pushed his hat back, then brushed his brown hair and rubbed the raw spot on his forehead.

"In the history of my days, this is not one of the better ones, Carlos." He patted the horse's neck. "Let's go visit with this posse."

The boulder was bigger than a privy. He held the horse behind it and listened for hoofbeats coming down the narrow pass. Frank cocked the massive hammer of the single-shot Sharps carbine but left it lying across his lap.

Surprise, boys. Let's see what's going on.

The first rider straddled an overo paint horse with one blue eye and one brown eye. The man in the suit, vest, tie, and round-brimmed hat reined up as Frank blocked the trail. He didn't draw his gun, but those on both sides of him did.

Buckskin Pass was no wider than three horses. The others bunched behind the front three.

"Mornin', boys. You're on Rafter F land. What can I do to help you?"

"This is government land," the man in the suit and tie called out.

"Yes, but it's legally leased to the Rafter F and posted. That makes you trespassers, unless you have some business with the Rafter F."

"I really don't have time to waste here. I do have business with the Rafter F. So, if you'll please move, you won't get hurt." The man had a curly black beard, but his lips were full, pink, and seemed to move a split second before the words came out.

When Frank sat up, a sharp pain shot through his ribs, and he slumped back over the saddle horn. "Are you threatenin' me?"

"I have no idea who you are or who you think you are. From your looks, I'd suggest a bath and a safer occupation. We are riding to the headquarters of the Rafter F to conduct some business," the man replied.

With his left hand, Fortune rubbed his forehead. He noticed blood on his fingertips. "You keep headin' this way, you'll end up in Rapid City, not the Rafter F headquarters."

The man in the suit glanced over at the heavy man with the drooping black mustache to his left. A Winchester 1895 carbine set across the man's dirty ducking trousers. "I know where the headquarters is," he growled to the suit-and-tie man. "I used to work for ol' man Fortune."

Frank Fortune studied the man. *You might have told your boss you worked on this ranch, but you never did.* "I'll save you all a trip to the headquarters. What do you want?"

The heavyset man spat a wad of tobacco over the nose of his horse. "You have no idea who you're talkin' to. The major here runs one of the biggest spreads in northeast Wyoming."

Frank rode closer to the man in the suit and tie. He made sure that the .50 caliber Sharps carbine in his lap was pointed right at the man.

"Yeah, and we aren't in Wyoming. I can see from the brand on your ponies that you are from the 'Axe-T.' Now, Mr. Suit-and-tie, what is your business on this ranch?"

The big man waved his revolver at Fortune. "He don't have to answer you. Get out of the way before I count to three."

"I'm not talkin' to you," Frank Fortune said. "It's just me and the major here."

"How in hades do you figure that?" another of the gunmen shouted.

"Boys, you all know that I have a single-shot Sharps here. So I get one shot, then you'll kill me. Right?"

"I reckon so," the big man conceded.

"But my gun is pointed at the major. A .50 caliber bullet will kill him on the spot. All of you know that. So that means that him and me are the only ones here who are guaranteed to die today. I reckon that means we should be the only ones talkin'.""

"You can't bluff me," the big man growled.

"That's because the Sharps isn't pointed at you, John Earl," the major blustered. "Now back off and let me do the talking."

"And I say we ride up to headquarters and have it out with ol' Frank Fortune himself," the man boomed. Several of the other men growled agreement.

"Shut up, John Earl," the man barked. He rode a foot closer to Frank Fortune. "I don't know if you've been wrestling a bear or what, son, but I like your style. A man who rides for the brand and stands up to twelve armed men has sand. If the day comes you're lookin' for a job, come see me. But the truth is, this is serious business, and I have to talk to your boss."

"Well, Mr. Thomasville, whatever it is can be discussed right here."

"You know me?"

"Mr. George Washington Thomasville? Yeah, I was up at the cattleman's meeting in Miles City that the railroad held."

Thomasville pulled a gold watch from his vest pocket and opened the lid. "I don't remember meeting you."

"I reckon you Wyoming men stick together. Not many from Dakota were there."

Thomasville let the watch slip back into his pocket. "Did you go up there with your boss, Frank Fortune?"

"You might say that."

"Look, I do have important things to discuss with Fortune. Could you lead us to the headquarters, so that we might talk to him?"

"That's a wasted trip. He's not there."

"Then are you second in command?"

Fortune raised his left hand to rub his neck, but the pain in his elbow was so great that he lowered it slowly. "Nope."

"Then I'm afraid you've wasted our time. And no, I don't think you'll shoot me. No one wants to die for someone else's fight."

Major G. W. Thomasville rode forward two steps. Frank brought the Sharps carbine up to his shoulder.

Like an orchestra ready for the conductor's baton, the dozen men brought guns up.

Each pointed at Frank Fortune.

"You are crazy," Thomasville shouted.

"You are right about one thing, Mr. Thomasville, and wrong about two. You're right that a man might not give his life for another man's cattle. But where you made your mistake was thinkin' that this ranch doesn't belong to me. I'm Frank Fortune, and I've never seen fat John Earl before in my life. He's never worked on this ranch."

Thomasville pulled a white handkerchief from his suit pocket and tugged off his hat. "You said I made two mistakes. What's the other?"

"Thinking that I'm out here alone." He nodded his head to the cliffs on both sides of Buckskin Pass. "I have a crew of men up in those rocks."

"Like hades, he does!" John Earl grumbled.

Frank Fortune kept his gun pointed at the Wyoming cattleman. "G. W., you tell me which man you'd like for my men to shoot first. I reckon that will prove my point."

"That's all a lie," John Earl huffed.

"How about the big boy?" Fortune suggested.

"I don't want any man killed," Thomasville breathed as he wiped the sweat from his forehead.

Frank hollered, "Howdy, if this fat man doesn't throw down by three, lead him down."

"That's a bluff!" John Earl yelled.

"One!" Fortune shouted.

"There ain't no one up there," John Earl blustered.

"Two!"

"John Earl!" Mr. Thomasville yelled.

The big man tossed his Winchester '95 carbine to the dirt.

"Now, if the rest of you will holster your guns and scabbard your carbines, me and Mr. Thomasville need to talk," Fortune announced.

John Earl pulled off his hat and waved it toward the cliffs. "And I say there ain't no one up there."

At the same moment that his felt hat flew from his hand, a rifle report echoed down from the rocks.

Every member of the posse shoved their guns in their holsters.

"Can we shoot them all now, Mr. Fortune?" a voice shouted from the cliffs.

"No, boys. They are just lost and needing directions."

"You really are Frank Fortune?" Thomasville asked.

"Yep. Now what is this business that almost cost both of us our lives?"

"Someone's been rustling my cattle and drivin' them over here. I intend to see that it stops. I heard that my cows have ended up being sold in Dakota. I hired me a few men here to see the rustling stops. I don't like losing cattle."

Frank felt his finger back off the cold steel trigger. "I know how you feel."

"You do?"

"Someone's been stealin' my cows, too, especially up around Buffalo Gap. There's a rumor that some of them are ending up in Wyomin'. I certainly want it to stop."

"Are you accusing me of stealing your cattle?" Thomasville huffed.

"Of course not." A slight grin crept across Frank's dirty, bloody face. "Are you accusing me?"

Thomasville paused. His smirk faded to a smile. "No, but I want some answers."

"So do I."

"Then we need to talk and compare losses."

"How about Wednesday?" Frank suggested. "I don't respond well to hunting parties, especially when they are hunting me. So you all turn around and go home. On Wednesday, you ride over here by yourself, Mr. Thomasville, and we'll try to figure out what enemy we're facing."

"We're checkin' all your bovines today, Fortune," John Earl grumbled.

"No, you're not," Frank growled back.

G. W. Thomasville held up his hand. "There's a time and place to make a stand, boys, but this is not it. We are retreating."

"You mean you're letting him bluff ya?"

"That ain't a bluff hole in your hat, John Earl," one of the men shouted.

"Wednesday?" Thomasville asked.

"Plan to stay for supper and spend the night."

"I march in here with an armed band of men and accuse you of rustling, and now you invite me to supper?"

"It's an honest mistake."

"Yours or mine?"

"That remains to be seen, doesn't it?"

"I'll see you Wednesday," Thomasville said. "How do I find this mysterious headquarters?"

"Ride out to Black Bear Butte, then look back at the tallest peak in the northern Black Hills. Imagine a straight line between those two points and ride for the hills. You won't see it until you're right up on it. It's down in a narrow valley, so keep ridin'."

"So you really are Frank Fortune?"

"Yep."

"And you're running a thousand head?"

"Closer to fifteen hundred."

"Just how in the world did a young man like yourself accumulate fifteen hundred head?"

"I live right."

Thomasville looked him up and down. "That's something we'll talk about next Wednesday."

George Washington Thomasville led the dozen men back up Buckskin Pass.

The last to retreat was John Earl. He dismounted to retrieve his carbine. "You purtneer cost me my job, Fortune."

"Not to mention your hat." Frank kept the Sharps carbine on the big man. "It was your lying to your boss that cost you. You never worked on the Rafter F.

38

I've never seen you."

"I worked for your Daddy one time." John Earl remounted his horse.

"You work for the railroad?"

John Earl slipped the carbine into the worn leather scabbard. "I worked in his lumber mill in Deadwood. Your daddy was Brazos Fortune, wasn't he?"

"No, he was my grandpa."

"No foolin'? How old are you?"

"Too young to look this worn out. Now, go on, get out of here."

Frank kept the carbine trained on the man until he disappeared up Buckskin Pass. Within minutes Howdy Tompkins raced his horse down off the mountain and galloped past Fortune. He turned and trotted back.

"What was that all about?" he asked.

"That was none other than George Washington Thomasville. He wanted to know if we stole any Axe-T cows."

"He accused you of rustlin'?"

"I think that's where it was headed before you and the boys sent them runnin'."

"It was just me."

Frank stared at the shorter man. "What?"

"The boys weren't at Cimmeron Flats yet, so I rode on back by myself."

"So we were bluffin' 'em?"

"I figured you and me could take 'em," Howdy replied.

"You hidin' behind a rock and me out in the open? One of us was bound to get hurt," Frank said.

"Don't underestimate yourself, Boss," Howdy grinned. "I figured you could have gotten two of them before they plugged you."

Frank Fortune tried to shove the carbine into his scabbard, but a sharp pain cramped his right shoulder. The gun missed the scabbard and tumbled to the ground.

Howdy stared down at it. "It could be that I was a little too optimistic."

CHAPTER TWO

THE BIG HOUSE at the headquarters of the Rafter F didn't look like a house. Tucked against the limestone cliff of narrow, treeless valley stretched a long log building. The structure was only twenty-four feet deep but one hundred and fifty feet wide. An eight-foot covered porch fronted the entire width. The heavy shake roof featured six stone chimneys.

Frank Fortune had purchased the building from the U.S. Army at Fort Meade and moved it piece by piece to the ranch. On the south end was a storeroom, his bedroom, a great room/office with the largest of the rock fireplaces, then a huge dining room, a spacious kitchen, and a pantry that combined for living quarters for the cook.

Each room opened out to the porch.

Each room had a door to the room next to it.

And even though all the ranch hands ate in the dining room and lounged on the porch, it was known as the big house.

Like huge bookends, identical barns stood fifty feet on both sides of the big house, one for animals, the other for wagons, gear, and a bunkhouse. Across the drive from the buildings, stout wooden corrals held the collection of ranch horses.

Riding east or west none of the buildings could be seen until a person crested the rim and looked down at Bear Butte Valley.

To many people, when they finally discovered the headquarters, it looked more like two barns and an army barrack.

For Frank Fortune, it looked like home.

He rode beside Butte Creek with his hat flopped over the saddle horn, glad to see no one in the ranch yard. The scratches on his back and chest burned with salty sweat. The pain in his elbow seemed greater the closer he got to the buildings. But his ribs ached the most, and every breath hurt. It was a deep, steady hurt.

Frank rode Carlos through the open double door on the south barn. He crawled off the horse, and a slight jar of his boot on the dirt floor caused a pain to shoot through his ribs. He tied the chestnut gelding to the feed trough and struggled to untie the cinch. Frank looped the right stirrup over the saddle horn, then shuffled around to the left side of the horse. He grabbed the saddle horn with his left hand and the cantle with his right.

He jerked the saddle off the horse. When its full weight hit his shoulders, a slicing pain rippled down his rib cage. Frank staggered to the back of the stall and dropped the saddle.

"You keepin' 'em in the dirt now, or is that a throw-away saddle?"

Frank had the Sharps carbine out of the scabbard as he spun around. "Uncle Sammy?" He leaned the gun against the stall. "You startled me."

The tall, gray-haired man with a drooping, thick mustache cracked a grin. "I reckon I did. But you didn't answer my question. Did you drop that saddle on purpose?"

Frank pulled the saddle blanket off the gelding, rolled it up, and wiped the horse sweat down. "What in the world are you doin' out at the ranch?"

Sam pulled his black tie loose and unfastened the top button on his white shirt. "I take it you know your pants are ripped."

Frank grabbed a brush and began to wipe down the horse. "Is ever'thin' alright in town?"

"And your shirt and vest are in shreds."

"The wedding is still on, isn't it?" A pain shot through Frank Fortune's ribs when he tried to smile.

Sam plucked a hay straw and chewed on it. "And your bandanna is bloody. You didn't take on a whole band of bronco Oglala Sioux, did you?"

Frank clutched his elbow to try to relieve the pain. "It's not Uncle Carty is it? He's been way too sick lately."

Sam plucked up the Sharps carbine and aimed it at the barn's rafters. "The way you came slinkin' in here, I surmise you had a wreck."

Frank led the horse over to the feed trough. "Mama didn't send you out here to hound me about the wedding rehearsal, did she?"

Sam Fortune began to laugh. "Little Frank, you are just like your daddy. So intense. Don't ever change. Ever' generation of Fortunes needs one like you."

Frank studied the gray hair and the neat but drooping gray mustache of his uncle. *Lord, I get the feelin' that's the way I'm goin' to look when I'm 48, aren't I?*

Sam picked up the saddle and shoved in on the stall railing. "Your ribs are busted." It was a statement, not a question.

"Yeah, I didn't know they hurt that much until the weight of the saddle hit me." Frank unfastened the front buttons of his ripped wool vest, then tossed the garment on top of the oat barrel.

Sam circled Frank. "Lookin' at that left boot, and the way your shirt and vest are ripped, I'd say you got bucked and your foot hung in the stirrup."

Frank tugged up the front of his shirt and surveyed the scrapes on his chest. "I didn't get bucked, but I might as well have. The results were the same."

Sam strolled across the barn and yanked a rope down from the wall. "It wouldn't happen to have anything to do with why I found this sixty-foot McGee looped to a dead poplar stump over near the forks at Claybank Creek?"

Frank held his elbow around in the daylight and tried to examine it. "I don't want to talk about it," he mumbled.

Sam looped the rope back on the wall. "I drove that old cow up out of there and out on to the prairie with the others."

"What were you doin' at Claybank?" Frank asked. "It's not on the road to Deadwood."

Sam rolled up his sleeves to his elbows. "Lookin' for you. Americus said you were out there. But you weren't."

Frank pulled his shirt off and tossed it on the oat barrel. "After the wreck, I had a little trouble up north I had to take care of."

"Your back looks like the boys who came out of the Andersonville prison after the war."

"I need some iodine, I reckon."

Sam climbed the ladder to the hay loft. "I hope your trouble didn't involve a purdy Mexican gal."

Frank handed a pitchfork up to his uncle. "Why do you say that?"

Sam tossed down a fork of hay. "Jamie Sue and your daddy threw a party for the señorita at the Merchant's Hotel last week."

Frank retrieved a wooden pitchfork from the next stall. "I did check out their camp, of course."

Sam tossed down a couple more forks of hay. "I trust that was before you looked like that."

Frank scooped up the downed hay and jammed it into the feed trough. "I don't want to talk about it."

Sam Fortune laughed as he climbed down the ladder. "She's a very smart gal. She would have given ol' Grass Edwards a run for his botany."

Frank scooped up the rest of the hay and jammed it into the trough. "We didn't talk much."

"Treat her good, Frank, 'cause your daddy surely does speak well of her mama and papa. 'Course, there's another reason for treatin' her good."

A shirtless and scraped Frank Fortune hiked out to the middle of the barn. "Oh?"

Sam stepped over by his nephew. "Little Frank . . . this is somethin' I wouldn't bring up in front of your mama and the girls, but . . . it is my opinion . . . havin' spent my younger years makin' the rounds and livin' too wild . . . that a man only gets to meet one or two truly beautiful unmarried women in his entire life. And in all my days, son, Señorita Rodriguez is only the second I ever met."

Frank held his ribs with both hands. "And the first?"

Sam slowly rolled down his sleeves. "If you'll remember, I married her within a few hours of meetin' her."

Frank ambled out the open double doors of the barn. "I have to admit, as far as beauty is concerned, I've been spoiled. I grew up with Mama, Aunt Rebekah, Aunt Abby, and Aunt Dacee June hoverin' around me. Then there's Amber, the twins, and the rest of the Fortune and Toluca girls."

"That's true, Little Frank. And I suppose it could get you to thinkin' that most women are heart stoppers. But I'm tellin' you, when you get to be an old man, you'll look back, and one or two gals will come to your mind, ones that time never erased their beauty."

"Now just what exactly are you tellin' me, Uncle Sammy?"

Sam stood beside Frank. They were the exact same size and build.

"I'm just sayin', it wouldn't hurt to visit with the

señorita, 'cause memories of her are goin' to haunt you the rest of your life. That's all I'm goin' to say about it."

Frank reached to the back of his denim trousers and scratched his leg through the long rip. "You rode seven hours from town to tell me that?"

"Five and a half hours. I got a fast horse. Didn't you see that new pony I turned out in your corral?"

Frank stared across the drive at the corrals. "I reckon I missed him. You always did like black horses."

"He's a snotty sucker, but I reckon he'll learn. Little Frank, I'm glad I don't have to tell Daddy Brazos that his own grandson rode back to the ranch without scopin' the corral for uninvited visitors."

"This is the twentieth century, Uncle Sammy. There isn't an outlaw in ever' draw."

"Still, a man ought to know his horses."

Sam and a shirtless Frank Fortune strolled over to the corrals. "I guess I was distracted."

"You see, she is a beauty, isn't she?" Sam laughed.

"He's a stallion, Uncle Sammy. You didn't buy a mare."

"I ain't talking horses, son. I mean Señorita Rodriguez is a beauty, and you were so enamored you forgot to look at the corrals as you rode up."

"I'll give you one part señorita, but there was one part pain and one part Major Thomasville."

Sam climbed up on the bottom rail of the corral and surveyed the peaceful horses. "What's George Washington Thomasville doin' over here?"

Frank shuffled over to the stock tank and splashed water on his chest and back. "I think he wanted to accuse me and the boys of rustlin' his beef."

"You sent him back to Wyoming?"

"Told him to come over Wednesday and we'd talk about our common problem. How do you know the major, Uncle Sammy?"

Sam Fortune perched on the top rail with his back to the horses. He still chewed on a hay straw. "I knew Thomasville before he was a major."

"No foolin'? I thought he was a major in the war."

"Nope. He didn't become a major until '77."

"He was in the cavalry?"

"He was in jail at Ft. Smith, Arkansas," Sam explained. "So was I, and we were goin' up before Judge Parker the next day. Thomasville concocted the scheme of bein' called Major."

"Why was he in jail?"

"Cattle rustlin', I believe."

"No foolin', he was a rustler?"

Sam pulled his felt hat off and ran his fingers through gray hair. "I don't think he was too good at it. He got caught."

"And why were you there?"

Sam slapped his knee. "I was in jail for borrowin' a carriage."

"Without askin'?"

"Yep, and a colonel's nineteen-year-old daughter just happened to be in the carriage at the time."

"Was she a looker, Uncle Sammy?"

"I can't remember her at all."

"Did Thomasville get off by pretending to be a major?"

"No, but he made such an uproar about being arrested just because he had been a confederate officer, that when he got out of jail, some of the southern boys got him a job drivin' Mexican beef to Montana. He worked crew boss on a few drives and ended up with his own spread. But don't hold that against him, Little Frank. Lots of us have pasts we ain't too proud of. Except for your daddy, of course."

Frank hung his hat on a fence post by the stock tank. "You're goin' to spend the night aren't you?"

"I wondered if you'd ask. Yes, sir, I believe I am. Might even spend a day or two."

Frank dipped his head under the stock tank water and raised up. The water burned its way across the wounds on his chest and back. "If you raid the kitchen, I imagine Americus has somethin' for you to eat."

Sam hopped down off the fence rail. "I just might do that."

Frank tried to wash dirt and grass off his chest. He flinched with every splash of cold water. "I think I'll change trousers. I reckon if I mend them careful, they would be good enough for wipin' rags."

"Or bore rags to clean that Sharps."

"Good thing I listened to mama and have two pairs of trousers," Little Frank laughed.

"Abby once accused me of bein' the only man she knew who owned more horses than he did shirts," Sam said.

Frank rubbed his clean-shaven chin. "Did she have a point to make, or was that just a random statement?"

Sam Fortune stared at him.

"What's the matter?" Frank asked.

"That's the exact same thing I asked her, word for word." Sam shook his head. "Lookin' at you and talkin' to you is like talkin' to myself twenty-five years ago, except your mustache isn't as rangy."

"Nor nearly so gray. We are both handsome cusses, aren't we? How do you account for that in the same family?"

The two men strolled toward the big house. "The way I figure it, about the time you were born, I was livin' reckless and dumb. The Lord must have figured I wouldn't live much longer and shaped you up for a replacement for ol' Sam Fortune, just to help Daddy Brazos with the grief."

"Just like the twins?"

"Yep, Daddy always figured he got a second chance with those girls. But I fooled him. I took the long trail home and got serious about things. Surprised ever'one, includin' the good Lord, I reckon, and stayed alive."

"Now, tell me somethin' Uncle Sammy . . . you bein' knowledgeable in these matters, and me bein' just a young man. I was ponderin' what you told me earlier about purdy women. Does the opposite hold true? Do you reckon women only get to meet one or two truly handsome unmarried men in their life?"

Sam let out a deep roar. "I'd suggest you ask Dacee June about that. Or Abby. But my prediction is, they don't spend much time lookin' for handsome men. They are lookin' for one that is noble, loyal, industrious, and a sweet talker."

"You think that's it?"

"Yep, that and one that is malleable like silver and gold, 'cause they will need to shape him up."

"So how do you think I rate?"

"Thanks to your mama and daddy, you have the first three qualities in spades. And I think with the right woman, you'd be malleable enough."

Frank paused by the step up to the porch at the big house. "And the sweet-talkin' part?"

Sam put his hand on Frank's bare shoulder, but when he flinched, he withdrew it. "Now, that's where I can teach you," he grinned.

"I don't want to get too good at it." Frank rubbed the stiffness from his neck. "I don't have time to get married until I'm thirty."

"Thirty? You don't aim to waste your whole life away, do ya?"

Frank waved his arm out at the open prairie. "I have a plan for ownin' my own property by the time I'm thirty."

"You got a plan, huh?"

"I've had it for five years. Last year I exceeded my projection by twenty-one percent."

Sam shook his head and roared. "You may look like Sam Fortune, but you are Bobby and Jamie Sue's boy all the way."

"You think I overplan my life?"

"I think Little Frank Fortune is goin' to get more accomplished by the time he's thirty than any man in the Black Hills. That's the way God created you. Don't change. What I'm sayin' is, maybe he created someone to help you achieve all those plans."

"You mean, besides Americus, Howdy, and the boys?" Frank said.

"Yep, and you will definitely need to know how to sweettalk."

Frank paused in front of the porch door that led to his bedroom. "I suppose you're goin' to teach me whether I want to or not?"

"It's my family duty."

"I never heard that Grandpa Brazos sweet-talked women."

"That's because you never saw him around your grandma."

By the time Howdy and the boys rode up to the headquarters, Frank had washed up, smeared iodine the best he could on his chest and back, and cleaned the blood off his face.

There was no blood or bruise on the elbow. Just intense pain.

He sprawled on a bench on the porch in front of the dining room. Sam reclined in a worn wooden rocking chair beside him.

"Always did like this rocker," Sam commented.

"So did Grandpa," Frank replied. "Most of my memories of him are down at the hardware store early in the mornings, sittin' in that chair. Grandpa gave me his carbine, and when Aunt Dacee June gave me the rocker, well, I figured I was the luckiest of all the grandkids."

"You're the oldest. You know, me, Todd, and your daddy have purtneer givin' up sittin' around that stove. Maybe come winter it will be different. Just too much to do. Todd is so busy. Don't know how those old men did it every mornin' for twenty years."

Frank brushed his fingers across his thick mustache. "It's what kept him goin' all those years, don't you think? It kept him pullin' himself out of bed every mornin'."

Sam leaned back in the rocking chair and stretched his arms out. "I reckon. We need a commitment to keep us goin' some time. Quiet Jim didn't last six months after Daddy died."

Howdy Tompkins, face dripping with water, was the first to leave the bunkhouse. A tall, heavy, black cowboy plodded alongside him.

"You got a new man?" Sam asked.

"Yep, his name is Jonas Lavender. He can ride Ida-hojoe to a standstill."

"I'm impressed," Sam grinned.

"And he can outeat Tree Roberts."

Sam slapped his knee. "Now I'm really impressed."

"You're a little wet, Howdy," Sam called out when the two men were still halfway across the dirt drive.

"Evenin', Mr. Fortune, glad you came out. Nah, ain't no reason to dirty a towel on my face just for supper." Howdy pointed his hat toward Frank. "Now the boss, he does look a little cleaner than last time I seen him."

Sam stood to shake hands with Howdy Tompkins. Then he reached out to the other cowboy. "Evenin', son, I'm . . ."

"You got to be the boss's father. You two is a spittin' image of each other," the black man said.

Sam grabbed his hand. "Thanks for the compliment, Jonas, but . . ."

"This is my uncle, not my father," Frank said.

"Sorry about that, I just assumed . . ." Jonas stammered.

"You're not the first to make the mistake," Sam roared. "We was sittin' up here talkin' about how unusual it was for the Lord to make two of the world's most handsome men and plop them down at the same location."

Jonas Lavender glanced over at Frank.

"Jonas, you better get used to teasin' when my family comes around. And Uncle Sammy is the worst of the lot at ridin' me," Frank said.

"Your name is Sam Fortune?" Jonas asked.

Sam nodded.

A white-tooth smile rippled across the tall man's dark face. "Ain't that somethin'. Shoot, that's a famous name down in the Indian Nation."

"You from Oklahoma?" Sam asked.

"Yep. There used to be a gunslinger down there when I was a pup went by the name of Sam Fortune."

Sam sat back in the chair and began to rock. "Did you ever meet him?"

"No, sir. But my mama knew him."

Frank Fortune laughed and shook his head. *Lord, did Uncle Sammy know ever' woman in the Indian Nation?*

Sam winked at Frank. "You don't say?"

"Yep. It was ol' Sam Fortune shot my mama," Jonas blurted out.

Sam quit rocking. His hand slipped down to his hip. But there wasn't any holstered gun to grip.

Frank struggled to his feet. "I find that hard to believe. Fortune men don't shoot women."

The smile dropped from Jonas Lavender's face. He glanced at Frank, then at Sam. His mouth dropped open. "I . . . I heard that Sam Fortune was dead."

Sam continued to rock. "You hear a lot of things down in the Indian Nation."

Jonas took another step closer. "Are you really that Sam Fortune?"

Sam leaped to his feet. "I reckon so."

Howdy Tompkins stepped between the men. "You two ain't causin' a row, are you?"

"I spent ten years lookin' for you, and gave up when I heard you got gunned down."

Sam stepped around Howdy Tompkins. "Son, that was a long time ago, and I truly don't remember shootin' a woman. That's the kind of thing a man remembers."

The smile broke back across Jonas's face. "Oh, don't get me wrong. I ain't mad."

"You aren't?" Howdy gasped. "And he shot your mama?"

"She didn't die or nothin'," Jonas reported.

Several other cowboys wandered toward the benches in front of the dining room.

"Maybe you can refresh my memory," Sam asked.

"My mama used to wash dishes and cook at a place called Thunder Toms down on the breaks near Mill City."

"Your mama is named Vinnie Mae and was wearin' a yellow dress," Sam said.

"You remember?"

"I remember that much, but I don't remember shootin' her. I truly don't."

The other cowboys gathered around them as Jonas waved his hands. "This is the way my mama tells the story. Syracuse Gilette and that bunch came into Thunder Toms and caused a ruckus, breakin' dishes, chasin' off customers, and threatenin' to shoot Ol' Tom if he didn't give them free food. He had mama cook some chops, and while she was servin' it, Tom slipped out the back door to find someone to help him throw the drunks out."

Sam Fortune rubbed his chin. "That sounds like Gilette, alright."

"Of course, there wasn't anyone that wanted to go against the Gilette gang. Ol' Tom was beside himself tryin' to get someone to help him."

"Meanwhile, your mama was inside?" Frank asked.

"Yep. That's when Sam Fortune rode up on a mule."

"A mule?" Frank hooted.

"I was havin' a bad day," Sam Fortune mumbled.

By now, every Rafter F cowhand was crowded around in front of the dining hall.

"Anyway," Jonas continued, "Ol' Tom called Syracuse Gilette out. Said he had Sam Fortune beside him and it was time for his bunch to leave. Mama said Gilette grabbed her around the waist and slapped a big ol' Bowie knife to her neck. She could feel the blade press into her skin. She said she heard the choir of heavenly angels and was prayin' for Jesus to take her home."

"I done that a few times myself," Howdy mumbled.

"Gilette stood in the doorway behind Mama and said he wanted Sam Fortune to ride out of town or he would slice her throat. She was so scared she pleaded for Mr. Fortune to leave."

"Nobody should treat a mama that way, no matter what color her skin," three-hundred-pound Tree Roberts rumbled.

Jonas looked around at each of the listeners. "Sam Fortune said he was leavin' and mounted his mule. He rode over to the front of Ol' Tom's place and with his left hand he tipped his hat to my mama and wished her well. While he did that, his right hand yanked out his revolver, and he shot Gilette right between the eyes. The knife tumbled, then he crumpled to the boardwalk. She said Sam Fortune just holstered his revolver, then rode off. Well, she felt a sharp pain under her ear and along her cheek as he fell."

"Gilette cut her with that blade?" Howdy asked.

"No, the doc told her later that day that he figured Sam Fortune's bullet must of glanced off Gilette's skull and grazed her. To this day she still has the scar. If anyone asks, she grins and tells 'em that Sam Fortune shot her. But I never in my life thought I'd meet ya."

"Jonas, I'm happy things turned out good for your mama. Is she doin' well now?" Sam asked.

"Yes, sir. That scared her out of the cafe work, and she moved to Galveston, Texas, to clean rooms at a fine hotel."

Although the dinner triangle was only ten feet down the boardwalk from the men, Americus Ash pounded on it like the boys were five miles away.

"I take it, it's dinner time?" Frank called out.

"It was dinner time an hour ago. Now it's time for left-overs. If the crew is goin' to be late, I'd appreciate someone givin' me warnin'."

Frank and Sam Fortune filed in at the back of the line.

Frank grabbed Howdy's shoulder. "You and the boys were late comin' in tonight. You didn't run across any more trouble?"

"Nope. The boys wanted to ride a circle to the north on the way back," Howdy admitted.

"Just to see if that Thomasville bunch had left?"

"Actually, they wanted to scope out a certain señorita I told them about."

"The whole crew rode north to look at some woman?"

"Some woman?" Howdy chided. "Sam, has he always been this dense, or did being drug by a horse too many times do this to him?"

"He's a lot like his daddy in that regard," Sam laughed. "He only thinks of one thing at a time, and it's seldom women."

"Anyway, it was all for nothing," Howdy shrugged. "She wasn't on Wildcat Mesa. We couldn't see them anywhere."

"What direction did the wagon go?" Sam asked.

"North for a while, but we didn't have time to track it."

"I told her to go east, then northeast," Frank said.

"She don't rightly look like a lady that takes to bein' told anythin'," Sam murmured as he followed Frank to the table.

All nine men circled the huge table and stood behind high-backed oak chairs until Frank got in place at the head of the table.

In unison every hat was pulled off.

Frank Fortune cleared his throat. "Lord, we're needin' strength and blessin's from this food. And I reckon we need your guidance and forgiveness as well. Some of us needin' more forgiveness than others . . ."

A round of scattered amens muted Frank's last words, "In Jesus' name, amen."

By the time most of the men jabbed their hats back on and were seated, they had food in their mouth. In less than fifteen minutes most of the food on the table had been devoured. Sam and Frank were the only ones sitting at the table drinking coffee when Americus Ash cleared the last of the dishes.

"OK, Uncle Sammy . . ." Frank began, "was Jonas's story accurate?"

"Most of it. Some parts were stretched."

"His mama wasn't a cook or dishwasher, was she?"

"Nope. But that's OK, Little Frank. When it comes to your mama, you got to find a story you can live with. The pain can be too deep if you don't."

"Did you really shoot Syracuse Gilette dead?"

"Twice."

"You shot him dead on two different occasions?"

"Yep. And he had the bald-faced audacity to refuse to die both times."

"You shot him in the head and he didn't die?"

"Some say that's because there wasn't anything up there to damage."

"Jonas was surely happy to meet you."

"Yeah, but he had me worried for a while. A reckless past is a horrible nightmare to live with."

"Don't those memories fade?"

"Most do. But some are like boulders in a stream. If the water's high, they are all covered up. But if the water level drops, ever' one of them boulders is exposed," Sam said.

"As long as the water is low, why don't you tell me why you were ridin' a mule."

"Speakin' of ridin', you haven't looked at that new horse of mine."

"You changin' the subject, Sam Fortune?"

"I reckon." Sam stood and carried his coffee cup. "Little Frank, do you have some things happen to you that you don't wish to recall?"

"Ropin' a stump, for one."

"You see . . . I spent too many years down in the Indian Nation ropin' stumps."

It was still dark when Sam Fortune wandered out to the horse barn the next morning carrying two cups of coffee. In the shadows of a dim lantern, Frank Fortune tossed a hoolihan over the chestnut gelding.

"Americus said you headed out before the coffee boiled," Sam called out. "I brought you a cup."

"If I ever wake up, I can't get back to sleep. Too many things to worry about." Frank led the big horse to the gate and tied him off at the post. He reached through the rail and took the steaming coffee.

"Sounds like your grandpa, that is until there at the

last. Todd figured Daddy slept so much those last couple of years to make up for all the sleep he'd missed. Said he reckoned Daddy didn't want to go meet Mama in heaven all tuckered out 'cause they had twenty-three years of catchin' up."

"These sore ribs kept me from sleepin'."

"That scrape on your forehead ain't exactly purdy this mornin'. You'd better hope that disappears before the wedding. I don't reckon your mama will let you in the church door lookin' all scuffed up."

"That wedding is goin' to be a madhouse, Uncle Sammy. I was hopin' just to go in and back out on Saturday, but Mama says I need to spend the weekend with them."

"The weddin' is a madhouse?" Sam Fortune took another sip of coffee and brushed back his gray mustache. "Why do you think I'm out here. Abby is still sewin' bridesmaids dresses. She and Rebekah have decided all the girls must wear one out of the same bolt of material. Amber and her Wade are coming in on the train with the baby. That means the house gets turned upside down. Your mama and daddy are repainting the entire church. Dacee June has the children's choir practicin' most ever' night. Some say it's the biggest day in Deadwood since the train arrived."

"I suppose having identical twin sisters marry identical twin brothers does make for a social event."

"I have a tough enough time tellin' one niece from the other. Now I'll never know which husband is which." Sam climbed up on the fence and stared out at the milling horses. "Where are you headin' out so early you need to rope in the dark?"

"I'm ridin' to the line up north. Need to take supplies to Chron and Reynoso."

"You ain't ridin' north to check on a purdy señorita, are you?"

"I ain't goin' to go traipsin' all over lookin' for her, if that's what you mean."

"Good. I'm glad I got that cleared up."

"But I need to check and see if any of my beef are missin'. Somethin' strange has been goin' on up there the past couple of weeks. And I should swing around to see if any of Thomasville's cows have strayed across the border."

"And visit with Dearyanna Rodriguez."

"I wish you'd quit sayin' that."

"OK. No more teasin'. See if you can rope that pony of mine while you are in there."

"You headin' back early?"

"Nope. I'm riding north with you."

"No reason for you to have to do that. I can take care of it. It's a long ride."

"Rope that pony of mine. I can tell when a cowboy is tryin' to toss a saddle blanket over my eyes."

Frank worked his way through the milling horses, the big loop of rope hanging at his side. *Lord, I've talked about this with you before. I moved out here to accomplish something on my own. I've got the best family in the Black Hills, but they can smother. How they can smother. I was really hopin' just to ride alone, to give me time to think. About my sisters getting married . . . about Thomasville claimin' we have his cows . . . about the future of the cattle business in the Black Hills region . . . about the future of Frank Fortune . . . about . . . OK . . . and about her.*

With one motion he brought the rope from the ground, over his head, and circled the neck of the tall black stallion.

I wonder just how far northeast they went?

Frank's mind wandered to the flashing smile of Dearyanna.

Until the big horse hit the end of the rope.

The horse bolted.

Frank's already scarred hands flared.

"Whoa!" he hollered. The horse dragged him through the remuda.

"Hang on, Little Frank. He likes to run a little if you rope him before daylight," Sam Fortune hollered.

Now he tells me?

"Run him out the gate. He'll calm down when he gets away from the others," Sam yelled.

Run him out the gate? I'm goin' wherever this horse lugs me!

Sam Fortune swung the fifteen-foot, five-rail gate open. The horse dove through the opening like a racehorse breaking from the starting line. Frank had two hands on the rope and was skiing on the heels of his boots across the Dakota dirt.

The panicked horse galloped past the lantern and into the dark straight at the bunkhouse barn. Lanterns inside the bunkhouse lit the porch as several cowboys in various stages of dress staggered out to view the commotion.

"Whoa!" Frank ordered.

The others dove out of the way when the horse kept barreling right for the bunkhouse door.

"You got ever'thin' under control, Boss?" Howdy Tompkins hollered.

Frank lost his footing and was towed as the horse cleared the steps and lunged through the open bunkhouse door. The sudden change in movement caused Frank to be whipped around the post that held the porch. He wrapped the rope a full circle around the twelve-by-twelve post and held on.

The horse was halfway into the bunkhouse when he hit the end of the snubbed rope. The entire front porch quivered. Then the horse quit straining and backed out of the bunkhouse, down the stairs, and stood quietly by the post.

Sam Fortune trotted up as Frank struggled to his feet and the other cowboys gathered around. He handed the end of the rope to his uncle.

"Here's your horse."

"Thanks, Little Frank. That's quite a style. Don't suppose you've taught that trick to all the boys, have you?"

"Shoot, no," Howdy said. "We're lucky to get 'em to go in the barn. Ain't a one of us can coax one into the bunkhouse!"

"That's the first time this old boy has been roped and held before daylight. I must have tried it a dozen times. I reckon he's scared of the dark."

Frank rubbed his raw hands.

"Say, Boss," Howdy jibed. "How about you ropin' that copper dun for me? I'm usin' him for my day mount. You don't even need to bring him inside the bunkhouse; jist tied to the rail will be fine."

Daylight broke with a low haze to the east. Frank couldn't tell if it was ground fog or thin smoke. A diamond-hitched sorrel gelding carried the pack, and Sam Fortune rode the strutting black stallion.

He trotted up beside Frank. "I reckon I need to ride the buck out of this ol' boy. Think I'll race him up to that rise by the sage and back," Sam announced. "How are you feelin', anyway?"

Frank held his finger and thumb about two inches apart. "If I felt this much better . . . I'd be dead."

"That line rolls off your tongue with the same flare as it did your grandpa. You pack more than just his carbine, Little Frank."

"I reckon we all do, don't we?"

"A good man has impact to the third and fourth generations. But the fact remains, you are banged up pretty good for a young man."

"I've been contemplatin' findin' me an easy, high-payin' job like ownin' a telephone company."

Sam snickered. "There's a lot of hard work in the telephone business. That's why I have to hire nine good men."

"I've got about that many workin' for me, and I'm still the one who gets all the aches and pains. I reckon I'm doin' it wrong," Frank said.

"Yep, you need to hire a foreman, and move to Cheyenne and raise kids."

"You reckon I ought to get married first?"

"I think that's the only way your mama would allow it."

"There is no way for a Fortune to be an absentee rancher, Uncle Sammy."

"You're right about that, Little Frank. Now let me run this ol' boy."

"You give him a name yet?"

"He ain't earned one. Good or bad, a horse ought to earn his name," Sam said.

"What was his name when you bought him?"

"Cuddles."

"What?"

"He was raised by a little girl in Custer City, and she called him Cuddles."

Little Frank began to laugh. "I can see it now. Here comes the notorious Oklahoma gunman, Sam Fortune . . . and his horse Cuddles!"

"Enough of that."

"Why, you could ride for ol' Buffalo Bill's Wild West Show. Maybe you could braid his tail with yellow ribbons."

"You're a whole lot closer to heaven than you think."

Frank held his aching ribs as he chuckled. "Go on, ride that unnamed horse."

Sam Fortune screwed his hat down tight and punched his spurs into the horse's flanks. The big stallion leaped ten feet forward and hit the prairie with a gallop. Frank watched the trail of dust disappear over the rolling prairie.

Sam Fortune running a telephone exchange never has made sense to me. But it's the life Abby wanted. I reckon a man needs to do what makes his wife happy. And Aunt Abby loves him dearly. He always says he wouldn't trade his life now for anything. Still I wonder, what if Abby liked ranch life?

The lead rope off the packhorse tugged on his raw, gloved hand as he trudged along in the cloud of Sam's dust.

I wonder if Señorita Rodriguez likes ranch life? She must live on one of those big ol' haciendas down in Mexico. But that's a long way from here. She surely wouldn't want to be that far away from home. Still, she does find this prairie has some interesting features. Shoot, we could take a train down a couple times a year and . . .

Frank reached over and patted his horse's neck. "Carlos, I'm makin' plans with a woman who hardly knows my name. I reckon I've been out here too long. I suppose a geldin' don't have thoughts like that. But that ain't a solution I'm fond of." He started to laugh, then grabbed his ribs. *I ought to go down to Hot Springs and soak until . . . Christmas.*

In the distance he spotted Sam running the horse back toward him. *Lord, Uncle Sammy looks good on a galloping horse. So did Grandpa. I always thought I did too, but now I don't know. A man is born to the saddle, Daddy always says. And there is no one who looks better in an ol' McClellan saddle with an officer's stride than Daddy. When the cavalry lost him, they really lost out. The entire clan is out of place in that narrow little gulch called Deadwood. But there we are. Well, not me. I escaped twenty-five miles away. At least until I go broke.*

Sam reined up and spun the horse, then trotted along-side Frank.

"How's your new pony?"

"Young, quick, and sorta stupid. Reminds me of me in my younger days," Sam laughed.

"You can name him Uncle Sammy."

"It beats Cuddles, but I'll think of something one of these days. Looks like you have company over to the east."

"A paneled wagon?"

"Yep and some outriders. But it must be three, four miles over there. I can't tell. You reckon we ought to just mosey in that direction?"

"It's out of the way. I need to go north," Frank said.

"But it is on your range."

Frank pushed his hat back and continued to plod forward. "Unfenced government land is hard to patrol."

"You reckon you need to fence it?"

"Only if I own it."

"So we'll just bypass the riders over there?"

"You figure there's trouble, Uncle Sammy?"

"I figure there's a señorita with flashing brown eyes and a smile second only to Abby Fortune."

"If you put it that way," Frank said. "I suppose we could circle in that direction. I mean, if you insist."

Sam Fortune laughed. "Oh, I do. And I insist we follow this draw east. That way they won't see us comin' off the trail, and you can be more honest when you say we were merely passin' through."

"Me? I don't need to talk to her. I thought you were

the one wantin' to visit."

"Little Frank, if I were twenty years younger and unmarried, I'd wrestle you for her right here."

Frank grabbed his ribs as he laughed. "Today, you might win, Uncle Sammy . . . but let me regain my strength and you're in for a tumble."

"Now, that's better. What do you say we meander up this draw and make a surprise visit?"

"I always knew you had a lot to teach me, Uncle Sammy."

"Son . . . what I could teach you, hmmmmm. But the Lord's been gracious and dropped a lot of it plum out of my memory."

The sun perched above the eastern horizon like a yellow-orange ball. The haze filtered the light and left the air with an early fall crispness. The draw that they followed had a tiny dry creek bed at the bottom and snaked east almost level. The prairie was so flat that it was almost impossible to tell if they were going up the draw or down it.

They rode single file with Sam leading the way, then Frank, followed by the packhorse. "Did you hear that Hank is thinkin' of goin' to that law college in Denver?" Sam called back.

"Doesn't surprise me," Frank replied. "Aunt Rebekah always had high hopes for him."

"She has high hopes for every one of us, just like your grandma."

"Who do you reckon will take the store? Aunt Dacee June won't let those girls of hers get their hands dirty."

"Maybe Casey," Sam replied. "Stuart is countin' the

days until next summer when he can come back out here and work for you. For that matter, Garrett wants to come out, but I don't think Abby could survive for three days without him. When Amber got married and moved, I thought that woman would die."

"Uncle Sammy, do you ever think there are too many Fortunes in the Black Hills?"

"Little Frank, I tried goin' it without family. Let me tell you, if you have to choose, stick with the family every time. But there is no way of keeping your grandkids all around. Within ten years every one of you will be married and raisin' your own families."

"Can you imagine those twin sisters of mine raising families?"

"Only if they live next door to each other."

"In identical houses. They are already talking about when they want to have their first child. They are hoping for delivery on the same day," Frank reported.

"I don't reckon their husbands will have any say in the matter."

Sam glanced back at Frank, and both men laughed.

"I don't imagine the Coulter brothers will get a word in edgewise," Frank hooted. "There are no twins on earth like Nica and Cilla."

"Life is never dull around them."

"Mama is dreading the day they are gone. She doesn't talk about it, but she comes out of her room with red eyes a lot."

"She needs grandkids to play with, Little Frank. That will help."

"You are in a hurry to push me, aren't you?"

"You're twenty-four years old. You ain't a young man much longer."

"And where were you and what were you doin' when you were twenty-four, Sam Fortune?"

"I was sleepin' on the dirt and stealin' cows from men like you. I'm hopin' you ain't as dumb as I was."

They rode for another half-hour without saying much, then Sam drew up by a clump of sage that lined off to the north.

"I'm thinkin' this is where we should cut north."

"It ought to bring us up near the buffalo salt lick," Frank reported.

"Are there many plants around it?"

"It's thick by the springs, but nothing around the lick."

"Then I imagine the botany student will be by the springs."

When Frank reached the top of the rise, he stopped to stare across the prairie and waited for Sam to catch up.

"No one's here. Do you reckon we went too far?"

"Nope. Where's Buffalo Lick Springs?"

"Right over there beyond the brush," Frank pointed. "That's where the wagon and horses were."

"So while we were bein' coy, they rode off?"

"Sort of looks that way. Let's ride over there and pick up their trail."

"So we can follow them out into the Badlands?" Frank asked.

"Actively pursuing a purdy lady ain't a crime, son."

"I am not actively pursuing her."

"Then what are we doin'?"

"This was your idea, remember?" Frank insisted.

"Humor your ol' uncle a little longer. Let's go look at the tracks anyway."

They circled the springs a couple times, then parked by the wagon trail to the east.

"I figure six outriders and a slow, heavy wagon," Sam reported. "Doesn't look like a scuffle. Do you expect trouble?"

"No," Frank replied, then yanked his Sharps carbine out of the scabbard, checked the breech for a cartridge, and laid it across his lap.

CHAPTER THREE

HOOFBEATS have a rhythm. A tune. A song. A message.

Often they tap out the heartbeat of the rider. And Carlos sensed Frank's concern. The chestnut gelding tucked his ears and clopped an anxious cadence on the hard dirt trail.

The packhorse hesitated. The lead rope tugged at Frank's raw hand. After a couple of miles, he spotted the paneled wagon and outriders descending into the salt flats to the east. By the time Sam rode up beside him, the wagon and riders had dipped into the horizon.

"Do you think they spotted us?" Sam asked.

Frank attempted to lean one hand back on the horse's rump, but the rib pain forced him to sit up straight. "I don't reckon so; they aren't headed this way."

Sam pushed his hat back above the tan line straight across his forehead. "How do you want to play this?"

"What do you mean?" Frank glanced back across the

prairie and could not see the wagon or riders.

"Do you want me to hang back and let you handle it? I don't want to interfere. She don't need two handsome men."

"I just aim to say hello."

"You got Daddy's Sharps carbine across your lap and the hammer pulled back. You're expecting more than a hello." Sam Fortune yanked his holster out of his saddlebags and strapped it on.

"It don't look like anyone is puttin' up a fight, so I don't know what to expect."

Sam pulled a bullet from his belt and shoved it into the one open chamber of the cylinder. "That's exactly why I'll drop back. When two go against six, we need some surprise."

Frank appraised the trail. "Maybe you should take the packhorse."

"Nope. You need him. That way you just look like you're passing through."

Frank pulled his Colt single-action revolver from his saddlebag and shoved it in his belt. "We surely are expecting the worse. I hope we're not embarrassed by all these weapons."

"Go on. And smile at the señorita."

"What if there's no trouble?" Frank asked. "What's my excuse for trailin' her down?"

"Tell her, eh, you wanted to invite her to a cookout at the ranch." Sam pulled his .38-55 half-magazine Winchester 1894 from the scabbard.

"What cookout?"

Sam checked the lever on the carbine, then lowered

the hammer to the safety position. I don't know, Little Frank. Shoot, with any luck we'll get in a gunfight, and you won't have to tell her anything."

By the time Frank rode twenty feet, the hammer of the pistol was jabbing his ribs. He shoved the revolver back into his saddlebags. When he rode over the rise, Sam disappeared into the eastern flanks of Salt Canyon. The treeless prairie offered no cover. When the distant wagon came into view, two of the outriders turned and rode toward him. Frank kept the plodding pace, but Carlos danced sideways like a dressage horse in front of royalty.

The two men blocked the trail, but Frank kept the horses trudging toward them. He tipped his hat with his left hand but kept his right on the receiver of the Sharps carbine, his finger on the trigger.

"Mornin'," he called out and kept riding.

A man with all the buttons busted out of his vest spat a wad of tobacco on the trail. "By the looks of that shiner on your head, you had a mighty fine time last night."

"I sorta got roped into it," Frank said and kept riding. "Where are you all headed? Maybe I'll just ride along."

"We can't have company," the other man announced. A short-barreled, large-caliber Winchester 1892 carbine lay in his lap. "We're on our way to Ft. Pierre with some prisoners."

Frank split the two and kept riding toward the wagon. "Are you two lawmen?"

They turned and rode close to Frank on each side.

"More like bounty hunters," the buttonless vested

man reported.

Frank studied the back of the wagon that rolled east about a hundred yards ahead of them. "You workin' for Major Thomasville?"

"Nope, but if he gets in our way, we'll haul him in too." The thinner man cut across ahead of him. "Now, you'll have to stop and take a different trail."

Frank spurred Carlos. The stout chestnut gelding bulled his way past the other horse. "Why do you want Thomasville?"

"For rustling beef, just like these Mexicans," buttonless vest said. "Ever'body up here on this range is stealin' beef."

"You got dangerous rustlers in the wagon?"

Buttonless glanced at the thin man, then back to Frank Fortune. "We caught 'em with fresh butchered meat."

The thin cowboy rested his hand against the grip of his revolver. "I said, you have to turn around."

"This is Rafter F land. Do you boys work for the Rafter F?"

"Nope. This is railroad land," buttonless vest said.

"Railroad land starts five miles north of here, just north of the stone cabin at Buffalo Gap."

"That don't matter," thin reported. "They're rustlers, and we done captured them. Where are you headed, mister?"

"To the stone cabin at Buffalo Gap."

"Swing a wide swath to the west then," buttonless insisted.

"No, I think I'll stay on the trail. Some spots are too sandy out there."

"Mister, maybe you don't understand." Buttonless reached to grab Carlos's headstall, but Frank pointed the carbine at the man's ample midsection.

"Careful with the Sharps," the man mumbled.

"Don't grab my horse."

Both men trotted ahead and blocked his trail once again. This time their guns pointed at him. "Mister, don't press our hand. You don't want to die today, do you?"

"I'll have to think about that. Who's your boss?"

"I am," the big man boasted.

"Sure, and I'm Stuart Brannon," Frank countered.

"You ain't Brannon. He's dead," buttonless added.

"He's alive, and you aren't the boss. I need to talk to the boss."

"He ain't goin' to talk to you."

Frank pointed the carbine straight in the air and pulled the trigger. The .50 caliber blast echoed like a cannon.

Both men threw their rifles to their shoulders and pointed them at Frank Fortune.

"What did you do that for?" buttonless shouted.

"I need to talk to your boss."

"Throw down that single shot."

"I don't think I'll do that."

"Then we'll have to shoot you."

"Even before the boss gets here?"

"I told you, he ain't talkin' to you."

"Is he ridin' that red roan?"

Both men glanced over their shoulders toward the wagon that was now stopped, only thirty yards ahead of them. Frank slipped another cartridge into the carbine.

"He is the boss, isn't he?"

Neither man lowered their guns, but they waited for a gray-haired man on a red roan to approach. "You boys havin' trouble back here?" he shouted.

"This hombre won't turn back," buttonless reported.

The man wore a soiled wool suit and tie, with a flat-brimmed straw hat. His eyes twitched when he spoke. "Son, we can't have you ridin' along. We have dangerous prisoners."

Frank rode straight toward the man. "You a U.S. marshal?"

"Pinkerton," he replied. "Contracted out to the railroad."

"This is private land," Frank said.

The man slid out a watch from his vest pocket and checked it as if waiting for a train. "This is railroad land."

"Don't give me that." Both horses now stood head-to-head. "These two old boys couldn't find a corncob in a dark outhouse, but you know better. You crossed into Rafter F when you left the Belle Fouche drainage at Buffalo Gap."

"I was pursuing rustlers." Straw hat jammed his watch back into his pocket.

"You weren't pursuing those three. Their wagon trail leads back toward the Black Hills."

"Them three is part of the gang," buttonless grumped.

Frank kept his eyes on the man with the straw hat. "Did you get permission from the Rafter F?"

"We haven't seen anyone to ask."

"What about the two riding the line up at Buffalo

Gap?" Frank asked.

"Wasn't anyone there when we came across the line at daybreak."

"So, you did know you were on Rafter F land?"

"I surmised that. But I also figured they had nothin' to hide and wouldn't mind some help corralin' rustlers."

"They mind," Frank replied.

"You work for the Rafter F? Why don't you ride and get your boss and bring him out here and let me talk to him?"

"It's a two-hour ride back. I'm sure you boys will be sittin' here playin' whist for hours and waitin' for me to return. Besides, you don't want to see the boss. He doesn't appreciate you harrassin' his guests."

The man glanced back toward the wagon. "Guests?"

"Two women and an old man. Hardly dangerous, are they?"

The man whipped back around. "You know them?"

"I gave them a Rafter F beef last night," Frank reported.

"They have a beef alright, but the brand was cut out of the hide. Only rustlers do that. We're takin' this bunch with us."

Frank stood in the stirrups and pointed the carbine at the man in the suit and tie. "And I said this if Rafter F land. Turn them loose."

"Whoa, son . . . relax."

"Don't worry, Boss," the vested one said as he kept his gun trained on Frank Fortune. "He already fired that single shot. He's bluffin' now."

He surveyed the big man, head to toe, then glanced

back at Frank. "It's not like the old days. Used to be I could hire men who were gun savvy. Now I'm lucky to find one that knows the right end to point a pistol."

"What are you talkin' about, Boss?"

"He had all the time in the world to shove in a cartridge when you two looked back here at me."

"We didn't see him load up," the thin man insisted.

"What?" Buttonless looked startled.

"I want to talk with this man alone. Bullard, you take Wesley and go back with the others."

"You goin' to be alright, Boss?"

The man with suit and tie looked at Frank Fortune. "Are you goin' to shoot me?"

"Not unless you provoke it."

"See there," the man replied. "I'm safe. Now get out of here."

The gunmen trotted ahead to the still-rolling wagon.

Frank sat down in the saddle and draped the carbine across his lap.

"You surely look familiar, son. Have we met?"

"Who are you?"

"Reid LeMay. And you?"

"Frank Fortune."

"Rafter F? That's it, this is Fortune's ranch. Never stopped to figure the brand before. You're Sam Fortune's boy. You look just like him. I knew ol' Sam down in the territory."

Frank surveyed the prairie to the east. "Sam's my uncle."

LeMay seemed to be studying his eyes. "Is this Sam's ranch?"

"No."

"Is he still alive?"

"Yep."

"That's amazing. I've never known a man in my life that more people took shots at than Sam Fortune. I haven't seen him in fifteen years. Where's he livin' now?"

"Deadwood." Frank continued to plod along toward the parked wagon.

Reid LeMay tugged his tie loose from the dusty, yellowed collar of his white shirt and rode alongside him. "Son, whose ranch is this anyway?"

"It's mine."

LeMay glanced across the prairie but kept his hand resting on the walnut grip of his holstered revolver. "No fooling? You run the place? Most young men with a lot of cows are good with a running iron."

"What are you insinuatin'?" Frank felt his finger tighten around the cold steel of the Sharps trigger.

"What I'm saying goes for other men. Your name is Fortune. One thing I learned in life: Don't underestimate the tenacity of a man named Fortune. I believe you, son. I'm sure you know that there's been a lot of rustling going on around here. It's increased in the past couple of weeks."

"Yeah, I've been losin' more than a few."

"The railroad's herd up north has been losing too many. We think maybe some Thomasville hands have been raiding some of them, but right now I'm looking for a Mexican gang. At least, a couple are Mexicans. Maybe some bronco Indians with them. I trailed them down this way."

"I haven't seen them."

They rode up on the five cowboys who surrounded the now parked wagon. Frank noticed the señorita and the old man and woman were in the front seat of the wagon. None of them looked at him.

He rode straight up to the five men. "That don't look like a rustlin' crew to me."

Wesley replied, "They were eatin' butchered beef."

Frank let the lead line on the packhorse drop to the dirt. "Did you ask them where they got it?"

"They don't speak English," Bullard huffed.

"They might have been hungry, but you can't believe those three are dangerous rustlers."

The big man rode next to Frank Fortune and waved his finger. "Them are just bait. Them ol' two is the camp tender and cook. And the señorita is either the ring-leader's girlfriend, or you know, just a workin' girl for the whole gang." He raised his eyebrows. "Either way, the others will come back sooner or later."

Frank pointed the Sharps at the big man's midsection that looped over the saddlehorn. "Dearyanna, this man has just insulted your virtue. Would you like for me to kill him?"

She brushed her long black hair over her shoulder. "Do you plan to bury him, or just leave his bones for the wolves and coyotes?"

Reid LeMay trotted up beside him. "She can speak English?"

Frank never took his eyes off the big man with the buttonless vest. "I was plannin' on gut shootin' him and just leavin' him on the prairie to die slow."

A slight smile revealed her white teeth. "Then, by all means, shoot him, Señor Francisco. I just do not want you to have to dig a huge grave."

The big man shot an anxious glance at his compatriots. "He ain't got a bullet in that gun."

"Apologize to the lady," Frank insisted.

"I ain't apologizin' to no Mexican rustlers." Bullard reached for his revolver.

Frank watched his eyes. *I'm goin' to have to shoot this man. Lord, Lord . . . he really is that dumb.*

"Back off, Bullard!" LeMay shouted.

"No, sir, I ain't!" the big man screamed. "I don't back down for no kid."

LeMay yanked his revolver and fired a shot into the ground in front of Bullard's horse. The horse reared and the big man tumbled to the ground.

He scrambled to grab his gun and hat. The rest of the gang had revolvers drawn.

"Why in hades did you do that?" Bullard screamed.

"To save your life, Bullard. This is Frank Fortune. Fortunes don't bluff," LeMay announced.

"I ain't never heard of Fortunes."

"You one of them Fortunes over at Deadwood?" Wesley probed.

"That's my family."

"I was in the Piedmont when your daddy flattened Cigar Dubois."

"That was my Uncle Todd."

"Who was the old man with him? He was a mean bobcat if I ever saw one."

"That would be my Grandpa Brazos."

"Apologize to the lady," LeMay insisted.

Bullard retrieved his horse. "I reckon I might've made a mistake, ma'am," he mumbled, then turned to LeMay and pointed his finger. "I only did that for you, 'cause I surely ain't afraid of a man without a bullet in his gun."

Frank rode closer to the wagon and tipped his hat to the women. "Señorita Rodriguez, are you and the others alright?"

Her brown eyes flashed. It was, for a split second, as if there was no one else on the prairie.

Frank felt his heart beat in his throat. *Oh . . . my . . . maybe Uncle Sammy was right.*

"Yes, we are fine. I believe that man has our hunting rifle."

Fortune waved the Sharps at Bullard.

The big man glanced at LeMay, then hiked over and handed the Winchester 1886 up to her.

"But I'm rather disappointed you showed up, Mr. Francisco Fortune," she said.

"Why?"

"It was rather exciting to be captured by armed men and to be treated like a common cattle rustler." A strand of her coal-black hair drooped down over her eye. "I didn't think this sort of thing happened any more." She brushed the hair behind her ear. "Do they work for Mr. Thomasville?"

"No, they work for the railroad. Do you know Thomasville?"

"Oh, yes," the señorita replied.

"I was not disappointed you arrived, Señor Fortune,

nor was Miguel," the old lady murmured.

"Thank you, ma'am," Frank tipped his hat at the older man and lady, then turned to Dearyanna. "How did I disappoint you?"

"I was already composing my book."

"Are you serious about being disappointed?" Frank asked.

"About missing the adventure? Yes. About the book, probably not. I don't have anything to write about. We were not in danger. Mr. LeMay saw to that."

"But they were going to haul you off to jail."

"Now, that would be something to write about," she smiled.

"What are you saying, that you want me to ride off and leave you with these bounty hunters?"

"Not now; my identity is ruined."

LeMay rode up beside him. "Señorita, is what Fortune said here true?"

She raised her eyebrows. "That depends on what he told you. You do know how cowboys lie about women."

"He said that was his beef you butchered and he gave it to you last night."

She clutched the Winchester 1886 rifle across her lap. "Yes, that part is true. He also thought I was a rustler at first. I wonder what looks so despicable about me? It must be my hardened glare." She squeezed her face into a frown.

LeMay scratched his gray hair. "I reckon you were just at the wrong place at the wrong time, ma'am. Some of the ranches north of here have been losin' cattle real regular, and me and the boys have been hired to stop it."

"So you capture everyone you find?" she asked.

"Only those with fresh beef on an unbranded hide."

"That steer had a brand last night," Frank said.

"I had no use for the branded portion," she reported.

LeMay jammed his hat back on. "Señorita, if you are eating fresh beef on the range, you should always carry the branded hide."

"He's right," Fortune added.

She folded her hands on her lap across the rifle. "What other rules should I remember?"

"Admit you speak English," LeMay said.

"When surrounded by six men with guns, I will use whatever defense I feel necessary."

He nodded. "I can't fault you there, señorita."

"We ain't ridin' off without the Mexicans, are we? That's money in the bank. There's a reward for ever' rustler we turn in," Bullard huffed.

"He's too young to own this place, anyway," one of the other men added.

"He ain't too young to rustle," another called out.

"Let's haul him in, too. Let's haul 'em all in!" Wesley shouted.

"I heard Howdy Tompkins say he worked for ol' man Fortune at the Rafter F. How do we know this is his place?"

"The boys have some legitimate concerns," LeMay probed.

"I don't reckon I have to prove anything on my own land. How do I know you are a Pinkerton man?"

LeMay began to laugh. "Here we are sitting out in the middle of the Dakota prairie fifty miles from town, prowlin' around for position. I think, boys, it's time to ride on."

"I don't ride off from a man with an empty single-shot," Bullard blustered.

To the east, Sam Fortune's black horse trotted toward them. "Who's horse is that?" Bullard asked.

Frank whistled between his teeth.

The horse trotted over to him.

"That's Cuddles," Frank said.

"Cuddles?" Dearyanna chuckled.

"The horse belongs to my Uncle, Sam Fortune. He must have taken position on the prairie. I was just wonderin' which one of you he has his gunsights on."

All the riders except LeMay pointed their guns east.

"If Sam Fortune is out there, it's a cinch he's not where you are lookin'," LeMay declared. He stood in the stirrups, then hollered. "Sam! Sam Fortune, it's me . . . Reid LeMay!"

Bullard spit a wad of tobacco on the dirt, then wiped his mouth on his sleeve. "You never told us that you knew Sam Fortune."

"Tell your uncle I said howdy." LeMay rode closer to Frank and lowered his voice. "Tell him that Ladosa buried Piney last spring up on the Cimmaron. He'll want to know."

Frank nodded. "I'll tell him."

"Come on, boys, it's time to ride north," LeMay called out.

"Sounds like a coward's way out," Bullard fumed.

LeMay bristled. "Now that is a subject I'm not too familiar with, but I reckon you are the expert on bein' a coward. I said we're leavin'. I'll bet you Frank Fortune has a bullet in the chamber. And I'll bet Sam Fortune is out there on the prairie hopin' we'll start somethin' so he can finish it. No one in the Indian Nation could finish a gunfight like Sam Fortune. Besides, you've overlooked the fact that Señorita Rodriguez has a rifle on her lap."

She checked the lever of the short rifle.

LeMay swept his hat in front of him. "Señorita, which one of these boys would you shoot first with that .45-70?"

"El Gordo gringo."

LeMay looked back. "That's you, Bullard."

"I ain't afraid of no Mexican." He pulled off his hat and waved it at Frank Fortune. "And I especially ain't afraid of him! He ain't got no bullet in the chamber."

The sound of the .50 caliber Sharps was a deep whomp, with cannonesque qualities.

Pain shot down Frank's ribs from the recoil.

A round hole the size of a dollar appeared in Bullard's hat.

His horse bolted north on a dead run, the rider grasping the saddle horn with both hands.

Frank had another bullet chambered before the others glanced back at him.

"I reckon that answers that question." LeMay tipped his hat. "Fortune, I aim to see this rustlin' stop."

"That's good, LeMay. I'm thinkin' the same thing. Just check in with the headquarters next time you start lookin' on the Rafter F. I'll send a crew with you. I'm meetin' with Thomasville next Wednesday to discuss the same thing," Frank reported. "You're invited, but you'll have to leave the boys at home. I don't aim for trouble."

"Where are you meeting him? In Deadwood?"

"Nope. At my headquarters on Butte Creek."

"I'll take you up on that." LeMay turned and shouted to the others. "Let's go turn Bullard before he reaches Canada."

He and the others cantered after the breakaway horse single file.

Frank shoved the carbine into the scabbard and stepped down out of the saddle.

"Is your uncle really out there with a gun?" the señorita asked.

He retrieved the reins of the black horse from the dirt, then gathered the reins of the sorrel packhorse. "I reckon so. This is his horse."

"And the horse's name really is Abrazos?"

"Yes, ma'am, if that means cuddles. Señorita, I don't want to ruin your research trip. But with cattle rustlin' goin' on out here lately, I'm not sure this is the safest place for you folks to be. You go out east of here, and it's so remote nobody reputable goes in there."

"Señor Fortune, do you have any idea how boring life can be when your madre sends two spies with you wherever you go?" She looked at her servants. "Latina and Miguel are very loving and pleasant spies."

"Are you doing research or just trying to get in trouble?"

The older woman began to laugh.

Señorita Rodriguez scolded her. "Now, don't you tell on me."

"The truth is, Señorita Rodriguez, the only ones that ride into the country east of here are men hopin' that no one pursues them. I would never let my sisters or mother ride out there. Not now, not ever."

"And which do you regard me, Francisco Fortune? As a sister or a mother?"

Frank chewed on his lip.

"Oh, look, Latina . . . I believe he is blushing."

"Pay no attention to her, Señor Fortune," Latina added. "She has always been this way. She is very spoiled."

"You see? They are spies!"

Frank stared at her long black eyelashes, then turned his head. "Señorita, I'm not exaggerating about the Badlands."

"That sounds like something from the old west. I understood that the frontier is settled and peaceable now."

"Where did you hear that?"

"I read it in a San Francisco newspaper."

Frank continued to survey the eastern horizon. *Uncle Sammy, are you out there laughin' at me?* "Señorita, when you pull the plug on the bathtub, all the dirty water races right for that one little hole before it disappears forever into the cesspool."

"Are you saying those Badlands are the drain hole of the west?"

"I reckon this part anyway. It seems to pull the worst from other areas."

"Then why did you choose to ranch out here?" she asked.

"Because no one else wanted to."

"Why is your uncle waiting to come in?"

"He's probably just givin' me more time."

"More time for what, Frank Fortune?"

"Eh, more time to miss him, I surmise."

The older lady nudged Dearyanna. "I think Señor Fortune is right. We should not keep going east."

"You see, now you have scared Latina and Miguel."

"There are several interesting hot springs on the ranch that produce an abundance of grasses and weeds. Perhaps you would like to study them instead," Frank offered.

"What are you saying, Frank Fortune?" she challenged. "That you would like for us to stay at your headquarters for a few weeks and take day trips from there?"

"Eh, well . . . I never . . . I guess." *Is that what I am saying?* "That would be one possibility."

"What do you think Latina? Miguel?"

"I think it would be better to stay with Mr. Fortune than fall into a cesspool," Latina reported.

"We have beef we can provide," Miguel added with a sly grin.

"Are you going to the headquarters now?" Dearyanna asked. "We could follow you."

"No, we are headed to Buffalo Gap. I've got supplies for the boys."

"Where is that?"

"About five miles north and west of here."

"If the headquarters is west and the gap is west, whatever possessed you to ride way over here to the east?" she asked.

"It was my uncle's idea."

"Yes, I see. You had nothing to do with it. Please tell him it was a very good idea. I do hope he is OK."

"To tell you the gospel, ma'am, he thought I was too bashful, and he wanted to force me to talk to you." Frank stared down at the saddle horn. *I can't believe I said that.* "I used to be shy when I was younger, and the family still thinks of me that way."

"Yes, I know how that is."

"You do?"

"I was a very skinny young girl, and my abuela still tries to fatten me up every time I go to her hacienda."

"No parts of you are skinny now."

"Thank you very much," she snapped.

"No, I meant . . . you are . . . you have . . . you look . . . you don't . . . ."

"Now, I can see the problem your uncle mentioned. Yes, you are shy."

"I spend a lot of time by myself, I reckon," Frank said.

"Since you need to go northwest and we southwest, perhaps we should get started. We will check out some of those hot springs of yours on the way to the head-quarters."

"Ride toward the hills and on the third ravine from here, follow it southeast for about three miles and you'll find July Springs. That might be a good spot."

She pulled off her black straw hat and laid it in her lap. "Perhaps we'll camp there."

"Then drive from July Springs toward Black Bear Butte, and you'll find a wagon trail at the base of some white limestone cliffs. Take that west and you will find the headquarters."

"Thank you very much. When will you be back at the headquarters?" she asked.

Frank pulled himself into the saddle and could feel his side cramp. "By tomorrow night, late."

She fanned herself with her hat. "We will spend a night at your springs. Perhaps we will arrive at the head-quarters at the same time."

He stared into her dark brown eyes. "Maybe so. If you get there first, tell Americus that I said to put you up in the big house." He raised his hand to the back of his neck and felt the sharp, searing pain in his elbow.

"When we get to your place, we will stay in the wagon. We have it furnished for overnight use."

Frank thought he caught a whiff of sage bloom, but there were none within sight. "My mother and father would never forgive me if I didn't have you stay in the house."

"Then I will not be the cause of family disunity. I will stay in the house. And Mr. Frank Fortune, I teased you a lot, but all three of us were glad you came and took care of the matter with Mr. LeMay. Thank you very much." She held out her deerhide-gloved hand.

Frank rode Carlos to the edge of the wagon and leaned across to shake her hand. When he did, he cracked his injured elbow into the iron railing of the wagon seat and jerked his hand back and yelped.

"Oh, dear," she said. When she sat back, her black straw hat tumbled off her lap. A gust of wind rolled it in the dirt in front of Carlos.

Frank held his elbow and bit his lip. "Sorry, señorita,

I injured that sucker yesterday and forgot how raw it is."

"I'm sorry to cause you pain."

The old man started to climb down out of the wagon.

"That's alright, Miguel," Frank called. "I'll fetch the hat."

Frank scooted Carlos to the left of the black straw hat. *If I wasn't so sore, I'd get down and hand it to her.* He kicked his left foot free from the stirrup, clutched the saddle horn, and reached down to retrieve the hat.

The huge hammer on the Sharps carbine slammed into his rib cage. He released his grip on the saddle horn to hold his aching side. When he did this, Frank tumbled off the saddle and landed on his back on the hard Dakota dirt.

A flash of blue and purple stars lit up the inside of his head. Stretched out among horse hooves, he gasped for breath. Miguel jumped from the wagon and ran around to him.

Still lying on his back, Frank handed the black straw hat up to him. "Here's her hat," he groaned. "Now, go on."

"Are you alright, Mr. Fortune?" she called out.

"Just my ribs."

"Did you injure them yesterday too?"

"Yep."

"Let Miguel help you to your feet," she insisted.

"Please go on, Señorita Rodriguez," Frank gasped. "If you stay any longer, I'll be dead."

"We can't drive off and leave you like this."

"Do it as a favor to my parents."

"This is absurd. We can't go off and leave you injured."

"Señorita, the only thing seriously damaged is my pride, and the sooner you are not staring at me the better I will feel."

"You are serious, aren't you?"

"Yes, ma'am, go on."

"I have never driven off and left a man lying on the ground before. At least, not a friend."

"I'd rather you were gone when Uncle Sam comes up."

"Yes, well . . . alright. I will see you tomorrow night at the headquarters, then."

"If I recover enough, I reckon we could go one more round. But after that, I'm not sure."

"You make it sound like a prize fight."

"Compared to how I feel, Miss Rodriguez, a prize fight would be a waltz."

Frank Fortune sat up and watched the paneled wagon drive to the southwest. He struggled to his feet and gathered the three horses when the señorita's wagon rolled over the rise in the prairie and disappeared from view.

He yanked the cinch tight on the chestnut gelding and could feel a sharp pain in his ribs. "I reckon I impressed her, Carlos. The first day I show up in ripped clothes. The second day I fall off my horse. If that don't turn her head, nothin' will. Maybe next time I can set myself on fire."

Frank rubbed his tender elbow and pulled himself up into the saddle. *And to think I invited her to stay at the* headquarters. *How did that happen? I don't remember invitating her. It just sort of transpired.*

"Well, Mr. Cuddles, let's go find that old man. He must be rollin' on the prairie, dyin' of laughter."

He rode straight east, then paused on the rise. Frank surveyed the prairie as far as the point where the brown grass turned to white dust and clay.

"Uncle Sammy, you can come out now. The shame is over!"

Somewhere to the north a hawk screeched, but he couldn't see a bird in the air. Leading the other two horses, he rode further east.

"Sam!" he hollered.

This is crazy. Sam Fortune doesn't just disappear. This is a strange day. Frank stood in the stirrups and scoped the grassland to the north. *I'm on my way to Buffalo Gap and find myself saving a señorita who didn't want to get rescued. Now I'm lookin' for a lost uncle who can't be lost. If I didn't hurt so bad, I reckon I'd think I was dreamin'.*

"Sam!"

I don't have any idea if he's north, south, east, or west of here. I don't think he's west. Nor probably south. East or north?

If I fire a signal, no tellin' who would come give chase. How far can a man wander on foot and why? Lord, my day is wastin' away. I know you had better things for me to do than ramble around out here. So, if you could just help me find . . .

A gray-haired man appeared down a steep gulch to the east waving his hat.

Never mind, Lord. I found him.

"Did you get lost, old man?" Frank hollered.

"Lost? I was just checkin' things out for you."

"That's the first time I ever heard that excuse."

"You didn't need me to help you up at the wagon. I just waited around until you spied out the situation."

"Are you telling me you're down in this ravine on purpose?"

"Is that your spring down there?"

"Sweetwater Spring," Frank replied.

"You better change the name."

"Why?"

"I'll show you." Sam Fortune pulled himself up on the black stallion. "Did my horse come help you out?"

The two men worked their way down through the brush.

"Are you sayin' that you sent Cuddles to help me on purpose?"

Sam's drooping gray mustache made his face seem like a permanent scowl. "Yep."

"You mean you didn't see what happened after your horse came trottin' in?"

"No, but I heard a pistol and the Sharps fire a second time. When there was no more shooting, I surmised you were in control or dead. Did you have to lead one down?"

"No, but I put some fear in him. They were bounty hunters."

Sam meandered along the path among the brown clump grass. "Who were they chasing?"

"They decided Señorita Rodriguez and her helpers

were part of a Mexican cattle rustlin' gang."

"The señorita? They don't sound too bright."

"One of them's bright enough. He was hired by the railroad to stop the rustling. He's a buddy of yours from the territory."

Sam Fortune reined up, "Who?"

"Calls himself Reid LeMay."

Sam immediately pulled his revolver from his holster.

"He claimed to be a friend."

"Him and Kiowa Fox were two of my closest friends."

"Why did you pull your gun at the mention of his name?"

"I thought Reid LeMay was dead. I put flowers on his grave in Silver City."

"Big droopin' gray mustache, short, suit-and-tie man, with straw hat."

"That's him. Where did he go?"

"He's workin' for Pinkerton, contracted to the railroad. They headed north."

"Are you sure it's my pal LeMay?" Sam asked.

"He said, 'Tell Sam that Ladosa buried Piney up on the Cimmeron last spring.'"

Sam Fortune pulled off his hat and wiped the corner of his eyes.

"Was she a looker, Uncle Sammy?"

"No, they were both plain. Ladosa's about the shortest woman I ever danced with. Piney was a happy gal who got beat up so bad by some men that she couldn't remember her name or where she lived. Ladosa took her in and cared for her for about fifteen years now. There's a big ol' house in heaven for gals like that."

"LeMay said you'd want to know."

Sam nodded his head. "Yep, that was Reid. We'll have to catch up with him later. First, you need to see somethin'."

Frank surveyed the gulch but saw nothing but brush. "What?"

"Take a whiff. What do you smell?" Sam said.

"A dead cow?"

"Six dead cows."

"Six?"

"All sportin' a Rafter F brand."

"Are they shot? Butchered?"

"Poisoned or diseased," Sam replied.

"But Sweetwater Springs is good water. I drink out of there all the time." When Frank's shoulders tensed, his sides ached. *This ranch is runnin' on thin margins already. Lord, this can't be why you led me out here.*

"I'd recommend you don't drink from it anymore."

The two men rode down the draw. Frank had the packhorse behind. The stench got so bad that both covered their noses and mouths with their bandannas. The horses tried to balk and were only persuaded forward by the point of a spur.

"It was always good water," Frank repeated.

"You think someone poisoned the spring?" Sam said.

"Why on earth? That don't make sense. Stealin' cows can bring you an income. Poisonin' them gets you nothin'."

Frank Fortune examined the bloated corpses of the six animals as he rode between them. Carlos strained at the reins, dancing away from each dead cow. "I reckon I'll keep this spring off-limits."

Sam peered over his bandanna. "Sorry to bring bad news, Little Frank."

"That's the cattle business, Uncle Sammy. Always one thing or another. Some days are plain discouragin'."

"Have you seen enough? The stench is bad."

Frank nodded, and they galloped straight north into a breeze.

"It hasn't been exactly a good day," he mumbled.

Sam Fortune reined up and yanked off his bandanna. He stood in the stirrups and shoved the handkerchief into his back pocket. "You mean it didn't go well with the señorita?"

Frank untied his bandanna and wiped his face. "I don't want to talk about it."

"Did you ever notice how many things there are that you don't want to talk about?" Sam rubbed his neck and shoulder, then spurred Cuddles, and they continued up the draw.

When they reached the top, they caught a west wind and paused to study the prairie. Frank glanced back down at the distant springs.

"That won't make it better," Frank muttered.

Sam glanced back. "Coyotes? I can't figure why they've left those cows until they bloat up bad. I guess they won't eat poisoned meat."

"They are drinkin' from the springs. Now there will be dead coyotes too," Frank offered.

"I read there is a place in Chicago you can send water samples to, and they can tell you what kind of water you got. Costs a bit, I suppose," Sam reported.

"This is government land. They should check into it. Except the only land agent is in an office in Ft. Pierre. I hate to lose that spring. This time of the year, it's the only water on the eastern border of the place."

"You better get some boys out here to fence the trail down there."

"I better find the two that are supposed to be ridin' the north gap. LeMay said they weren't on patrol or at the cabin."

"Herdin' an unfenced border is a boring job, Little Frank."

"The cattle business is a borin' job, Uncle Sammy. That's why I'm out here. I like borin'."

They trotted the horses across the brown grass prairie.

"You mean to tell me you found the señorita boring?" Sam jibed.

"You goin' to keep trollin' until you fish that out of me?"

"That's my duty."

"To who?"

"To the entire Fortune family. They sent me out here to check up on you and the señorita," Sam roared.

"I thought you just came out for my fine companionship."

"Whatever gave you that idea?" Sam said. "So now you have to tell me about you and la bonita señorita. Are we goin' to run into her again up here?"

"No, she went southwest."

Sam led the way and didn't look back when he talked. "Back to Deadwood?"

"She went to the ranch headquarters."

"Oh?"

"I figured it was provin' not to be all that safe out here, and she sort of . . . invited herself to the ranch."

"She did? You mean, she's goin' to stay with you for a while?"

"She ain't exactly stayin' with me. She's stayin' at the headquarters."

"In the big house?"

"I didn't think Mama would think it hospitable if I made 'em sleep in the barn," Frank murmured.

"Ain't that nice. Little Frank doin' all that just for his mama. So you have a beautiful señorita staying with you. It's a good thing I came out here. You'll need a chaperon."

"A chaperon? What for? She has two servants, and there's a dozen cowboys at the ranch. Besides that, she don't have too good an impression of me."

"Let's see, your clothes weren't ripped. What did you do this time?" Sam hooted.

"Here's the thing I can't figure. I rode into a hostile situation with six armed men, and me and Cuddles there dispatched them with a few words."

"And a couple of bullets."

"OK, with two bullets, but no injuries. Now that ain't bad. It's not too big a deal in the Fortune family. Aunt Dacee June can do that much with a glare. But for most folks, that's a fairly successful mornin'."

Sam searched the distant prairie as he plodded north. "I have a feelin' there's more to the story."

"Then, all I have to do is be pleasant with a fetchin'

señorita, and I fall flat on my backside."

Sam turned Cuddles around so they were face-to-face. "What did you say this time?"

"What do you mean?"

"You said you fell flat. Did you say something wrong? Make a social mistake? Boy, I need to know more than that."

"I didn't say I fell flat. I said I fell on my backside."

"You fell?" Sam hooted. "You actually tripped over a rock and fell?"

"Actually, see, my ribs were hurt, and I reached over to retrieve her hat and fell out of the saddle."

"You fell out of the saddle?" Sam laughed. "I can't believe I missed seein' that!"

"That was after I cracked my bad elbow on the iron rail of the wagon while I was tryin' to shake her hand."

Sam leaned across the saddle horn. Laughter rolled out so deep he waved his hand. "No . . . no . . . wait . . . I don't think I can take any more."

"I was hopin' for a little more understandin' from you," Frank grumbled.

Sam sat up, folded his arms, and took deep breaths. "OK . . . I ain't goin' to laugh any more."

"Good. I figure I'm safe until I get back home."

"Maybe you should stay up north and ride the gap yourself," Sam chided.

"I've been seriously considerin' it. If it wasn't for that meetin' on Wednesday night with Thomasville and LeMay."

"Reid will be there?"

"Yep."

"Now I have to stay for sure. I'd like to visit with him about Piney and Ladosa." Sam reached over to Frank. "Give me that lead rope. I'll take the packhorse for a while."

"I can do it."

"You look like your ribs are botherin' you."

"I been hurt worse than this," Frank muttered.

Sam leaned over and jerked the lead lines from Frank Fortune's hand. "Sometime's it's frightenin'."

"What?"

"You not only look like me. You sound just like me."

CHAPTER FOUR

THE LINE CABIN at Buffalo Gap was a nine-by-fourteen-foot stone building with no windows, but the shake roof was new. The heavy wooden door had been sawed in half to make a dutch door. A stone chimney rose above the roofline. A stone corral joined the cabin with a stone shed about half the size of the cabin.

The cabin and corrals appeared empty.

"Maybe your boys are out workin'," Sam suggested as they rode into the bare dirt yard.

Frank stood in the stirrups to survey the landscape. Scattered white clouds drifted across the Dakota blue sky. "Could be, but they normally take shifts. That leaves someone here to act as sentinel and watch the horses."

Sam scratched his back with the front sight of his .38-55 rifle. "If there was trouble, it might take both of them."

"There's plenty of reason to tackle a job together. But the back-up horses are gone. No matter what the situation, two men only need two horses." Frank thought he caught the whiff of ashes. "I don't think that fireplace has been dead all that long."

Sam rode over and studied the dirt in front of the open corral gate. "I reckon they could have needed relay horses."

Frank slid down out of the saddle and tied off Carlos to a post about five feet in front of the porchless front door. "The ranch just isn't that big. Relay to where?"

"So what's your take on the layout?" Sam rode to the front of the stone cabin.

Frank pulled off his hat and fingered the knot on his scraped forehead. "If that railroad posse rounded up my spare horses, the boys might have gone after them."

Sam shoved his half-octagon-barrelled rifle back into the leather scabbard. "That don't sound like something Reid LeMay would permit. Not these days, anyway. Maybe they got tired of the job and just rode off."

"Three of those ponies are mine."

"Some of 'em rationalize that as back pay. What do you know about these two ol' boys?"

"Both have been with me about a year. I fed 'em through the winter and kept 'em on all summer. I think they'd stick with me. I try to rotate them every couple of weeks. If it was winter, I'd say cabin fever had somethin' to do with it." Frank led the sorrel packhorse up to the door of the cabin. "I'll unpack this ol' boy. One way or another, these supplies are needed here."

Within minutes Sam circled back to the cabin. "What's it look like inside?"

Frank leaned across the closed bottom half of the dutch door. "Like someone rode off with coffee still boilin' on the fire. He was in a hurry. But it was after breakfast. They cooked eggs in the skillet."

"Maybe they walked off, instead of rode off," Sam suggested.

Frank swung open the bottom of the door and strolled out to the dirt yard. "What do you mean?"

"There's three sets of hoofprints leading to the east." Sam pointed his hat in that direction. "And one man walkin'."

"Going after the horses?"

"Could be. But there's a fourth set of hoofprints in the footprints."

"One is walkin' ahead of the horses?" Frank asked.

"Yep. Or both of them. The tracks are mixed. Maybe he's leadin' the horses. He's wearin' boots."

"There's no water that direction." Frank hiked to the edge of the house and stared east. "It doesn't make any sense."

"Unless one of the boys got captured and was forced to hoof it in front of the horses," Sam proposed.

"Captured? By whom?"

"LeMay has a posse. So does Thomasville."

"Neither of them are to the east. No one's to the east. There isn't a ranch for a hundred miles in that direction."

"You're plannin' on tracking them down, I suppose."

Frank licked his chapped lips and could taste bitter

dust and salt. "Yep."

Sam Fortune studied the scattered clouds. "You bringin' that packhorse?"

"Soon as I saddle him." Frank plodded back toward the storeroom. "If there's a man on the prairie, he'll need a horse. I assume there's still a spare saddle or two here." He stopped and looked back. "Uncle Sammy, were the ponies runnin' wild and free, or did they have them in a line?"

"Some of both," Sam hollered back. "At least one seems to be off from the others."

The small, dark little shed smelled of old dirt and sweat-dried leather. Frank tossed the blanket and saddle on the packhorse, yanked the cinch, then slipped a bit in the brown horse's mouth. He looped the reins over the tall, narrow saddle horn, and kept the lead rope dangling from the halter. When he swung up into the saddle on Carlos, his side cramped.

Sam led them out of the yard, where they picked up the trail to the east.

Frank rode up alongside of him, leading the third horse. "Was there ever a time in your life that you had it under control?" he asked his uncle.

"You mean everythin' goin' exactly the way I planned it to go?" Sam brushed down his drooping gray mustache.

"Yeah. Did you ever have a time like that?"

The crow's feet around Sam's eyes tightened. "Once."

"Did you like it?"

A tight-lipped smile broke across his face. "Nope."

"That's what I figured."

The two men and three horses plodded east in silence. The treeless prairie of brown grass stretched east without any sign of diversity.

Or cow.

Or horse.

Or people.

Frank rode up alongside his uncle again. "Tell me again about the excitement of running a telephone exchange."

Sam peered out from under the wide brim of his felt hat and laughed. "It's tough work, Little Frank. Why, just last Friday the wind brought down a pine on top of the line to Central City. I had to go out there with a crew at daybreak and set two poles and restring the wire. Took me until noon to get it workin'. Meanwhile Zenith Mitchener had her baby, and they couldn't telephone any of her friends in Deadwood with the news. I thought Grandma Mitchener would cane-whip me for sure. Gruesome. Folks can get real testy when the telephone don't work. I had to rest up all weekend from that one."

Little Frank grinned and shook his head. "The infamous Sam Fortune gettin' done in by angry grandmas."

"Little Frank, no matter what happens out here on the ranch, it's better bein' here than there. You got ups and downs. In town, it's just routine."

"Some days routine would be nice and peaceful. The image of those bloated, bleeding cows is hard to shake. And now, men and horses missing."

"There's only a short hop between peaceful and boring. If you want routine, you can move up to Lead and work in the Homestake. Ever' day, ever' shift's the same routine."

Frank took a deep breath and let it out slow. His ribs didn't hurt as much when he took small breaths. "You're right, Uncle Sammy. Every day I get to spend out on the prairie is one I'm thankin' the Lord for. Don't you go tellin' my mama or daddy, but I never could get used to Deadwood. All those years in the wide-open desert of southern Arizona spoils a person, I reckon. The gulch is so cramped."

"Especially when it's packed with your relatives."

"I suppose so."

"Abby and I figure most of you grandkids will move out." Sam picked his teeth with his fingernail.

"Not without a guilty conscience. Grandpa pioneered it, and we feel tied to his legacy."

"Now, don't you ever use that for an excuse to stay. Daddy pined for a ranch ever' day of his life. But from the moment he buried Big River Frank up on Mt. Moriah, he couldn't leave. Said he owed it to Big River, then to Yapper Jim and Grass Edwards."

To the north Frank heard another screech of a hawk, but the sky looked empty of birds. "They are all up on Mt. Moriah now."

"They put their lives on the line for each other, time and again. There's a bond there that's hard to explain. I know a little how it was. 'Cause I had a tough time leavin' Kiowa in a shallow grave in Oklahoma."

"I miss that, Uncle Sammy. I don't have brotherhood like that. Oh, I've got Howdy and the boys, but most of 'em come and go. I don't expect them to risk their lives for me. They are hired men."

"Little Frank, you never know who you got on your side until the crisis comes. Maybe the frontier is settling down. We hire sheriffs and brand inspectors and Pinkerton men to look after us. Besides, there ain't much threat left."

"Uncle Sammy, you ever reckon you were born too late? I always figured I was just one generation behind. I would have liked to be around trailin' those big herds after the war."

"We are always one generation behind. Daddy lamented that he was twelve at the battle of San Jacinto."

Frank watched the sun reflect off the bare white clay rolling hills in the distance. "We keep riding east and we'll wish we were anywhere but here. We're losin' the grassland. You still have a trail?"

"Yep, but it seems to be slantin' to the north."

"We'll be on railroad land soon, if we aren't already."

"What's on up this direction?"

"Owl Butte, then nothin' until Cheyenne Agency."

"What do you mean, nothin'? No towns?"

"No towns, no roads, no houses, no trees, no brush, no grass, no water . . . nothin'. It drops off into Devil's Wash at Hades Canyon. Some say it's the mouth of hell."

"Then no one would ride there on purpose," Sam said.

"Except maybe Indians runnin' away from the reservation. They can always find water down in there."

"It would be peaceful and quiet, at least until you ran across some desperadoes or died of thirst. If your boys didn't want anyone following, wouldn't this be the way to come?"

"Yep. But if they were getting bored of riding the high line, why would they ride out here? You'd think they would hightail it for a town."

"Especially if one is on foot. How far out here do we ride?" Sam asked.

"Until we find them," Frank replied.

Sam Fortune shook his head. "I knew you'd say that. Or . . ." He stood in the stirrups and stared at the northeast horizon. "Or until they find us. Is that a rider up there?"

Frank pushed his hat back and squinted his eyes. "I think so."

Sam rode the big black stallion to the south and continued to parallel Frank by about fifty feet.

"Can you tell yet?" Frank shouted. He checked the chamber in the Sharps carbine and released the massive hammer down to the safe position. Still leading the sorrel packhorse, he continued a slow pace straight at the oncoming horse.

Sam Fortune held up two fingers.

Frank studied the distant image. *Two horses? No, two riders on one horse. That's Reynoso and Cron. And one horse?* He stopped and waited for them.

Sam Fortune rode closer. "Looks like they are coming back."

Frank watched the gray gelding plod closer with two men perched on his back.

"I told Reynoso that you'd come lookin' for us," Cron shouted as they approached.

"No, you said Howdy would come look for us. We

didn't know El Padron was coming up," Reynoso replied.

Frank rubbed dirt out of the corner of his eye. "Looks like you lost some horses."

"That's all my fault," Cron admitted as he slid down off the back of the horse.

"Climb aboard Yellowboy and you can explain going back to the cabin. Don't know if you two met my Uncle Sam Fortune before."

"No, sir," Mike Cron tipped his hat. "Mighty fine to meet you. You own the hardware store in Deadwood?"

"That's another uncle. I own the telephone exchange," Sam explained.

"You puttin' telephone lines out here?" Cron pressed.

"Not for another hundred years. Just helpin' Little Frank trail you two down."

Mike Cron swung into the saddle of the sorrel gelding, relieving Frank of the lead rope and reins.

"You care to explain this situation?" Frank probed.

The four men rode side by side across the rolling prairie to the southwest. "It all started with Reynoso's chili," Cron mumbled.

The Mexican spat tobacco on the dirt between them. "You blamin' it on me?"

"No, I just said that's where it started." Cron pulled his fixings out of his vest pocket and began to roll a quirley. "Reynoso rode a night check to the east tanks, and I was tossin' and turnin', tryin' to sleep. He had so much garlic and onions in the chili last night that my stomach was cryin' for mama, if you know what I mean."

"You had to make a few trips to the privy?" Sam asked.

"One, as it turns out."

"Oh?" Frank asked.

"I got to sittin' down there in the pitch dark without so much as a sulphur match lit. I was tired from ridin' that west ridge all day straight into the wind. The truth is, I plum . . ."

"He fell asleep in the privy!" Reynoso hooted.

"I was tuckered out."

Sam shook his head. "Chili will do that to a man."

"No, I was tuckered out from bringin' three back down from the Wyomin' line yesterday."

Frank looked back at Mike Cron. "We got strays up there?"

"Three with Rafter F were in Fox Creek Canyon mixed in with Thomasville's," Cron reported. "It was almost as if they was brushed up. It was just breakin' daylight when I woke up. I was feelin' much better and hiked back up to the cabin. That's when I noticed the horses gone."

When Frank slumped his shoulders, pain flashed across his rib cage. "Someone stole three horses while you slept in the privy?"

"At first, I figured that Bonner just nosed open the gate latch and led the other two out. You know what a pill that horse can be. So I grabbed a cup of coffee in one hand and my carbine in the other and hiked after the tracks, expectin' to see them just over the rise."

"By the time I got in," Reynoso continued, "I spot the horses gone and figured Mike is taking them out to Wildhorse Draw to pasture. I cooked some breakfast for us, but when he didn't show, I came out to look for him."

Mike Cron's mustache stretched across his face and hooked up with his sideburns. "Not until you ate both breakfasts."

Reynoso leaned back, his hand on the rump of the horse. "Ain't about to let good food waste."

"You kept trailing the horses on foot?" Frank pressed.

Mike Cron rubbed his dark, unshaven chin. "I kept thinkin' I'd spot 'em just over the next rise. We ain't never had trouble up here, so I didn't even worry about that."

"But you never did spot them?" Frank said.

"Nope. Reynoso caught up with me on the flanks of Owl Butte. We doubled up and followed the tracks to the ridge of Devil's Wash. Those three ponies plowed right off the side of Hades Canyon."

"They had to be chased or ridden to go off that embankment," Frank offered. "Free rein horses would never take that route."

"We weren't about to take it either, especially two to a horse," Reynoso added. "We turned around and headed back."

Sam Fortune turned his horse toward Frank. "Sounds like Indians, to me. Who else would ride off the side of the ridge?"

"Why would they travel this far to steal horses?" Frank pondered. "It would be easy to get them closer to the agency."

"Ain't nothin' easier than stealin' a man's horses while he's in the privy," Sam whooped.

Cron pulled off his dirty gray hat and scratched his matted brown hair. "Boss, you want us to go after them, now that we got two horses?"

"Nope. There's no way to catch braves once they drop down into Devil's Wash." *I just want a fence around this entire ranch and ever'one and ever'thin' to stay out and leave me alone to raise some cows. That's what I want.* "I'll telegram the agency and have them look out for three Rafter F horses. I can't believe they would break out and steal horses way over here. The Cheyennes own some fine horses. The three they took weren't all that good."

Sam spurred his horse to a trot. "Maybe it's just the principle. Lettin' you know they can still do it if they want to."

"It's been a great day, and only just past noon. So far I've lost six cows, three horses, and a fair amount of my pride. At this rate I'll be busted by Saturday."

"You got a wedding to go to on Saturday."

"You truly know how to cheer up a man, Uncle Sammy."

"You want us to swing north to the river and try to pick up their tracks?" Reynoso asked.

"Not today. I don't want you ridin' across railroad land. A posse from up north crossed Buffalo Gap and rode into the ranch unchallenged. I don't want that to happen again. I'll send Happy up here with some more ponies in a day or two. In the meantime, take your horse to the privy with you."

"You're jokin', ain't you, Boss?" Cron said.

"You want to work the north line on foot?"

"Eh, no. I reckon we'll take the horse to the privy," Mike Cron mumbled.

. . .

They arrived back at the stone cabin at Buffalo Gap by mid-afternoon. Like a lighthouse on a rolling sea of brown prairie grass, it was the only object over three feet tall within sight.

Frank paused in front of the wooden gate at the stone corral. "Mike, you and Reynoso settle in those new supplies and cook up some supper. Uncle Sammy and me will take a brisk ride out on the drift line west to make sure things are calm in that direction."

Frank spurred Carlos, but the chestnut gelding refused to trot.

After about twenty minutes, Sam pulled up beside Frank. "You reckon these horses will tire before we get back?"

"Carlos is already tired. A drift line is no fun for animal or man."

"You're goin' to have to fence this place, Little Frank. That's all there is to it."

"I can't afford that, you know that."

"Don't try it all at once. Fence a little bit one year, and a little more the next. Which is your worse line to protect?"

"The cows want to drift north, but the people wander in from the west mainly," Frank explained.

"Then start right up here at Buffalo Gap. Fence east and west until money runs out."

"That would be about noon Saturday."

"You know that Todd will get you the wire at his cost. Rebekah's family has connections with that steel mill."

"I know. Even then, it's a tough sled to pull. I'd have

to buy fence posts too." Frank rubbed the base of his back and sat straight up in the saddle.

"I got an old pal with a saw camp up in the Big Horns who makes telephone poles for me. He's always complainin' that the trees are gettin' too small for poles. They might make good posts."

"I'll think about it. Seriously, I could go broke before I ever get it fenced. Besides I can't fence government land unless they sell me the place."

"Maybe you need a different ranch."

"The only one they'd lease to a kid is one no one else wanted."

"You're not a kid any more, Little Frank. You're an experienced rancher."

"Yeah," Frank murmured. *Yeah, an experienced rancher who's still called Little Frank.*

They rode the divide west as the sun slipped lower. At first, the ridge angled a gradual slope in both directions. When they hit Cheyenne Hills, the south slope steepened. They meandered the rim and peered over the top of scrub pines.

"Is it this way all the way to Wyomin'?" Sam asked.

"The last ten miles are flat, but that isn't Rafter F."

"Then there isn't too much need to ride this ridge. Cattle won't come up here, except in a storm."

"I made 'em ride to Soldier Point anyway. You can see Wyomin' from there."

Sam stood in the stirrups. "You got some mules out here?"

"Mules?"

"There's two mules down that draw."

Frank leaned across the saddle horn in time to spot two dark brown mules drift into the brush and trees of the draw far below. "It's a steep draw. How in the world did they get down there?"

Sam cleared his throat. "You didn't answer my question. Do you have some mules?"

"Not up here." Frank scratched Carlos's ears and patted his neck.

"Then I reckon we should go down and investigate. Did you ever notice how mules smell different than horses?"

Frank took a deep breath. "Smells like sundown on the prairie to me."

"Yeah, but there's a mule scent in the air." Sam pointed to the gradual slope behind them. "You want me to swing around and take the low side?"

"You don't think Cuddles wants to plunge off the side of this?" Frank laughed.

"If you have rustlers down there," Sam said, "they will try to escape by the easiest possible route. That's the downhill side toward the dry creek bed. One of us needs to circle around and down."

"You didn't answer my question," Frank hooted.

Sam Fortune frowned. "No, I don't think Cuddles will do too good going off the side."

"Carlos will take the plunge. I don't know what else he'll do, but he'll take a shot at it. Did you see anyone around the mules?"

"Nope, the mules could have just drifted up here. There are wild mules all over these plains, I reckon. Is there a trail down there?"

"The old Owl Creek road. But it's washed out in so many places, no one goes down there any more."

"If someone is up here on purpose, chances are they are hidin' out. And that means they won't be happy to be found," Sam cautioned.

"Then we better take this nice and slow."

"Give me some time to work down the side and cut off their retreat." Sam yanked his Winchester from the scabbard.

"How much time?" Frank asked.

"You got a watch?"

"Nope."

"Neither do I." Sam started down the incline to the east. "Take yourself a twenty-minute siesta, and I'll meet you down there."

Frank studied the treeless, rocky ridge as Sam dropped out of view. "Come on, Carlos, we aren't goin' to park up here on the ridge. Let's find some cover."

He rode down the gradual slope north to a clump of buck pines no more than eight feet tall. He tethered the chestnut gelding to the biggest, then loosened the cinch.

"He said a siesta, partner. Right now we could both use a big pile of hay. You'd eat it and I'd rest on it. These bones ache too much to sleep." He pulled his Sharps carbine and toted it with him.

Frank used a stand of clump grass for a pillow and stretched out on the dirt with his legs running down the slope. The sinking sun in the west did reach over the crest of the divide. He reclined in the windless shadow of the mountain.

His back cramped, and he scrunched around to relieve

the pain. He swung his arm around, then caught it just before it crashed into the carbine.

No more. I will not injure myself any more for one day. He tugged his felt hat down over his eyes. *Lord, this don't feel right. I'm not able to get control of things. I've been runnin' from one crisis to another for so long, I don't even remember why I'm doin' this. All my life I heard Daddy and Grandpa Brazos talk about how they should get back into the cattle business. And all my life I determined that I was the one to do it. I quit baseball so I could ranch. I quit college so I could ranch. I quit workin' the cattle pens at Rapid City so I could ranch. I quit . . . I quit Marla Jolene . . . so I could ranch.*

Now I don't remember what I really want. It never has been money. Or power. Or fame. I reckon, Lord, I just want to look up to the heavens some day and say, "Grandpa, I did it!"

He reached over and fingered the cold, slick steel receiver of the carbine. *I'm still packin' your Sharps .50 caliber, Grandpa. You had it in Brownsville after the war. You had it when Grandma died. You had it when you left Ft. Worth with the boys of the Texas Camp. You had it in Custer City when Gen. Crook ran you all out. You had it in '76 in the gulch. It stopped outlaws, repelled Indian attacks, and brought Uncle Sammy home. I've heard all the stories a hundred times. Some say I should hang it over the mantle and pack a lever action. But I can't do that, Grandpa. This carbine is a symbol of a dream, a dream that Fortunes will be back on the ranch where they belong. So, until I completely lose that dream, I'll carry this old gun. Mama doesn't understand. Daddy finds it obsessive. Uncle Todd just shakes his head. But Uncle Sammy knows. And Aunt Dacee June knows.*

Frank let out a long, deep sigh.

I have to succeed. There are no options. I can't live with anything less. Lord, help me.

Deadwood is such a noisy place.

A narrow gulch crowded with people.

A lower end of town with gunfire, fireworks, shouts, and screams, day and night.

The constant thunder of the stamp mills rolls like waves down the gulch.

But the prairie is peaceful. A rustle of wind. A distant cry of a hawk. The shuffle of horse hooves.

A man can rest on a prairie.

When Frank woke, he sat straight up and grabbed his carbine. His hat tumbled off and rolled downhill a few feet.

"Carlos! What time is it? I can't believe I went to sleep."

Frank struggled to his feet. Pain shot through his ribs when he grabbed for his hat.

"The sun's all the way down, but at least it's still daylight. Come on, boy, let's go find that ol' gray-haired uncle. I'm stiff all over from sleeping on the dirt. I need to learn to sleep standin' up like you do."

He untied the horse and trotted him up to the divide. Frank jammed his left foot in the stirrup and yanked himself up.

The saddle slid to the side. He tumbled to the dirt.

Carlos shied away a few feet.

This is not happening to me. This is a dream. This is a very, very bad dream.

Frank sat up and laughed.

Pain shot through his sides.

He held them with both arms.

And laughed.

"I would write this day in a book, Carlos, but no one would believe it." He struggled to his feet. "Come on, boy. This time I'll cinch it down."

With the saddle reset and cinched down, Frank pulled himself up. He rode Carlos back to the drop-off on the south side of the divide. He could not see the mules below. The bull pines made the mountainside a mosaic of shadows.

"Let's do it, partner. You can take this grade. Let's see if I can."

Carlos balked at the first kick in the flanks with the spurs, but the second kick drove the horse over the granite gravel edge.

Frank leaned so far back that his stirrups were even with the gelding's neck. Dust fogged around them. He felt Carlos sliding his rear hooves off the mountain slope. Where he did find traction, the chestnut horse galloped ahead, each step sending a jarring pain from Frank's sides to his head.

Within a minute they stumbled out of the rock and hit dirt.

And trees.

Carlos continued to gallop.

"Whoa, boy . . . slow it down now." Frank yanked on the reins, but the horse thundered straight at the trees.

"I said, that's enough! Whoa!" Frank leaned forward and grabbed the horse's leather headstall and yanked it to the right.

Carlos jerked it back straight, almost unseating Frank Fortune. The horse's ears tucked back as he slobbered at the bit.

"Whoa!" Frank shouted.

They roared down the mountain.

He can't stop. He's got momentum, and can't stop. He's scared to death. We got to get out of these trees.

The scrub pines got bigger as they stampeded down the slope. Frank hugged the horse's neck to form a low profile. The leather-wrapped saddle horn pressed into his aching ribs. He let the tied reins drop to the horse's neck and reached up and clutched the headstall on both sides near the horse's ears.

There's no reason to pull on your mouth now, boy, 'cause you couldn't stop if you wanted to. Ahead in the shadows, Frank spied two mules, a horse, and an old paneled wagon.

As they rumbled closer, he saw his uncle sitting on a log that had fallen across the trail.

Little Frank yanked back on the headstall. "Whoa!" he screamed.

Sam Fortune jumped up and waved his hands and hat. Carlos didn't slow.

"Heyaaaah!" Sam yelled.

The horse barreled at him and the downed tree.

"Move!" Frank shouted.

Sam dove behind the log just as Carlos leaped.

When he hit the dirt on the other side of the log, Frank

didn't have time to look back. He wrenched hard on the left side of the halter to guide the runaway horse out of the trees, but they continued at full speed down off the mountain. The sandy dry bed of Owl Creek was fifteen feet wide, but Carlos cleared it with a few feet to spare. There were no brush or trees on the south side of the creek bed, and the horse galloped out into the open prairie.

About a hundred yards out on the Dakota plains, Carlos slid to a stop. Only Frank's belt catching on the saddle horn kept him from sliding over the horse's head. He leaped to the ground and grabbed the horse's slobbery head. White sweat beaded out from under the saddle blanket.

"You alright, boy?" Frank gasped for breath. "How in the world did we keep from killin' us both?" He unsnapped the bit and pulled it out of the horse's mouth. He tied the reins to the bottom buckle on the headstall and looped the bit over the saddle horn.

"No more yankin' on that mouth, partner. Let's walk awhile."

Frank hiked toward the old Owl Creek road, leading the horse. He had just crossed the creek and approached the first stand of stumpy trees when Sam Fortune trotted out on Cuddles. The two unhaltered mules meandered behind him.

"Glad to see you alive!" Sam shouted.

"And you as well!" Frank hollered.

"I move mighty quick for a gray-haired old man."

"I reckon that was too steep for Carlos. He couldn't regain control until we were out on the plains."

Sam pulled out his red bandanna and wiped dirt off his forehead. "Yeah, I noticed."

Frank waited for Sam to ride closer. "What's the deal with the mules? Did you find anyone?"

"Are you goin' to walk him all the way back to the cabin?"

"I might. What's that wagon up there?"

"Here's what I can tell," Sam said. "Someone drove the wagon up that hillside pulled by the mules."

"That's too steep to take a wagon, and the old road sloughed off. There's no way to make it."

"That's true, but they didn't know that. By the time they got to the log across the road, the mules were so burnt out, they abandoned the wagon. Looks like they rode the mules a tad farther, but I imagine the mules just quit," Sam reported.

Frank walked Carlos on a diagonal up the hillside. "Did you see any signs of someone up there?"

Sam rode along beside him. "Three tracks lead up the mountain. Once they reach the granite slide, they disappear."

"What kind of tracks?"

"Some shoes. Some moccasins. Small feet."

"Indians?" Frank asked.

"Nowadays, who knows?"

"You think maybe boys or maybe women?"

"I don't think women would be up here. Just small feet. I know some Sioux with small feet."

Frank kept plodding along, leading the lathered chestnut gelding. "You wouldn't think Indians would drive a wagon. What did it say on the wagon? I didn't take time to read the panel."

"It's an old one with faded letters. But it says, 'Miss Fontenot's Photography Shoppe, Cantrell, Montana'."

"Miss Fontenot? Must be her old wagon."

"It's beat up. They busted an axle and made the mules drag it for a while."

"She's been married over ten years now. Doesn't go by Fontenot anymore." Frank stopped to stare up the slope. "When I heard she was married, it was one of the saddest days of my life."

"She was a little old for you, wasn't she?" Sam laughed.

"When a boy is twelve or thirteen, age don't even enter into it."

"Miss Lydia Rose Bishop . . ." Sam grinned. "She was my fourth-, fifth-, and sixth-grade teacher."

"Was she a looker, Uncle Sammy?"

"I thought she was an angel from heaven. She married a man named Austin Hamond when the war broke out and was a widow within six months. Last I hear she moved to St. Louis. But I still remember her. I can't remember one other teacher, but I remember Miss Lydia."

Frank rubbed his chin and stared back up the hill. "Did you say there were three of them with the wagon?"

"Yep."

"They could have been the ones who stole the horses at the corrals."

"I reckon so. What do you want to do now?" Sam asked.

"Go eat. I'm hungry. What about your mules?"

"My mules!" Sam sputtered. "I ain't leadin' them any-where. They can follow if they want to. Maybe they'll turn and head back for home, wherever that is."

"They didn't come all the way from Montana, that's for sure."

Sam pointed at Frank's horse. "It's goin' to be a long time before supper if you walk all the way."

"I'm not stickin' that bit back in Carlos's mouth." Frank tightened the cinch, then crawled back in the saddle.

Sam leaned over and handed him his hat. "I found this about halfway down."

Frank jammed the hat on. "OK, that was our brisk ride. Now we can go back to the cabin."

"Brisk?" Sam blustered. "The Missouri Valley and Elkhorn Railroad doesn't have a train engine that fast."

The table at the stone cabin was barely big enough for two, so they dragged the benches outside and ate supper by the light of scattered clouds and a half-moon. Cron and Reynoso took the two crude bunks inside. Frank and Sam smoothed out bedrolls on the dirt just beyond the front door. They left their boots on and stretched out on top of the canvas-covered blankets.

"Sorry I can't offer you more, Uncle Sammy."

"Little Frank, I tossed in this bedroll because I hoped to get to use it. I spent the best part of ten years sleepin' on the ground half the nights of the year. I get to missin' it at times."

"You ever regret comin' to Deadwood?" Frank asked him.

Sam rolled up his canvas jacket. "Never, not even for a minute." He laid back on the coat pillow. "Comin' to Deadwood was the best decision I never made."

"Never made?"

"I only went to Cheyenne out of courtesy for a murdered friend. And I came to Deadwood as a favor to another. But I reckon the Lord was leading. That's the way he does it sometimes. We stumble along and one day wonder how in the world we got to where we are, and it's been his leadin' all along. I don't reckon you ever wonder how you got here?"

"Not more than a dozen times a day."

"Do you regret it?" Sam challenged.

"Not yet, but I might some day. It's takin' a lot out of me, and ever' once in a while I have a little chat with myself on whether it's been a good investment."

"You're a young man. It's a good time to try some things."

"I'm gettin' old fast. Take today. It covered about ten years in most men's lives."

"But you weren't bored, were you?"

"Not for a minute," Frank said.

"Do you know how many men would trade you in a flash? I'm one of them."

"No trade," Frank replied. "I don't want to run a telephone company."

"Neither do I, Little Frank."

"What's holding you back, Uncle Sammy? Why aren't you ranchin'? Is it Abby?"

"Nope. That woman is stubborn and strong willed and opinionated, but she's also lovin', supportive, and the purdiest gal God ever created. She'd move with me any-where I had my heart set. But I stayed away from my family for way too many years. I don't aim to do that again."

"You mean, if the whole clan decided to move, you'd go with them?" The back of Frank's head hurt. He scrunched his coat pillow to a more comfortable posi-tion.

"Yep, I believe I would," Sam murmured.

Frank studied the clouds blowing past the half-moon above. "Now, there's an idea . . . lock, stock, and barrel the Fortune-Toluca clan moves out of Deadwood."

"The Last Fortune in the Black Hills," Sam laughed. "Has sort of a catchy ring to it."

Frank sighed. "It's not going to happen."

"Nope. It's gettin' tough to get the whole family together for anything."

"Except weddings." Frank's mind drifted to Patricia and Veronica.

"Did you hear Dacee June wanted to get the old boy who made the elephant cake to whip one up for the twins?"

Frank glanced over in the darkness at his uncle. "You got to be kidding me."

"Your mama vetoed it."

"Good for Mama."

"But there's a little tension."

"Between Mama and Aunt Dacee June?"

"You know how Dacee June likes to plan things."

"She'll have three weddings of her own to plan."

"She already has those organized," Sam said.

Frank closed his eyes as he thought of his nieces. "They are only eleven, twelve, and thirteen."

"She's had those girls' weddings arranged for years."

"A rather stubborn family, aren't we?"

Sam began to laugh. "Now, that, Little Frank Fortune, is the most understated thing I've heard all day."

Coyotes yip.

Wolves howl.

Night owls screech.

Corralled horses whinny and snort.

Sam Fortune snores.

When Frank woke up with a pain in his side, he could hear all the sounds, muffled by a dark sky with clouds blocking the moon and most of the stars.

He sat up and held his sides. The pain lessened, and he sat there for a moment rocking back and forth with his eyes closed. *I need to sleep more. But here I am in the middle of nowhere, and the night noises keep me awake. Too many worries, I reckon.*

I don't sleep good at home, either.

I don't know why that is, Lord. Mama says I'm too young to sleep poorly. I'm too young for a lot of things. Too young to have a ranch of my own. Too young to be in charge of a dozen men. Too young to be this far in debt.

Here's the funny thing, Lord.

I feel old.

Way too old.

Frank laid back down and sprawled his arm over his ears. He attempted to block out the snores when he heard the horses shuffle in the corral.

The addition of the mules had made the horses restless. Frank had listened to them position around most of the night. Just the sound of horse hooves striking packed clay soil.

Only this time it was different.

Just a little different.

He moved his arm and tried to filter out the snores so he could concentrate on the horses. His mind wandered to the canyon. To Miss Fontenot's wagon. To the señorita. To dead cows by the well. And back to horse hooves.

Rhythmic! There's a pattern to one of those horses. He's bein' led! They don't mill in formation.

The wool blanket dropped to the dirt as he used the Sharps carbine to push himself to his feet. He stayed close to the cabin as he scooted toward the stone corrals.

I won't give them any silhouette to take a shot at. They must have come back. They were just waitin' to steal more horses. Who was it that we trailed to the Badlands? Maybe they just hid out there during the day. Maybe they had something in that wagon and buried it. Now they are on their way back. Maybe it's just some compadres. Maybe they're a gang of rustlers like LeMay said. Someone is in the corral leading a horse out. I can't see him, but I can hear him, that's for sure.

Frank dropped to his hands and knees and crawled along the corral to the west.

At least there is only one gate. He'll have to bring the horse out this way.

He tried to muffle the sound of pulling the huge

hammer back on the carbine. He reached into his vest pocket and fingered two more .50 caliber cartridges, then he pointed the gun toward the closed gate.

Uncle Sam is right. I can smell those mules.

I'll call them to throw down as soon as that gate opens. But they could dive back behind the wall and we could get into a gunfight. I don't know if there is one or two or three. I only hear one horse led. But if I wait until he's clear outside, there's a chance he could swing up into the saddle and get away.

I could shoot the horse, if he tries that.

But what's the difference between stealing a horse and having a horse dead? Either way, I lose.

Frank continued to squat down and try to get his eyes focused on the gate. The carbine was at his shoulder. His finger was on the slick, cold steel trigger.

Maybe I'll just lame him at the gate. But what if there are three of them? Where will the second shot come from? Can I wing a man with a .50 caliber bullet? It would take two days to get to a doc. Wingin' him with a bullet that size just means a slow death instead of a fast one.

Lord, I don't want to shoot anyone. I never have. There's a whole lot of difference between threatenin' to shoot someone and actually shootin' someone. I don't want to shoot anyone. I just don't want them stealin' my horses neither.

Frank held his breath as the wooden gate slowly creaked open. He couldn't make out horse or man.

Is he on horseback already? Is he on foot? He has to be on foot to open the gate. Doesn't he? I can't see. I can't tell. I only hear one. Are others waitin' for me to make a move? I should have woken up Uncle Sammy. But I can't admit that I can't handle the problems on my own.

Frank crept closer. The gate opened wider.

I have no idea if I'm going to shoot him or coldcock him, but he isn't takin' my horse. I'm just too tired to put up with any more. Too tired to care what happens to me. I'm one of the Fortunes of the Black Hills. You don't steal my horse from under my nose, pure and simple. I might not catch the other two, but I can make sure this hombre doesn't ever steal another horse.

Not more than five feet away, Frank brought the carbine barrel even with what he thought was the man's head. The man closed the gate.

Frank Fortune's trigger finger flinched.

But he didn't squeeze.

His shoulders slumped.

His side ached.

His head throbbed.

I can't do it. I just can't shoot a man I can't see, even if he is stealin' my horse.

Maybe I'm in the wrong business.

A sulphur match flared. The man's unshaved face glowed orange as he lit the stub of a quirley draped from his pinched lips. Narrow eyes widened as he stared down the barrel of Frank Fortune's carbine.

"Mike?" Frank shouted.

The lit match tumbled to the dirt. "Don't shoot!" Mike Cron yelped in the dark.

When he did, the poorly rolled cigarette dropped from

his lips and tangled in the folds of his half-open shirt.

"Ahhhh! It's in my shirt . . ." Cron howled.

Moonlight broke from behind a cloud. Frank could see the cowboy ripping off his shirt. The horse shied back to the corral wall, and Frank grabbed the abandoned reins.

"It's in my pants leg!" Cron shouted.

Frank saw the man shove his ducking trousers to his knees and continue to dance down the hillside.

"It's in my boot now," he hollered. "It's burnin' a hole in my foot!"

Cron sat in the dirt and yanked off his boot.

Frank saw the glow of the still lit cigarette drop to the dirt as Cron struggled to his feet, still brushing sparks of burnt cloth off his body.

"Boss, I thought I was a dead man when I seen that barrel six inches from my nose."

Frank walked over to Cron, leading the horse and carrying the man's shirt. "Mike, what on earth are you doin' sulkin' around in the middle of the night, leadin' my horse out of the corral?"

"I wasn't sulkin'. I thought that packhorse was to be mine."

"It is, but what are you doin' at this hour?"

"Jist followin' your orders," Cron insisted. "You said any time we went to the privy we was to take our pony and tie him to the door handle."

"But I didn't mean when I was sleepin' out next to the corral."

"Oh, yeah . . . well, I was sleepy and not thinkin' too clear. I got a horrible stomachache."

"How about the quirley burns?"

"I'll live. I've been burnt worse than this. Did I ever tell you about the time I was in the Heavenly Delight Dance Hall in Denver when it burned to the ground?"

"No, and I don't want to hear about it tonight. Go on and take care of your business. You only need to take the horse if you're here at the camp by yourself."

"How about them mules? Do we need to lead them to the outhouse too?"

"No, I'm hopin' someone comes along and steals them, then they won't eat up our feed. I'll put this pony back. Sorry about startlin' you, Mike."

"Startlin' me? Boss, for a split second, I reckon I heard the heavenly choir sing."

Frank led the horse back to the corral and turned him out with the others. The clouds had broken free. When he got back to the rock cabin, Reynoso stood in the doorway. Sam Fortune sat up on his bedroll. Both held revolvers.

"Was there trouble out there?" Sam probed.

"Nope."

"Who's out there?" Reynoso asked.

"Mike."

"What's he doin'?" Sam questioned.

"Goin' to the privy," Frank explained.

CHAPTER FIVE

THE DAKOTA SUNRISE cast mile-long shadows across the plains as the two riders rode south. To the west the daybreak turned the Black Hills a dark green. Frank knew that in Whitewood Gulch, Deadwood would still be waiting for the sun.

Sam chewed on a slice of elk jerky when he rode up alongside. He pointed the jerky like a stick. "You figure today will be as excitin' as yesterday?"

"I surmise today will be plum borin'," Frank replied.

Sam's words smacked with jerky juice. "I don't think Mike Cron will let anyone steal your horses again."

The still, early-morning air smelled of sage.

"It's heart stoppin' when I think how close I came to pullin' the trigger on Mike," Frank said. "That was way too close."

Sam pulled the jerky out of his mouth like a man savoring a fine cigar. "The 'what if's' of life can eat at us worse than a cancer. It's best to drop them like a horseshoe fresh out of the forge."

Frank gazed south across the rolling prairie. "Sam, do you ever regret shooting any of the men you shot?"

Sam gazed down at the saddle horn, then finally mumbled, "Most all of them."

"Really?"

"Oh, they played their hand and came at me. At the time I figured I had no choice. Lots of 'em deserved to die. But I always wished someone else was around to shoot them. Takin' a life eats at a man's soul and spirit, Little Frank. I think that's why lots of men had trouble with drinkin' after the war. No matter how justified your actions, it steals something from a man's humanity. They never look as mean and despicable when they're dead. Don't reckon we were created to take another's life."

"I've never heard you talk like that before."

"You never asked. Besides, I didn't think that at the time. Lookin' back, things seem clearer. It doesn't mean I won't pull the trigger again. If that's my best option, I'll do it in a heartbeat. Any hesitation and you've lost the battle. 'Course, there are one or two I wouldn't hesitate to shoot all over again."

"I've considered it on occasion. It would have to be with this Sharps. I never could get used to packing a pistol on my hip. Gets in my way when I'm workin' cattle."

"Just as well. Those were the old days. No lawmen. No laws. It was a rough life. Don't ever wish for it to come back. I like things better now, in that respect."

Sam Fortune led the way down a long draw in the rolling prairie. As they reached the base, six white-faced hereford gave them momentary notice, then returned to grazing.

"Those steers look brushed up to me," Frank said.

Sam folded up the last of his jerky and crammed it into his mouth. "You mean, someone built a brush fence? How did those steers get in there?"

"I supposed they could bull their way through the thicket," Frank replied.

"One might, maybe . . . but not six. They look trapped."

Frank rode to the front of the brushy barrier. He slipped off Carlos and tugged on the brush, which opened up. "It's a corral, alright. This brush isn't planted."

"Any chance they blew in like that?"

Frank stared up at his uncle.

"No, I reckon not," Sam mumbled.

"The draw steepens back up the mountainside. Kind of a natural barricade. I guess they want to steal more than six."

Sam surveyed the prairie to the west. "If someone brushed them up, they'll be back."

Frank untied the wide leather latigo on Carlos's cinch strap. "Yep, I reckon they will."

"We can hide the horses up the draw," Sam suggested.

Frank pulled his Sharps carbine from the scabbard. "Go hide the ponies, Uncle Sammy. I'll close this brush back up, and we'll wait until they make a move. I need to find out who's pennin' my steers and why."

Frank surveyed the hidden draw and brushed his fingertips across the painful, swollen lump on his forehead.

The six steers were happy.

And full.

They settled down on the tall brown grass behind the temporary brush gate, ignoring the intruders.

The Dakota air was cool, but the draw blocked the wind as Frank scrunched around, sitting cross-legged in the dirt behind several waist-high sagebrush that housed a clump of yellowing, leafed sunflower plants.

Sam Fortune tossed him a piece of elk jerky. "You want me to sit across the way so we'll have position on them?"

"We can see them comin' for a half mile or more, so I reckon we can sit down together. Who knows how long we'll have to wait." The jerky was tough. Frank soaked it in his mouth before he ripped off a chunk.

Sam stretched out full length on his back. His two-day beard was as gray as his mustache. "You surmise they will come from the west?"

"Yep. We came from the north, and they weren't up there. The headquarters is south. The end of the earth is east. So it has to be from the west. But I still can't believe they would be bold enough to ride out here and brush up my cows in daylight. They got to figure someone will ride along and try to stop them."

Sam pulled his hat down over his eyes. "I agree, it don't seem possible. Maybe there is another explanation. How long do you figure to sit here?"

Frank shoved the rest of the jerky in the pocket of his leather vest. "We should stay here 'til evenin', but I don't think I have that kind of time."

Sam peeked out from under his felt hat. "You got company showin' up at the ranch." He winked. "Don't forget the señorita."

"In that case, maybe I should stay out here all week," Frank grinned. "I don't think I'll live through another face-to-face with that lady. But, we will leave at noon. If there's no activity, we'll drive these six steers south a few miles. I'll send a couple of men up here tomorrow to see what they can find. I thought Howdy said that Tolle and Meyers were riding the west line today and tomorrow. I'll have them keep an eye out. I might just have them camp right here in this draw tonight. I wanted them to drive every cow back from that western line. I didn't want to have any bovines wander over near Thomasville's."

Sam chewed on jerky. "You ever notice once you get

convinced someone's stealin' your cows, you see evidence at ever' sagebrush?"

"You sayin' we're sittin' out here for nothin'?"

Sam propped himself up on his elbows. "It surely looked like somethin' when we rode up. But now it just don't make sense."

Frank began to laugh. One of the steers turned to stare at him. "I suppose if one of the boys rode up, it would be tough to explain what I'm doin' here."

"You're the boss. You don't have to explain anything." Sam sat up and jammed his hat on. "Tell 'em we were studyin' ants."

Frank sat up straight and gently rubbed his ribs. "Ants?"

"Like the big ol' ones crawling up your pant legs."

Frank hopped up and danced around, brushing off his denim jeans. "Why didn't you tell me I was sitting in ants!"

"I did."

Frank meandered back and found a different place to sit.

He and Sam talked of Deadwood, gold mines, Texas . . . and dead cattle by the springs. Clouds moved in slowly and parked. Whatever drift of breeze reached the draw now died. The air warmed and trapped the sweet pungent aroma of dried sage blossoms.

The clouds lofted high and filtered the sunlight. The lack of wind warmed Frank's body. He began to doze. Sam mentioned something about the twins.

Frank opened his eyes. "What did you say?"

"I hear the twins are arguing who will walk down on

your daddy's right arm and which on the left."

"Mama suggested that I walk one of them down, but they pitched a fit." Frank studied the prairie. "This is crazy, Uncle Sammy. Let's drive these steers south with us. I've wasted enough time."

"I agree with you, there. Want me to go gather the horses?"

Frank struggled to his feet. His left foot was asleep and he hobbled around, clutching the Sharps carbine in his right hand. Sam moseyed toward the brush gate, then dropped down to his haunches. He motioned Frank down and held up two fingers.

Frank crept toward his uncle. "Two men?" he whispered.

"Yeah, about three hundred yards west. They'll be coming over that swell any minute now."

"Let's get back by the sage," Frank suggested.

They crawled to the sunflower-encircled sage and hunched down.

"Were they drivin' more cows?" Frank asked.

Sam slowly cocked the lever on his rifle. "Nope."

Frank pulled back the giant hammer on the Sharps.

"If you look right across over that yucca, you might see them before they see you."

Frank rubbed the dirt, grime, and sweat off his face and watched as two riders broke into view.

"It's just Tolle and Meyers!" he whispered.

He started to rise up.

Sam held his shoulder. "Just wait," he murmured.

"They've worked for me since February."

"Then waiting two minutes won't hurt. Let's see how

they play this. Which one is which?" Sam asked.

"Tolle has the vest, Meyers the black hat." Frank waited and watched as the two cowboys rode up to the front of the brush fence.

"All six of them are still here!" Tolle shouted to his partner.

"That's good." Meyers stayed back on the prairie.

Tolle rubbed his narrow, unshaved chin. "You reckon there's enough dry wood back there for a runnin' iron?"

Meyers stood in the stirrups and studied the draw. "Ought to be some wood up by them sages." He sat back down. "I don't know why Thomasville wanted us to rebrand them. They can do that themselves."

"That's the deal. Five dollars a head, branded over and delivered to John Earl at the Minnesela Road," Tolle said.

"Easiest money I ever made."

"Anyone back there on the prairie?" Tolle called out.

"Nope."

"Come on in here, and let's burn some hair."

"You sure you don't want me to stand guard out here?" Meyers asked.

"While I do all the work?"

"What if Howdy or the old man ride up?"

"They sent us out so they don't have to come. Howdy said that there señorita was comin' to visit. The ol' man will be hurryin' back to greet her."

"I look forward to seein' her myself."

"Then get your sorry sack of bones in here and help me get this done with," Tolle insisted.

Meyers rode closer to the brush gate. "I don't know,

Tolle. I don't like the feel of this."

"If you don't want to do it, ride on out of here. I'll make all thirty bucks myself," Tolle barked.

"Shoot, I don't mean I don't want to rustle 'em. That don't bother me. It's just that there's been folks ridin' over this ranch for two weeks. It's not predictable like it used to be. Who knows who will come ridin' up? Do you figure we should wait until after dark?"

"Not if you want to see that señorita."

Tolle gathered an armload of sage wood in the clearing where the cattle chewed their cud. "Once they smell burnt hair, they will get restless. It will take both of us to hold them."

"We really goin' to drive them over to the road this afternoon?" Meyers asked.

"We're supposed to be up here drivin' cattle. That's what we get paid to do."

Meyers slipped off the saddle and walked his horse into the draw. "Fortune won't miss 'em. He don't know how many he's got, anyway. A man that young don't need to get rich too quick."

When Tolle smiled, he revealed cigarette-stained teeth. "Now you're talkin'."

Meyers pulled out his blue bandanna and wiped off his forehead. "Shoot, if someone comes along, we're just startin' a nooner fire."

"They are goin' to pay us cash on the spot. We'll have jingle in our pockets before dark. If I save up a hundred dollars, I'm goin' to Texas," Tolle declared.

"And I'll ride with ya, as far as Las Vegas, New Mexico," Meyers added. "We'll need more wood than that."

Frank glanced over at his uncle. Sam pointed to the front of the brushy draw and held up three fingers. "Three minutes," he mouthed without uttering a word. Then he crawled east along the brush row.

Frank kept his right hand on the cold steel receiver of the Sharps carbine but rubbed his temples with his other hand.

Lord, this just about makes me cry. I try, Lord. I try to treat 'em fair. I pay six bucks a month more than most of the ranches. Got a good cook, plenty of food, and a decent bunkhouse. They have no ticks or fleas in their mattresses and no lice, unless they bring 'em with them.

I never ask them to do anything that I'm not willing to do myself. No one gets rich cowboyin', that's for sure. But no one gets rich havin' his cattle rustled either. How many more will steal from me? I thought I knew them better than that. I thought they knew me better. I'm young, and I'm not hot-tempered. Maybe ranchin' isn't for me. He wiped his hand across dry, chapped lips. *But I'm goin' to make it. And the likes of Tolle and Meyers won't stop me. They must have figured I wouldn't hold them to account.*

They figured wrong.

Lord, I'm havin' a hard time with this. Keep me from doin' somethin' I'll regret. And keep me doin' those things I'll regret not doin'. And I'm surely thankin' you that Uncle Sammy is here.

Tolle's holster still hung around the saddle horn of his tethered horse. Meyers had a tie-down string looped over the hammer of his.

Frank Fortune stood up behind the sage and sun-flowers. His legs felt cramped. Sweat rolled out from under the brim of his dusty felt hat.

The hammer was back on the carbine.

The gun pointed toward the two.

His finger on the trigger.

"Throw down your gun, Meyers!" he shouted. "Right now."

"Boss!" Tolle shouted. "Eh, you're in time for lunch."

"Throw down your gun, Meyers," Frank repeated.

"I knew somethin' was wrong here," Meyers grumbled.

"These six kept driftin' west, so we brushed them up for a day or so," Tolle insisted.

"Meyers, if that pistol isn't on the dirt by the time I count to three, this .50 caliber slug is comin' at you."

"Why shoot me? What about Tolle?"

"You're the only one packin' a gun at the moment. One."

"You can't shoot me!" he hollered.

Tolle dove for the revolver hanging on the saddle horn.

Sam Fortune stepped in front of him; his .38-55 pointed and cocked hovered at Tolle's temple.

"Meyers," Tolle whined, "we're dead men."

"Who's the old man?" Meyers stammered.

"Sam Fortune," Tolle replied.

Meyers slammed his revolver into the dirt.

"Boss, what are you doing?" Tolle pressed.

"Pull off your bullet belt and toss it down too."

"I don't understand," Tolle griped as he pulled off the

bullet belt and holster.

Frank marched closer, his gun at his shoulder. "What did we hear these two say, Uncle Sammy?"

"They were goin' to rebrand your cattle and sell them to Thomasville for five dollars a head."

"That's crazy!" Meyers shouted, his wild eyes searching the draw.

"Yes, it is," Frank said. "I treat you boys good. Carried you all through the summer, even though there wasn't much work, and this is how you thank me."

"You misunderstood us!" Tolle shouted.

"And you underestimated me. No one rustles Rafter F cattle. Sit down."

"What?" Meyers choked.

"Sit down, both of ya," Frank ordered.

"We need to talk this through," Tolle whined.

"The time for talkin' is over. Uncle Sammy, shoot their legs out from under them if they don't sit down."

Sam aimed his rifle at Meyers. "Happy to," he murmured.

Both men plopped down in the dirt.

"What are you goin' to do?" Meyers asked.

"Uncle Sammy, you've been on the grand jury. What do you think they would say if we hauled two bodies back and claimed they were shot rustlin' Rafter F cattle?"

"Justifiable homicide," he said.

"Wait! You can't shoot us," Tolle pleaded. "We ain't stolen or rebranded anything yet. You can't kill someone for talkin' about it."

"If you two are dead, no one will know what you did

or didn't do, will they?" Frank replied.

"This ain't funny, Fortune," Meyers said.

"No, it's sad. You two are the sorriest, most worthless drovers on the prairie." Frank retrieved Meyers's pistol and emptied the bullets.

"That's my pistol," Meyers protested.

"But I furnished the bullets. I'm takin' 'em back, along with those in your bullet belt. You came to the ranch with nothin' but what you wore. That's the way you are leavin'."

"You firin' us?" Tolle replied.

"That was your choice, boys. Keep them pinned down, Uncle Sammy. I'll get the bullets from Tolle's gun."

When both bullet belts were empty, he hiked over to where the men sat and tossed the guns at their feet. "You worked two days this week." He tossed two silver dollars in front of each man. "Now you've been paid up."

Frank hiked up the draw and untied Carlos and Cuddles. He swung up in the saddle and rode back, leading Sam's black stallion. He roped the brush at the mouth of the draw and dragged it back. Leaving Cuddles by the other two horses, Frank rounded up the six steers as Carlos pranced from one to the next. Then he drove them far out on the prairie.

He trotted back to the draw.

When he let out a deep sigh, his side ached. *Lord, I don't know which hurts more, my side or my heart. I reckon it's about time somethin' went my way. Unless, of course, you're tryin' to tell me to get out of the ranchin' business. That's a possibility I'm just not ready to accept.*

Frank rode back into where the cowboys sat on the dirt. "Uncle Sammy, mount up and bring those ponies with you. I'll cover these two."

"You ain't goin' to leave us out here without horses, are you?" Tolle sniveled.

"Nope. You're not welcome on Rafter F land. Next time I see you here, you'll be shot as the rustlers you are."

"We need our horses to get off the place," Meyers said.

"Your horses? Those are my horses, my saddles, my bedrolls. Ever'thin' you brought to this ranch you're wearin' right now. And that's the way you'll leave. Get up."

"What are you goin' to do?" Meyers asked.

"Escort you off the ranch."

"You goin' to make us walk five miles?" Tolle griped.

"If I have to leg-shoot you," Sam Fortune grumbled, "you'll be crawlin' five miles."

"I've got my possibles bag in that bedroll," Tolle said. "You ain't goin' to steal my things, are you?" He and Meyers shuffled out of the draw onto the prairie.

"When you get to the property line, you can retrieve your possibles," Frank said.

"It will take an hour to walk there," Meyers complained.

Frank stared up at the sun. "Closer to two, I would imagine. You better get goin'."

"You can't drive us like this. We ain't cattle," Tolle said.

The blast from Sam Fortune's rifle sprayed prairie dirt behind Tolle. He broke into a trot. "That ain't funny!" he shouted.

"I'm glad we agree on somethin'," Sam mumbled, and kept both men shuffling west.

The Dakota sun peeked in and out of high gray clouds as the men trudged along. Frank took the north flank, Sam the south. Each man led one of the saddle horses.

The west wind picked up, and Frank tugged his hat down in front. His carbine lay in his lap, pointed at Meyers.

"It's right neighborly of Thomasville to hire your boys to steal your cattle," Sam shouted across.

"I've been ponderin' that myself. Tolle, did you say Thomasville himself made you that offer? Or was it just John Earl or one of those gunslingers he's hired?"

"I don't have to tell you nothin'."

"That's right. And I don't have to give you a drink out of the canteen. I suppose we'll just decide if we are playin' 'have to' or not."

Tolle stopped and turned around to glare. "You wouldn't deny a man a drink of water. That ain't Christian."

Frank glanced over at his uncle and back at Tolle. "Nope, you're right about that. I wouldn't." He pulled the canteen off his saddle horn and tossed it to Tolle.

The tall, thin cowboy took a deep swig and let the water roll down his chin and drip on his neck. He handed the canteen to Meyers. "I didn't see Thomasville. Shoot, I don't even know what he looks like. It was that big ol' boy, John Earl, who set it up. But he said Thomasville approved."

"I can't figure why a man runnin' 20,000 head would want to rustle beef." Sam took the canteen from Meyers and draped it over his own saddle horn.

"Keep movin', boys," Frank urged. "A couple more miles to the Minnesela Road."

"And then what?" Meyers asked as he resumed plodding east.

Frank brushed his spurs along Carlos's flanks, and the chestnut gelding surged forward. "I figure you can go north, or south, or just wait for John Earl to show up. Don't reckon he'll be real pleased with your work, though."

Meyers broke into a trot. "It's still twenty miles to town from there."

Sam kept Cuddles the same pace as Carlos. "You know, that's a fact I would have thought you had considered before you took up a life of rustlin'."

"We didn't take it up for an occupation," Tolle panted. "We just wanted some extra money."

"I'd encourage you to find a different line of work," Frank said. "There's not much future in rustlin'."

Tolle gasped for breath. "You don't know what it's like to spend your life ten dollars in the hole all the time."

Frank kept the pace steady. "And you have no idea what it's like to be $10,000 in the hole all the time."

"Ten thousand?" Tolle stumbled to one knee, then pulled himself up. "I ain't never seen that much money in my life."

"The trouble is . . . neither have I," Frank countered.

. . .

The Minnesela Road was no more than parallel wagon ruts across the treeless prairie. But it did mark the approximate boundary of the Rafter F.

"Boys, as I said before, I don't want to see you on Rafter F land again. I will feel justified to shoot you on sight," Frank declared.

"You really goin' to leave us out here?" Tolle asked.

"Yep."

"Do we get some bullets?" Meyers quizzed.

"Nope."

Tolle stared north, then south. "What do we get?"

Sam reached in his saddlebag. "I'll contribute four sticks of elk jerky."

Frank waved the Sharps carbine. "Give them that canteen, Uncle Sammy. It's the fullest one we have."

Sam tossed it down. "Water and jerky, boys, it could be worse."

"I want my possibles," Tolle demanded.

"Go get 'em." Frank nodded at the horse Tolle had been riding.

The lanky cowboy stepped up to the back of the horse and jabbed his hand into the rolled canvas.

Sam Fortune stood in the stirrups and pointed his Winchester 1894 rifle at Tolle's head. "Take it out slow."

"Wha . . . what?"

"You heard me, take your hand out slow. I don't want to see you pull a pistol out of there," Sam growled.

"I ain't rich enough to own two pistols." Tolle yanked a buckskin pouch from inside the rolled-up blanket.

Frank noticed the other cowboy's eyes widened.

"Meyers, you got any personal belongings?"

"In a cigar box back at the ranch."

"I'll have one of the boys take it to Deadwood next time in. Where do you want it left?" Frank asked.

"At the Piedmont, I guess. I got some letters I don't want to lose."

"In that case, I'll personally take it to the Fortune and Son Hardware. I know it will be safe there."

"I appreciate that." Meyers pulled off his hat and wiped his forehead on his gray shirtsleeve. "It wasn't nothin' personal, Frank. We just needed the money."

"It's personal to me, boys. Ever' single cow and calf can spell the difference between success and failure. I don't aim to fail."

"You really ridin' off?" Tolle pressed.

"You didn't leave me any option. I hope you make it to Texas . . . or New Mexico . . . or wherever. But I think your days around here are limited."

Frank turned Carlos south and spurred the horse to a trot. Sam rode beside him. Both men led saddled horses.

"You reckon you've seen the last of that pair?" Sam asked.

"That's my guess. I don't think the other boys on the place will put up with it either."

"How do you know the whole crew isn't in on the same thing?"

"No, no . . . I know my men better than that."

"You knew Tolle and Meyers better than that until a couple of hours ago," Sam reminded him.

Frank shook his head. "If the whole crew was rustlin' cows, I wouldn't have any left."

"How many do you have left?" Sam asked.

"Last count was near fifteen hundred."

"When was that count? At the spring roundup?"

"Come on, Uncle Sammy, I keep better track than that. We had a loose runnin' tally at the end of August."

"Did you count ever' head personally, or did the likes of Tolle and Meyers do some of the countin'?"

"Are you saying . . ."

"Just a thought. You might want to round them up a little early this fall. At least push them all to the southeast."

"I've thought about it. There's not much water down there. I just thought I was better at sizin' up my men, that's all."

"We all make mistakes hirin'. Daddy had and Dacee June only has a knack of gettin' it right all the time. Dacee June claims men are easy to read but women are impossible. I don't know if they are that difficult, or she just doesn't want us to try. You can just about go to the bank on her assessment of any man. Daddy was the same, but us boys always laughed and said that was because one look at the anger of Brazos Fortune put the fear of God in any soul."

Frank kicked Carlos, and the gelding broke into a trot. "All my life, growin' up, people would ask me if I was ever scared around Grandpa. I had no idea what they were talkin' about. I still don't know."

"I never knew a man who loved or dwelled on his grandkids more than Daddy Brazos," Sam said. "You kids made his life tolerable. Every one of you were handsome, beautiful, talented, smart. 'Til the day he died, he thought he was the luckiest man on earth. Not bad for a man who lost his twins when they were twelve and his beloved Sarah Ruth twenty-three years earlier."

They rode in silence for several long moments.

Then Frank cleared his throat. "I reckon I'll need to talk to the whole crew when we get back."

"Can you run things two short, or will you need to go hire some more?"

"I'll do alright until roundup. I was just keepin' them on to be fair. Strange, isn't it? I'd have been better off thinnin' the crew and rehirin' for the roundup."

"Treat 'em like you want to be treated. That's the only way we can live with ourselves and the Lord," Sam said.

"This is a rough business."

"You thinkin' about quittin'?"

"No, but I'm thinkin' about a one-man operation."

"Just you, Mama, and the kids. That ain't a bad plan."

"I suppose I ought to wait until there is a mama and the kids." Frank couldn't help but grin.

Sam spurred Cuddles into a trot and pulled ahead of Frank. "In that case, we better hurry back to the headquarters. You might have purdy company waitin' for you."

Frank led the way, once they broke down the trail into Bear Butte Valley. His carbine lay across his lap. His right hand cradled the receiver and the reins. His left hand tugged the lead lines on one of the extra horses. Sam Fortune rode behind him leading the other horse.

Frank spied two columns of smoke from the big

house, even when they were two miles away. As they plodded closer, he saw Jonas Lavender jump off the bench in front of the bunkhouse and dive inside. By the time they rode up even to the corrals, Howdy, Jonas, Tree Roberts, and Pete Mesquito waited for them in the bare dirt yard.

"Are those Tolle and Meyers' horses?" Howdy called out as they approached.

Frank rode slowly past them. "Yep."

"Are they dead?" Tree Roberts ventured.

He and Sam kept going straight toward the barn. "Nope."

The men paraded behind them.

Howdy trotted up next to Carlos's head. "Where are they?"

"Last I saw them, they were standin' alongside the Minnesela Road."

Jonas Lavender jogged to the barn door and swung it open. "What are they doin' up there?"

"Waitin' for a ride," Frank snapped.

"A ride? Did you give 'em some days off?" Howdy pressed.

"I gave them a lifetime off." When he reached the middle of the barn door, Frank turned around and stared down at the men who looked up at him.

"Boys, here's the deal. Me and Sam caught Tolle and Meyers with six of my steers brushed up and runnin' iron fire. They blurted out that they were plannin' on rustlin' Rafter F beef. So I fired them on the spot, took my ponies, saddles, and bullets, and left them at the road. I don't know which I hate worse, losin' money or disloyalty. But I won't put up with that. I won't put up with it for one minute. I expect ever' one of you to ride for the brand every minute you're on this ranch. If I have to make a stand, I expect you to be on my side ever' time. Now, if you aren't ready to make that kind of commitment, I'll make it easy on you. Get off the ranch before mornin'. A couple of you have your own horses and saddles, and that's fine. You just draw your pay and ride on off. The others, I expect you to walk off the ranch, 'cause if you take one of my horses, I'll track you down like a horse thief. Do you understand that?"

Howdy's face flushed brilliant red. "You don't think we'd steal on you, do you, Boss?"

"No, I don't, Howdy. But up until a few hours ago, I didn't think Tolle and Meyers would steal off me neither. I'm just soundin' a warnin'. I won't put up with this."

Sam Fortune stepped to the ground. "I reckon Little Frank let Tolle and Meyers off easy. No one ever got arrested or fined for shootin' a rustler in the act of over-brandin' cattle. They are alive, boys."

Howdy and the others said nothing. They drifted one by one back toward the bunkhouse.

Frank pulled the saddle off Carlos, while Sam took care of Cuddles.

"Was I too uncharitable to 'em, Uncle Sammy?"

"Some things need to be said."

"I don't have any reason to suspect any of them."

"It goes with the territory. You aren't one of the boys. You're the boss. There's a gap between the two. You just widened the gap a tad, that's all."

"Howdy looked real hurt."

"Find time to talk to him private. You had to say it in front of all of them."

They hung the saddles in the barn and stepped out to the dirt yard.

Sam pointed to the cowboys gathered on the bench in front of the bunkhouse. "Looks like a meetin' goin' on."

"Maybe I should go talk to Howdy now," Frank offered.

"Give 'em a chance to think and talk it through. Sometimes a crew will cull themselves. That's better than you havin' to say any more," Sam insisted.

Americus Ash, still wearing his white canvas bib apron, scurried down to Frank and Sam. "What's this I hear of Tolle and Meyers?"

Frank rubbed his temples. "They were stealin' my cows, Americus." His forehead hurt. His elbow hurt. His sides hurt.

The old man shook his head. "Don't that beat all? I never figured 'em for that."

"A lot of men will do whatever they think they can get away with. The Bible says there's sin in ever' man." Frank glanced back at the bunkhouse. "Fear of gettin' caught keeps most legal systems workin'."

"That's a cynical view," Americus mumbled.

"It's honest," Sam said.

Frank yanked off his bandanna and wiped caked dirt off his neck. "We'll have some empty spots at the dining table tonight."

"Not really," Americus wiped his hands on the soiled apron.

"How's that?" Frank asked.

Americus raised bushy gray eyebrows. "The lady, of course."

Frank's heart raced. "She's here already?"

"She got in a couple of hours ago. She was tired, so I told her she'd be welcome to take a nap in your room."

"Ohhhhh?" Sam laughed.

"Did I do the wrong thing? I didn't think you'd want her in the bunkhouse."

"Are all three of them in my room?" Frank asked.

"She was by herself, I think," Americus said.

Frank glanced south of the barn and could see a wagon tongue, but not the entire wagon. "I bet she had Latina and Miguel stay with the wagon."

"Who are they?" Americus asked.

"Her servants," Frank explained.

"She has servants?"

"Ladies like that usually do."

"I've been away from town too long," Americus said. "I thought only rich folks had servants."

"Don't let the fact that she's been out on the prairie a few days fool you. She comes from a very prominent family," Frank said.

"You see, I know nothing about women. Are you goin' to fire any more? I need to know when to cut back on supper," the cook said.

"I don't want to fire any at all." Frank nodded toward the bunkhouse. "It's up to them."

"Are you goin' to hire two more?"

"Not until roundup." Frank took several steps toward the big house, then paused. "Is she . . . you know . . . still nappin'?"

Americus shrugged. "It's your room. I wasn't about to go in there. But I think I heard her in the great room lookin' for somethin' to read."

"I surmise she reads in more than one language," Sam said.

"That doesn't surprise me," Americus replied. "I figured her for an educated lady."

"Maybe Americus knows more about women than he lets on," Sam hooted.

"Did you tell the boys she was here?" Frank asked.

"Nope. I got busy in the kitchen. Besides, I didn't know exactly what the deal was, so I figured you could introduce her."

Frank scratched his neck. "I reckon she'll be here for a while."

"She asked for only one night."

"That reminds me, I've got two men comin' in on Wednesday night. I want to cook some decent chops on that night. Nothin' fancy is needed, just some good meat."

"Over an open fire?"

"That's the best way." Frank stared off toward the house. "I reckon we should go check on the señorita."

"We?" Sam yelped. "Oh, no. You have to go in there alone. I'll go over and listen to the boys."

"Warn them we'll have a lady for supper. Some of them might want to clean up."

"I'll tell them. Now go on."

"I think I'll go invite Latina and Miguel up to the big house, first," Frank murmured.

Sam grabbed Frank's shoulders and pointed him toward the headquarters house. "Boy, if she didn't bring them in the house herself, she doesn't want them in the house. Comprende? She wants to be with El Padron, by himself. Get on up there."

"You don't think it's improper?"

"I don't know," Sam grinned. "Just what do you intend to do!"

"Nothin'," Frank mumbled.

"Doin' nothin' is never improper. Trust me. Now go on. You can do it."

"How do I look?"

"It's too late to do anything about that."

"Should I wash my face?"

"You're a rancher. It's alright to look like a rancher."

"This is the same shirt that I was wearin' when I saw her yesterday."

"Where are your clean shirts?"

"In my room."

"Ask her to close her eyes and hand you a fresh shirt."

"Yeah, I suppose I can do that."

Sam Fortune let out a long, slow whistle. The crowd at the bunkhouse stared at them. "I was joshin' you, Little Frank. Just be polite, and try not to fall off your horse this time." Sam shoved him toward the big house.

"You would remind me of that. Maybe I ought to go talk to the boys again."

"Have you ever seen anything so pathetic, Americus?"

"Not since Thunder Stewart got bushwhacked by a twelve-year-old girl," the old man mumbled.

Frank wiped his forehead on his shirtsleeve and straightened his vest. "I don't know if I should bother her. Maybe I'll wait for her to come out."

"You want me to go talk to the señorita?" Sam asked.

"Would you?"

"No. Now if you don't head over there, I'll march you at gunpoint."

"You would, wouldn't you?"

Sam shoved him toward the big house. "Go on!"

"Don't you have to get back to Deadwood soon?"

"Not with you entertainin' a purdy lady in your bedroom."

"She ain't in my . . . I mean, I only have two rooms . . ."

Sam Fortune reached for his revolver, then glanced over to see all the men at the bunkhouse watching him. "Have fun, Little Frank."

"I'd rather face a pack of angry armed men than that one woman."

"With any luck, you'll get to do both."

Sam meandered over to the cowboys in front of the bunkhouse.

Frank Fortune wavered in the middle of the dirt yard, staring at the long, low building.

I know, Lord. I make things too serious in my mind. I've always done that. I guess I'm like Mama in that way. She's just a lady, a beautiful lady. And she's a friend of my parents. She's the daughter of friends of my parents. And she's out here to study the prairie. It's just by chance that she's here . . . in my bedroom. I mean, my house.

Frank inched toward the front door. *I'll just say, "I hope you found everything comfortable, Miss Rodriguez." I mean, Señorita Rodriguez. I wonder if I should call her Dearyanna? "I'll be in the barn if you need me. Supper will be in less than an hour."*

Frank paused with his hand on the cold brass door-knob.

But why should I go sit in the barn? I have some book work to do. I'll just slip over to the desk and work on those accounts. Maybe I'll read up on cattle poisons. I need to figure out what happened to my cows at Sweet-water Springs.

As if sneaking up on a sleeping baby, Frank pushed open the front door. "Eh, excuse me, señorita, I, eh, got, eh, invoices to dispatch!" he blurted out as he barged into the room. *Why did I say that? It's not even true.*

The room was empty.

"Ma'am?" His eyes surveyed the rock fireplace, the leather sofas facing each, the rolltop desk in the corner, the rocking chair, the saddle stand.

She's not here. Maybe they left. Maybe they went back to Deadwood, and I can . . .

Sounds of a lady humming filtered from the slightly ajar door to his room.

She's in my room! But that's where Americus put her. It's OK, of course. I don't think I straightened it up this morning. I didn't make my bed. I haven't made my bed in a month. This is not good. This is embarrassing. Mama would die if she knew I welcomed the señorita into a messy house. What am I goin' to do? What can I say? This is pathetic. Maybe I should just ride up to

Buffalo Gap.

Sweat beaded on Frank's forehead. He pulled off his hat and rubbed the swollen knot on his forehead. *She has already seen me battered. So at least that's no surprise. I'll just say hello, then go talk to the men. I need to talk to Howdy.*

Frank shuffled over to the partially open door.

Hat in hand, he held his breath, then leaned close to the door. He could still hear the soft humming. He peeked through the two-inch opening of the door.

She must be over by the mirror. I had a shirt hanging over the mirror. Or was it my long underwear? No, no, no. I can't believe this.

Using two knuckles, he rapped on the door.

The humming continued.

He took a deep breath and held it. *I really need to go talk to Howdy.*

This time Frank rapped a little louder. "Excuse me, ma'am."

The humming stopped.

He continued to lean into the door as he heard light footsteps approaching. He brushed his hair back with his fingertips, forced a smile, and rolled the brim of his hat with his hands.

The footsteps halted.

He waited.

His head almost touched the oak door.

"Ma'am, is ever'thin' satisfactory?"

"Yes, quite so." The voice had a light, breezy tone.

The door started to open, then slammed shut, like a heavy paddle cracking against the swollen lump on

161

Frank's head.

He let out a cry and staggered back. When his boots hit the rag throw rug, his feet slipped out from under him, and he clutched the back of the couch to keep from sprawling on the floor. Pain shot through his sides.

Frank struggled to steady himself as a lady with brown hair in a long beige dress hurried to his side.

"Oh dear, I'm terribly sorry. My foot hit the door and shoved it closed," she explained.

Frank labored to stand.

The woman had a round face. Brown eyes. Upturned nose.

And pale skin.

"Who are you?" he blurted out.

"Obviously, not the woman you were expecting to be in your room."

"I . . . I . . . I thought . . ."

"And I thought your cook would explain. Please forgive me if I have intruded."

"No, no . . . I just . . . I mean, that's fine. Eh, who are you?"

"Are you Frank Fortune?" she asked.

He stepped back and felt his legs jam against the back of the brown leather couch. "Yes, ma'am."

"Oh dear, did I put that lump on your forehead?"

"No, ma'am, I did that the other day. You just sort of . . . well, I reckon you aggravated it a tad."

"Let me make you an astringent poultice and . . . I'm sorry, Mr. Fortune, that's the schoolteacher in me, I suppose."

"You are a schoolteacher?"

"Yes, we haven't been introduced. I'm Miss Estelle Bowers." She held out her hand.

"Happy to meet you, Miss Bowers." Frank felt his shoulders relax.

"Seriously, Mr. Fortune, an astringent poultice will bring down that swelling. I notice you had some Dr. Bull's in your room."

"That's horse liniment."

"I am well aware of that, but it works quite well. I've used it often at school. You had a bottle on your dresser. Let me fetch it."

"My room is a mess," he blurted out.

"Yes, it was. But I tidied it up a bit. I trust you don't mind. It's a nasty habit I learned from my sister."

Frank trailed her to the door. "You made my bed?"

"And dusted, swept, and put up a few things. I believe the shirt hanging on the mirror was beyond saving. I hope you weren't in it when it got ripped like that."

"I took a little tumble the other day."

"Do you have any linen bandages?"

"Eh, no. I don't reckon so."

Estelle marched back across the room carrying the liniment. "I'll just apply a little of this. I think it will help."

"Actually, I'm fine . . . now, who did you say . . ."

"Nonsense. Just sit down, and let me apply a little of this. Perhaps out in the great room?"

"Oh."

"Schoolteachers need to be discreet about being in a man's room," she grinned.

It was a pleasant grin.

A very pleasant grin.

"Yes, ma'am." Frank shuffled back out to the great room and plopped down on one of the leather couches.

"Lean your head back. I'll stand back here," she instructed.

"Yes, ma'am."

"And don't call me, 'ma'am'. I'm Estelle Bowers. But please call me Essie." She patted ointment on his bruised forehead.

"What are you doin' here?" he asked.

"Close your eyes so this doesn't sting you."

"You didn't answer my question, Essie," he insisted.

"Well, Frank, let's see. I told you I'm Essie Bowers, originally from Scottsbluff, Nebraska. I have been teaching at the Girls Boarding School for Indians on the Wind River Reservation."

"That's a long ways away," he said.

"Yes, it is. Three of my girls decided to leave the school and try to find their families up at Cheyenne Agency. They stole horses at Greybull."

Frank opened one eye and studied her face upside down. "Did they have a paneled wagon with two mules?"

She closed his eye with her finger. "Yes, have you seen them?" She continued to apply the liniment.

"No, but I found the wagon and mules."

She stopped rubbing. "You mean, they are on foot?"

"No, they stole three horses from my corral at Buffalo Gap."

"Oh, dear. I'll pay you for the horses, Frank."

"Essie, you don't owe me anything. They are branded horses. Did you come to bring them back by yourself?"

Why am I calling this lady by her first name? I haven't known her for three minutes.

"I didn't follow them to bring them back. I just want to make sure they get to their families safely. They are dear girls. Tomorrow, could you show me where you saw them last?"

"I reckon so. But you can't take a wagon down in the Badlands."

"Perhaps I could borrow a saddle horse."

"You can't go into that country by yourself."

"Frank Fortune, we have known each other less than five minutes. Are you telling me what I can and can't do?"

"Yes I am, Essie Bowers."

"OK."

He peeked at her with one eye.

She pursed her lips. "Good. We have that established. I won't ride down into the Badlands by myself."

"Thank you."

"But you will need to apply this liniment, without fail, to the worst part of this bruise every day for a few days."

"Essie Bowers, we have known each other less than five minutes; are you telling me what I have to do?"

"Yes, I am, Frank Fortune."

"OK. We have that established."

Frank reached up and touched the middle of his forehead with his fingertips. "I presume right here is where it needs most attention."

"Yes, but also . . ." Essie took his hand in hers and gently slid it over to the left a little. "Right there . . ."

The front door swung open.

"Oh, my . . . am I interrupting?" a woman gasped.

With Essie's fingers still clutching his, Frank stared at the woman in the doorway.

"Señorita Rodriguez?" he mumbled.

CHAPTER SIX

FRANK LOWERED HIS HAND as Essie Bowers continued to clutch his fingers. Her hand was warm. Strong. Calloused, yet tender.

"I was just . . ." He sat up on the couch. Essie stood behind him.

Dearyanna Rodriguez slowly licked her narrow lips. "You don't need to explain to me."

Estelle Bowers reached over and plucked a small piece of straw from Frank's matted hair, then brushed it down with her fingers.

Frank glanced back at her, then at the lady in the blue satin dress who filled the door with color and fire. "No, it was just that we were . . . eh, we . . ." Frank stammered.

Señorita Rodriguez's flawless complexion revealed no emotions. "It's obvious what you were doing."

Essie dropped his hand and folded her arms across the front of her beige cotton dress. She bit her lip, then blurted out, "What did you mean by that?"

Like a sudden summer hailstorm, the señorita's brown eyes sprayed everything in the room. "Honey, there's no reason to get all puffy. It seems dear Francisco invites many ladies to the ranch."

Frank leaped off the brown leather sofa. "That's not

true. I didn't invite Essie here."

Dearyanna Rodriguez raised her thick, black eyebrows. "Oh?"

Frank shifted from one foot to the other. "Tell her, Essie. I didn't invite you, did I?"

Estelle waltzed around the couch and stood next to him. "No, Frank didn't invite me. But I'm not sure what difference that makes. Your innuendoes stand, don't they? And I don't believe we've even been introduced."

Sweat rolled down the back of Frank's neck. "Oh, this is Señorita Dearyanna Rodriguez of Sonora, Mexico." Then he turned to Estelle. "And this is Essie . . . eh . . . Essie, eh . . . "

Essie never took her eyes off the señorita. "Bowers," she said.

"Essie Bowers," Frank blurted out.

Dearyanna marched straight over and held out her hand. "How very nice to meet one of Francisco Fortune's old friends."

Essie paused.

Frank held his breath.

Essie shook the señorita's black leather-gloved hand.

"I presume you work in Deadwood?" Dearyanna hung onto Essie's hand.

"No, I don't." Essie patted the top of Dearyanna's hand. "Do you work in Deadwood, honey?"

Señorita Rodriguez dropped Essie's hands. "Not hardly." She waltzed over to the fireplace and untied the chin ribbon on her flat straw hat. "This is a beautiful room, Mr. Francisco Fortune. It reminds me so much of my father's hunting lodge near Santa Fe."

"Thank you." Frank rubbed his chin and could feel sweat, beard, and grime. "It's home to me."

"I don't want to interrupt you two any more. You can get back to that little thing you were doing." The señorita's leather boots tapped across the worn wooden floor.

"I was playing nursemaid to Frank's head wound," Essie explained.

"Yes, I'm sure you were, dear. That was one of my favorite childhood games, too." She laid her finger against her cheek. "But I don't believe we played that down at Ft. Huachuca when we were young, did we, Francisco?"

"You've known each other a long time?" Essie inquired.

"It seems like our families have been close forever," Dearyanna added. "Anyway, enough of that. I'll stay out in the wagon with Miguel and Latina."

"You are traveling with friends?" Essie asked.

"Servants," Dearyanna replied.

"No, wait," Frank protested. "I invited you to stay with me as long as you wanted, and I . . ."

"You did?" Essie said.

"But, of course, being old family friends."

"How convenient." Essie raised her thin brown eyebrows.

"What did you mean by that?" Dearyanna shot back.

"My goodness, Frank, this is a rather sticky business, isn't it?" Essie closed up the liniment bottle. "I haven't had this much fun since my sister, Jolie, got married. Look, señorita, I am only staying one night, then I have to find my girls."

"You have children?"

"No, and I don't have grandchildren, either," Essie snapped. "So, since I'm not the one moving in for an extended period, let me sleep out in my wagon. It wouldn't be the first time."

"She is not moving in," Frank mumbled. "Well, just for a few days or weeks or so . . . I think."

"This conversation is going too far," Dearyanna replied. "I'm afraid I got carried away with the teasing. Please forgive me. Now, if you don't mind, Francisco, I would be happy just to take this room and sweet Essie may have your room."

"You're right. I said more than I intended, also. Now," Essie protested, "I believe I should take this room since I'm only going to be here one night. That would leave La Dona Rodriguez to settle into your bedroom."

The señorita glared at her.

"Oh dear, that sounded rather coarse. Please excuse me. What is your idea, Frank?"

He searched the room.

But not their eyes.

"I would be happy to have you both use the house. These two rooms are yours. I think maybe Essie is right. Since she's only staying one night, perhaps this room would be more compatible for the evening."

Essie took his arm and patted his hand. "I think you made a very wise decision."

Dearyanna laced her fingers and tilted her head. "Oh, Mr. Fortune," she batted her long black eyelashes, "you are such a charming, decisive man." Then she dropped her hands and started to laugh.

"It's rather difficult to stop, once we get started," Essie added.

The señorita tugged off her black leather gloves. "You are very good at it."

"Oh, you are much more accomplished than me," Essie insisted. "You have a certain multinational depth that I could never duplicate."

"Yes, and I didn't even have to resort to Spanish."

"That would have crushed me for sure."

"What are you two talking about?" Frank said, turning his head from one to the other.

"The fine art of the insincere compliment," Essie said.

"The what?"

"Strange how they can go through life so clueless," Dearyanna remarked.

"I suppose they have to make up for it in other ways."

Dearyanna slipped her arm into Essie's. "You ought to see what a fine horseman Francisco is."

"Really?"

"It's stunning. Why, he nearly took my breath away when he leaned over in the saddle to fetch my hat off the prairie soil."

"When was that?"

"Yesterday. He single-handedly rescued me from a posse of dangerous gunmen. Francisco, didn't you tell sweet Essie about our encounter yesterday and the day before?"

Frank stared down at his boots. "Eh, no, we just met."

Dearyanna twirled a blue satin handkerchief. "I keep forgetting that you just met. It seems as if you have known each other much longer."

"That's exactly my feeling," Essie grinned, then strolled toward the door to the bedroom. "I'll move my things out into this room."

Dearyanna followed her. "And I'll get Latina and Miguel to help with my trunks. My, this is very tidy. Most men leave their room in a mess."

"Is that so?" Essie said.

"That one was very good," Dearyanna smiled. "I especially liked the little-girl tonal inquisitiveness. It was professional. I couldn't have done it better myself."

"Thank you, dear. Coming from you, that is a fine compliment."

Frank stopped at the doorway. "Make yourselves at home, ladies . . . I need to . . . eh . . ."

Both women paused and stared at Frank.

"Eh . . . you know . . . do some chores."

He barreled out the front door.

A wave of cool fall air rolled across Frank's sweaty face.

Four men waited for him, huddled in the dirt yard.

"Well?" Sam Fortune pressed.

Frank shot a glance at each of the men and hiked toward the barn. "Well, what?"

"You got two women in your house, and you say, 'Well, what?'" Sam chided. "The men want to know which one you chose."

"Which one I chose? I'm not choosing women. They are just spending the night, that's all."

Howdy Tompkins held his hat in his hand. "Both of

'em stayin'?"

"Yes. One is in the great room and one in my . . . eh, other room."

"And just which one is in the 'other' room?" Sam teased.

"Sounds like the old man is lookin' for trouble," Howdy said.

"Who stays where is up to them." When Frank stopped hiking, the others did the same. "Howdy, I need to talk to you alone."

"I figured that."

"Jonas, you and Pete and Tree, I just want to say . . ." Frank searched around. "Where's Tree Roberts?"

"He quit," Jonas reported.

"Took his horse and saddle and five bullets. Said you could deduct the cost of the bullets from his pay, but he wasn't ridin' out with an empty gun. He took Meyers's possibles box and said send his pay to the Piedmont in Deadwood."

Frank rubbed his neck. "Why did Tree leave?"

Howdy stared at the dirt between them. "Said he couldn't work for someone who thought he was a cow thief."

Frank pulled off his hat and scratched the back of his head. "Boys, let me apologize for soundin' so condemnin' when I rode up. I was upset about Tolle and Meyers. I still am. I was hurtin', not just at the loss of cows, but at the loss of men I thought were friends. But that's no reason to accuse any of you. That wasn't a very Christian attitude, and I'm sorry."

"I appreciate you sayin' that," Jonas replied.

"Kind of late for Tree," Pete added.

"I'll apologize to Roberts next time I see him. You boys let him know he has a job here, any time he wants."

Pete nodded. He and Jonas ambled back toward the bunkhouse.

Sam glanced across the yard at the old man dragging a large green trunk. "I think I'll go help Miguel with the señorita's belongings. Looks to me like she is movin' in permanent."

Frank and Howdy drifted toward the corral.

"Howdy, I'm feelin' bad about what I said to the men and especially to you. You've been here with me for almost the whole time. I had a hundred head and a canvass tent when you signed on. I'm grateful for you stickin' around. The whole thing caught me off guard today. I just didn't know what to say or do."

Howdy brushed hay off his shirt sleeve. "That's alright, Frank. I've been ponderin' it myself. I reckon if it happened to me, I'd say somethin' stupid, too."

Overhead a red-tailed hawk squawked. Both men looked up. "Thanks for bein' honest. Howdy, can we take care of this place three men short?"

Howdy Tompkins rubbed his unshaven chin. "If we put only one up at Buffalo Gap and only one man along the Minnesela Road. We can do it till roundup, anyway. Does Sam plan on stayin' long?"

"Only a few days. We got dead cows at Sweetwater Springs, Howdy. We've got to fence it off until we can figure out what happened."

"Me and Jonas can do that first thing. You want Pete

to ride up to the Minnesela Road?"

"I'd rather you ride up there than Pete. If Thomasville's behind any of this, I'm not sure Pete will stand up against them by himself."

"And you think I will?"

"I know you will, Howdy Tompkins."

"Yeah . . . well, you read that one right. I do appreciate the confidence. You'll take care of chores here tomorrow?"

"I'll get Sam to do them. I promised to take Essie to the Badlands. I'll swing by Sweetwater Springs and show Pete and Jonas what to do."

Howdy stared back at the big house. "Is Essie the señorita or the sturdy one?"

"Sturdy one?"

"Looks like a farm girl to me. I didn't mean that in a bad sense," Howdy said.

Frank watched Sam Fortune as he visited with Estelle Bowers. "Essie's a schoolteacher from Wyoming."

"I heard about the señorita, but I didn't know about the schoolteacher. Where did you meet her?"

"In my room, just now."

"She just showed up?"

"It's a long story."

"Things are changin' quick around here, Boss."

"You noticed that? Good. I was worried it was just me. After we get Sweetwater Springs quarantined, I think we'll move all the cattle down to the lower part of the ranch."

"The best grass left is up there," Howdy said.

"I know, but it's crazy on that northern line. The railroad gang comin' south. Thomasville from the west."

"I thought you didn't want to abandon any part of the ranch?"

"You know I don't, Howdy. I'm goin' to move them down, count them up, and see how many we've lost."

"You figure we lost some since the August count?"

"Meyers and Tolle counted some of those in August. I can't be too sure of their addin'."

"Sounds like an early roundup."

"We've got a month of grass left down here."

"After that, we'll have to move them back north. And it will be cold then," Howdy declared.

"Either that or we'll sell them."

"The whole herd?"

"I'd rather sell them than be picked clean one bite at a time. But keep all of this to yourself. The boys only need to know one day at a time."

"You can count on me, Boss."

"I know it, Howdy. Thanks."

"Now, are you goin' to need any help?"

"Talkin' to the boys?"

Howdy grinned. "No, I meant talkin' to the ladies."

Frank laughed. "It's strange, Howdy. I don't think I've hardly had a lady visitor in four years who wasn't related to me. And now I got two of them."

"Are you braggin' or complainin', Boss?"

"I don't know, Howdy. But I reckon I'll find out."

"You want me to talk to Pete and Jonas about tomorrow's assigns?"

"Appreciate it. Have we got enough fence posts?"

"Plenty of posts, but not too many rails. How

big a space?"

"Just across the trail down the draw until I figure it out."

"Ah, ain't ranchin' a fun business?"

"Too dumb to quit, Howdy."

"Where are you headed now, Boss?"

"To the barn."

"You got some work in there you need help with?"

"No."

"Are you . . .?"

"See you at supper, Howdy."

"Yep," he said. "You will. I'm stickin' around to see how this plays out."

"You mean whether I can make it with this ranch?"

"Whether or not you can survive them two women," Howdy whooped.

When the sun set behind the bluff, the barn darkened, while the corrals remained in daylight. Frank inhaled the familiar aroma of old hay, old leather, old manure. He climbed the ladder to the loft.

The big double door was open to the yard below, but he plopped down on the grimy, straw-covered floor far enough back to not be seen from below. Horseflies buzzed in the log rafters above him. He gazed east at the Dakota prairie and the shadow of the cliff behind him as it crept like the tide sweeping the eastern edge of the little valley.

He plucked up a piece of straw and chewed it with disinterest.

My life is out of control, Lord. Cattle dyin', horses

*stolen, men rustlin', neighbors harassin' and women . . .
Lord, . . . well, Lord bein' with those two reminded me of
bein' with the twins when they were twelve. That's when
I would go someplace and play baseball.*

*Lord, I'm a simple man. I can do one thing at a time.
I want to raise cattle. I don't want to bother anyone; I
don't want anyone to bother me. I came out here 'cause
nobody wanted this land. Too remote. Too worthless.*

*I can still hear Daddy say, "Well, no one will bother
you out there, Little Frank." You were wrong, Daddy. It
took a little over four years, but you were wrong. I think
I could make it out here if I was on my own. Uncle
Sammy's right. I need a fenced ranch.*

I need a fenced life.

*Fence in my life, put a padlock on the gate, and only
give the key to a few, Lord. Mama, Daddy, Uncle
Sammy, the twins . . .*

A wide smile broke across his face.

*Maybe not the twins. I'm jokin', Lord. My entire life
would have been hollow and boring without my sisters.*

Of course, right at the moment, boring might be nice.

Frank pressed against the barn post and closed his
eyes. The rough-cut timber pressed into the back of his
vest and shirt. *Lord, that first year I moved this barn out
here, I used to sit up and count my cows. I could see
them all from here.*

Do you ever sit and count your cows?

Your people?

*I reckon there's no need, since you never lose track of
them.*

OK, I'm gettin' scattered. I'm a cattleman. I have

some cattle problems. And I better take care of them.
  After I get a nap.

Frank swatted a horsefly away from the back of his neck. Then another. And another.

He opened his eyes and could see that the entire little valley was flooded with evening shadows.

It wasn't a horsefly but a pebble that bounced off his neck.

He glanced back down into the barn. "Howdy, are you the one . . ."

A wide smile beamed from the lady in the yellow cotton dress.

"Everyone seems to be waiting for the 'ol' man.' I presume that is you, Frank."

He rose slowly to his feet. "Essie, I'm only twenty-four."

She brushed her bangs off her forehead. "And I'm twenty-two, which my sister, Jolie, considers to be an old maid."

Frank stared down through the shadows. "No matter what my age, if I pay the salaries, I'm the old man." *Sturdy? What was Howdy talkin' about? She looks a lot like Mama when she was younger.*

Essie began climbing the ladder to the loft.

"What are you doing?" Frank scurried around to the top of the ladder. "I'm on my way down."

"I want to see what's so fascinating up here." Essie's words bounced with each step.

"It's just a loft."

She paused halfway and caught her breath. "But it is

where you go when you want to be alone. Isn't that why you are here?"

"I had some ranch problems to think through."

He reached his hand out and helped her up the top step.

She released his hand slowly. "And you have two tempestuous women in your house. I imagine you aren't used to that."

"I have identical twin sisters. I'm used to almost anything."

"Oh my, that would be a challenge. Do you have other siblings?"

"Just the twins."

"I have an older sister, Jolie, who's married and has three children. She plans on having six, and she will, of course, because no one and nothing stops her from her goals. My brother Lawson is also married. He's farming in Nebraska. My brother Gibs is U.S. deputy marshal in El Paso. They are all married, but me." Estelle Bowers hiked over to the open barn door.

"Careful, Essie, that's a fifteen-foot drop."

"Did you ever jump off the roof of your house, Frank?"

"What?"

"When we first moved to Nebraska, we had a sod house. And one time my brother Gibs and I jumped off the roof of the soddy. I landed in the mud and ruined my dress."

Frank sidled out next to her. "What did your mama say about that?"

"Mama plowed that day and didn't say anything. But

my sister Jolie pitched a fit. She practically raised me, you know. Even now, she will write me a letter and tell me how to organize my shoes. That's just the way she is. Your uncle said that your whole family is in Deadwood. I read in a book that Sam Fortune was the only man hauled into court who made Judge Parker laugh."

"Was that in a book?"

"Yes. It's called *Folklore of Early Oklahoma*. What was it that made the judge laugh?"

"On a dare Uncle Sammy stole the judge's favorite horse and rode him all over town, then snuck him back into the judge's corral. The judge couldn't get him for stealin', so he fined Uncle Sammy twenty dollars for horse borrowin' without permission."

"What made the judge laugh?"

"Uncle Sammy paid the fine and handed the judge a bill for twenty dollars for horse breakin' and trainin'. He said he had the horse ground broke and standin'."

"What did Judge Parker do?"

"He laughed and paid Uncle Sammy the twenty dollars. Told him he had two other horses that needed to be borrowed some time."

"You have a colorful family, Frank."

"I'm the plain one."

Essie started to laugh.

He stared at her.

"Oh, I'm not laughing at you. I was laughing because all my life, I've been called the plain one. My sister is quite beautiful. But you know what, Frank?"

"What?"

"I like me. I know a lot of people who don't like themselves." She slipped her arm in his. "Now, come on, I told you everyone is waiting for you so we can have supper."

"Everyone?"

"Except the señorita. She is still in her room. Well, in your room. I think she is waiting for you to usher her."

"She surely is . . ."

"Beautiful?"

"Yep, that's what I was goin' to say, only . . ."

"Only you said to yourself, should I tell Essie that I think Dearyanna is beautiful?"

"Something like that."

"Well, you are right, Frank Fortune. She is one of the most beautiful women I have ever seen. She reminds me of Jolie. I spent my life being the 'other' Bowers girl; no one could quite remember her name. But Jolie is a wonderful sister and still my best friend. There's a lot of freedom in people not having very high expectations for you. Do you know what I mean?"

"Not really."

"Your family has high expectations for you?"

"I have high expectations for myself. I'm the oldest of the grandkids . . . well, not counting Amber. She's my Uncle Sammy's step-daughter. Now, there is another beautiful woman."

"Thank you very much," she grinned.

"Oh, I meant . . ."

"Frank Fortune, I know exactly what you mean." She peeked over the edge of the barn door and stared at the ground.

"Careful." He tugged on her arm and pulled her back

away from the edge.

"You worry too much about me." Essie spun around and slipped her hand into his. "Come on, we better go back before La Dona Rodriguez finds us in the hayloft."

Her hand felt good, and Frank continued to hold it as they strolled over to the ladder.

"Let me go down first and help you down," Frank offered.

"Thank you very much, Mr. Frank Fortune, but little girls learn quite young that they always go down the ladder first."

"Oh . . ." Frank could feel his face blush.

"I'm certainly glad Señorita Rodriguez doesn't see you blushing. She would really be upset, wouldn't she?"

Essie waited for him at the bottom of the ladder.

"I guess it got a little dark while I was up there." He reached out and took her arm. "Can you find your way to the door?"

"Frank, are you searching for an excuse to keep holding my hand?"

He dropped her arm. "No!"

Essie began to laugh. "You are so fun to tease. Come on, your crew really is waiting. They said they don't eat until El Padron blesses the meal. I like the way you have them all sit at the table in your house."

"Usually it's just the boys and me."

"Will you still be able to show me where the girls rode down in the Badlands? It's quite alright if you can't. I know you have company."

"I plan on it, if you don't mind me swinging by Sweet-water Springs with the boys. I have to fence off the place. I had some cattle die. I think the water got poisoned."

"You mean, someone actually tampered with it?"

The evening air felt fresh when they strolled out of the barn. "I don't know, but six of them are bloody and bloated."

"Bloody?"

"It's gruesome. I don't want to talk about it."

"Nostrils, mouth, ears?" Essie pressed.

"Yeah. You seen that before?"

"Anthrax."

"Are you serious?" he asked.

"It must be anthrax. I've seen it before."

"Is it in the water?"

"It's from bacteria."

"Where does the bacteria come from?"

"From other animals. Maybe the spores float in the air. I don't know."

Still arm in arm, Frank paused halfway to the big house. "How do I stop it?"

"You can't, but keep your men away from it. It can kill people too, you know."

Frank felt the hair on his neck bristle. "I rode through it two days ago."

"You are alive, so you don't have it."

"Essie, how do you know about this?"

"We had an outbreak in Wyoming last fall. Three men and one woman died. They lost about one hundred head of cattle, too."

"Will you go by the springs with me, then?"

"Certainly."

"Thanks, Essie."

She pointed to the door from his room that led out to the covered porch. "You'd better go fetch the señorita. The men have been anxious for another glance."

"Why don't you go get her for me?"

"Oh no, I'm sure she will not be happy unless El Padron comes for her."

"How can you be so sure?"

"Because if I were that beautiful, I'd demand it myself."

He took a big breath and let out a deep sigh. "OK, I'll do it."

"Good. Now, wait a minute." Essie pulled her handkerchief from her sleeve and wet it with her tongue. She wiped his face. "You had a smudge."

"Thank you."

Essie grinned and wiggled her nose. "You're welcome." With her fingertips she brushed his hair behind his ears. "There . . . except for that yellow lump on your forehead, and needing a shave, you look very handsome. Now, go be the charming Mr. Frank Fortune."

"No one has ever called me charming."

"I just did."

He made a face at her.

"What's the matter?" she asked.

"Essie Bowers, how long have we known each other?"

She laughed. "We were neighbors when we were kids, weren't we?"

"I figure about an hour."

"Posh, we've known each other for two hours and

twelve minutes," she corrected.

"That long, huh?"

"Yes."

"It seems like longer, Essie. And I mean that in a good sense."

"Thank you, Frank. What a sweet thing to say. Now go, she's waiting for you."

"How do you know?"

"She's hungry, just like the rest of us."

Frank rapped his knuckles against the door. "Señorita Rodriguez?"

He listened to boot heels tap their way across the wooden floor. He stepped back from the door.

It swung open with the patience of a cat just waking up.

"Are you ready for supper?" he asked.

"Yes, I am, thank you." She stepped out onto the porch. Her blue satin dress swished with each step.

"I suppose it will sound repetitive if I say you look very pretty tonight," Frank began.

"Repetitive? I don't believe you've ever said that before."

"I suppose I was just thinkin' it."

"How flattering. You are very charming." The señorita clutched his arm. "I feel like I need to apologize."

He paused by the door to the great room. "What for?"

"I am afraid I wasn't very pleasant to Miss Bowers. She is your guest and I'm sure, a pleasant enough lady. She caught me by surprise when I walked in. I behaved poorly."

"That's alright. She caught me by surprise too. When Americus said there was a lady waiting, I assumed it was you."

She took his arm as they strolled down the covered porch toward the dining room. "Do you know this is the first time we've seen each other without some awkward scene?"

"Yes, but I'm well aware the evenin' is just beginning."

"Do I make you nervous, Frank Fortune?"

He felt his mouth go dry. "Why did you say that?"

"I have had men say that I make them nervous. And I don't know why that is. I thought perhaps if I made you nervous, you could explain it to me."

"I reckon it is difficult for some men to be at ease with such a beautiful woman."

"Do they want to impress me with their words?"

"I'm sure they do."

"Do you want to impress me, Frank Fortune?"

"Wh . . what kind of talk is that?" he sputtered.

"Well, do you?"

"What I want is to live up to my image of me."

She clapped her hands. "Oh, yes. I like that. And what is your image of you?"

"A man who is relaxed and himself, no matter who he is in the presence of."

"You certainly look that way right now."

"Thank you." He reached for the door handle.

"Just a moment." Dearyanna tugged a small silk scarf from her sleeve. She licked it, then wiped his cheek. Then she ran her fingertips through his hair.

"There, that looks nice."

Frank just shook his head.

"Two can play that game, Mr. Francisco Fortune."

"You were watching, weren't you?"

"Yes, I was."

He pushed open the door. A chorus of sliding chairs greeted them as each man stood, and the two ladies remained seated.

Dearyanna Rodriguez's blue satin dress swished ahead of him. "My, what a handsome crew, Mr. Fortune!" she said.

Happy, Jonas, and Pete sat at the far side of the table. Sam was at the kitchen end. Americus and Miguel were in front of the door. Estelle Bowers sat next to Sam and Latina next to Miguel. At the end, near the door to the great room, were two empty chairs.

Dearyanna dropped his arm and swished toward the kitchen end of the table. "You must all forgive me, but I will take a very spoiled Mexican girl's privilege and change the seating arrangement."

She swooped between Essie and Sam.

"Miss Bowers and I simply have much to talk about and must sit next to each other." She tugged on Essie's arm. "I insist. Please come sit with me."

A blushing Essie Bowers followed the raven-haired señorita.

"Looks like you're stuck between me and Pete, Little Frank," Sam hooted.

"At least Pete is good company," Frank responded.

Latina insisted on helping Americus serve the food, and soon most were slicing meat and dipping it in brown gravy.

Sam loosened his tie.

"Nice of you to dress for supper," Frank said.

"I figure some member of the Fortune family should be presentable. Although it don't seem to matter much. Those two gals seem to be ignoring this end of the table."

Frank studied the grins and whispers of Dearyanna and Essie. "Don't that beat all? They were tryin' to poke out each other's eyes earlier."

"How did you settle things?"

"The señorita is in my room. Essie is in the great room."

"Where's Uncle Sammy and El Padron goin' to sleep?"

"I hear there's two empty bunks in the bunkhouse. And plenty of hay in the loft."

"There's even a little hay still stuck in the back of your hair," Sam murmured.

Frank reached to the back of his head. "There is?"

Sam began to laugh. "Nope. But you surely looked like a kid with his hand in the cookie jar."

"Essie fetched me while I was sittin' in the loft."

"Isn't that nice of her?"

"She's a very friendly girl," Frank said between bites. "She thinks the cows over at Sweetwater Springs may have died from anthrax. Have you ever seen anthrax, Uncle Sammy?"

"Nope, but I ran across a patch of it in New Mexico after some sheep had died."

"What do you mean, a patch of it?"

"It seems to infect the soil. That's what the government thought anyway. They built a huge bonfire and tried to burn it out of the dirt."

"Did that work?"

"I don't know. At the time I was tryin' to keep ahead of Marshall Chola and a lady named Fire Bucket Red."

"Did you succeed?"

"Yes and no. Do you want me to ride out there with you two?"

"What for?"

"Chaperon."

"With Essie?"

"I didn't know there was a difference," Sam jibed.

"What I need is for you to stay here and see that the boys get the place straightened. I've got your ol' pal Reid LeMay and Major George Washington Thomasville comin' in. I'll need someone to keep them apart."

"We just captured two of your own men stealing cows for Thomasville and you're invitin' him in for supper?"

"There is somethin' crazy about that story, Uncle Sammy. I want to find out what's goin' on. Besides, if he's guilty, I figure he won't show."

"So you think they will tear into each other?"

"Could happen. Reid said they'd shoot at Thomasville's men if they ran across them."

"And you are runnin' off with a pretty lady."

"No, I told you I'm goin' to take Essie . . ." he glanced across the room. "Maybe you're right. Maybe I should take both of them with me."

"Both of them?" Sam choked back the words. "It is

much safer to be with Reid and Thomasville than those two women."

"That's absurd. Look at how well they are getting along."

"They are just sparrin', son. They are testin' the length of their jab and tryin' to discover a soft spot."

"Señorita Rodriguez gets in her jabs, no doubt. But Essie don't seem that type."

Sam gawked at his nephew and chewed his meat real slow. "Those, Little Frank, are the most dangerous ones of all," he mumbled.

Latina and Miguel volunteered to help Americus in the kitchen. Sam, Howdy, Jonas, and Pete headed for a whist game in the bunkhouse. Señorita Rodriguez and Essie Bowers adjourned to their rooms.

Frank hiked across the road to the corrals alone. The charcoal gray sky faded to black, and the clouds muted the starlight. Lantern beams sprayed out from every window in the big house.

Frank leaned his back against the corral fence and studied the building. He pulled his shirttail out of his trousers and slipped his rough, calloused hands up his sides. He rubbed his rib cage gently and took deep breaths.

This day has been so hectic, I hardly remembered the pain. But now I feel so stiff. I'd love to take the train down to Hot Springs. Soak and sleep for about a week. I'll do that when roundup is done . . . if my ribs hold out that long.

In the dark, he pulled off his vest and laid it carefully

on the fence rail. Then he tugged his long-sleeved cotton shirt over his head. The cool evening air felt good on his bare chest and back. He clutched the shirt by the sleeves, wrapped it tight around his rib cage and tied them.

At least I can stand straight this way. There must be an old sheet in the house someplace that I can use. I've got way too much work to do to feel bad.

Frank turned around and leaned against the leather vest hanging on the corral fence. He could hear the horses mill but could barely see their shadows.

I've got to get busy with the ranch. These other things are diversions. The ladies, the stolen horses, Uncle Sammy, even this meeting with Thomasville and Reid. I need to take care of the cattle. Everything else can wait. I'm a cattleman. At least, I hope I am. Not a politician. Nor a ladies man.

Frank smiled and shook his head.

The only thing more scary than a friendly woman . . . is two friendly women. Well, Essie isn't scary, but, my, she is friendly. Dearyanna, on the other hand . . . Lord, I can't even breathe when she gets close. My heart races. I can't even remember to put one foot in front of the other. All the time I imagine she's laughin' to herself over the rawboned, clumsy cowboy.

Wouldn't that be somethin'? To go back to Deadwood with Señorita Dearyanna Rodriguez on my arm?

Frank began to laugh out loud.

Now would that ever turn heads. Mama and Daddy would be happy. The twins would want her in the wedding. Aunt Dacee June would tease me something hor-

rible. And the rest of town . . . they would say, "Frank Fortune found himself a gold mine alright."

A sudden waft of fresh spring flowers hit him. Frank shook his head.

This is exactly what I was talkin' about, Lord. It's a distraction. I've got a dwindlin' herd to worry about, not . . .

He heard footsteps in the yard behind him.

Light footsteps.

And a woman clear her throat.

Frank glanced over his shoulder. He could see a vague silhouette. "Evenin', Essie."

"I'm afraid you guessed wrong, Francisco."

"Dearyanna, wait there!" he blurted out.

"Oh my, you can't have company, can you? You thought I was Miss Bowers, so she is not out here. But I did hear you laugh."

"I'm by myself. I need to put my shirt on."

"You were waiting for Estelle with your shirt off?"

"No. I wasn't waitin' for anyone, it's just . . ."

"Don't untie your shirt. I can see it. Your ribs hurt, don't they?"

Frank tried to focus on her face, but the light from the big house kept her in the dark. "I think I bruised them bad the other day."

"I think you must have broken several."

"You could be right," he murmured. "I just don't want to admit it."

She meandered up next to him and stared out at the darkened corral. "I don't suppose you intend on going to the doctor."

"Not for a week. You've seen how hectic things are here. I have to keep on top of things."

"Would it be best if we left? We don't have to stay here. The wagon is quite comfortably furnished. I would like to stay for the supper tomorrow night," Dearyanna offered.

"No, I think it's best that you are here."

"Are you saying you'd like me to stay?"

"Yes, I am."

"Thank you. I would like to stay here a few days. As hectic as you think it is, it is peaceful for me."

"Peaceful?"

"Do you follow politics, Mr. Frank Fortune?"

"I don't get the newspaper ever' day, but I know that Bryan is runnin' against President McKinley again. My Uncle Todd's a friend of Roosevelt's, so I do get some news. And I heard that Galveston was flattened by a tidal wave or hurricane or something. We still got kin down in Texas."

"What do you know about Sonora, Mexico?"

"There are some pretty women down there. Well, at least one."

"Oh, my."

"What's the matter?" he asked.

"Francisco, why is it my heart leaped when you said that?"

Frank swallowed hard. "It did?"

"And why does my mouth get dry and my throat constrict when we talk? It is very strange, Francisco Fortune. I am not used to such phenomena. Perhaps I should ask a doctor."

"It does sound like a disease."

Dearyanna began to laugh. "Yes, I suppose that was all very foolish. And I do not like being foolish. There is political unrest in Sonora and in all of northern Mexico. Some in the government want to take away our ranchos."

"Why?"

"Because we are too successful." Dearyanna stared across the dark corrals. "When my grandfather started ranching in the Mariposa Valley, there was not a settlement for one hundred miles. The first winter my grandmother was killed by Indians. My father's oldest brother was eleven, and he got lost and froze to death. But grandfather persevered. In the winter of '86 and '87, ninety percent of his cattle died. My father took over the rancho in '90. He has worked hard. He almost died of pneumonia three years ago. And this summer my youngest brother was murdered."

"What?"

"He was shot while selling cattle in Nogales."

"That's horrible."

"I spent four years going to college in California. Every time I went home, the situation seemed worse."

"You came up here to get away from it?"

"It was my father's idea, but I didn't argue."

"I'm surprised. I couldn't tell you had gone through all of that," he said.

"People are not always what they seem on the outside, Mr. Francisco Fortune. But I believe you are."

Frank folded his arms across his chest and rested his hands on his bare arms. "Yeah, I'm a lousy poker player.

Everyone can read me."

"You are very worried about your cattle and your ranch."

"Yes, I am."

"I can relate to that, you know."

"I reckon you can. I just hadn't thought of it before."

She leaned her satin-covered shoulder against his muscled arm. "What can I do to help you?"

"What do you mean?"

"I am going to be here a few days. I do not want to be a hindrance. Can I help you here at the ranch?"

"Oh, no, I don't need you to . . ."

"You are at least three men short. Would you like Miguel, Latina, and I to take care of the chores here at the headquarters while you and the men round up the cattle? Or would you like us to go camp at the north or west lines and keep the strays from being rustled off?" Dearyanna's voice was soft, yet confident.

"Are you serious?"

"Of course. Why do you ask?"

"It's just . . ."

"Seems out of character for me?"

"I suppose that's what I was thinking."

"You think it over. Let us help in some way. It is good for me to think of someone else's struggles. My own can be way too depressing."

"Thanks, Dearyanna."

"Now, Francisco, I am going to go look in my things for a wrap for those broken ribs of yours."

"No, you don't have to . . ."

"Frank Fortune, don't you ever let anyone help you?

I'm sure I have something to wrap around your ribs, and you can wear the shirt over it. I insist you let me play nurse. After all, you let Miss Bowers play nurse. There I go again. Forget I said that."

"Pain has overcome my reluctance. I would be happy to get my ribs wrapped."

"Good. Let's see how wide they can be." In the dark, the señorita put her hand on Frank's bare shoulder, and the other against the shirt tied around his midsection. "Oh, my . . ." She pulled her hand back.

"What's the matter?"

"My . . . my . . . my . . . Francisco, how you do make a girl's pulse race. I think I had better go find those wraps."

Frank watched as she scurried back toward the big house.

"Oh . . . my . . ." she murmured once more.

His smile stretched to his ears, and his cheeks hurt from the grin. *I can't believe this. Maybe it's a dream. Perhaps I'm asleep. Did the most beautiful raven-haired woman in the world just say "oh, my" when she touched my shoulder?*

This is crazy, Lord.

Frank let his eyes close and began to whistle. He was still whistling when he heard footsteps.

"Dearyanna?"

"Good guess, Frank, but wrong."

"Oh. Hi, Essie."

"You're expecting someone else?"

"No . . . eh, well yes . . . perhaps."

"Frank, would you like for me to leave?"

"Of course not."

Essie leaned against the fence next to him. "How are your ribs tonight?"

"They hurt."

"Is that why you have your shirt tied around them?"

"Yes. Sorry to be so informal."

"Frank Fortune, you don't have to apologize. We've known each other much too long for that."

"How long has it been now?"

"Either four hours or four years."

"Why does it seem that way?"

"My sister Jolie said one time that the Lord picks out special friends for all of us. When we first meet them, we recognize his intervention immediately."

"Do you believe that?"

"Not until today," she murmured. "Anyway, I wanted you to know that I fixed the big room up with a screened-off corner that will be fine for me. There is no reason you and your uncle can't use those wonderful leather couches."

"We can use the bunkhouse, even the loft."

"I won't hear of that. Frank, you are staying in the big room."

"OK, as long as I don't compromise anyone's opinion of the schoolteacher."

"Good. That's settled. Now what time are we going to head out in the morning?" Essie asked.

"I'd like to go early. I need to get back before supper. I have company coming in."

"I know Mr. Thomasville," she said.

"What do you think of him?"

"I think he's alright, although I wouldn't stand next to him with his shirt off in the dark."

Frank chuckled. "Essie, you have got to be the easiest gal in the world to talk to."

"Now, Frank Fortune, I bet you say that to all the girls."

"Nope."

"Can we get on the trail before daylight?" she asked.

"I imagine."

"Do you have a horse I can ride?"

"Of course. I've even got a side saddle or two."

"How nice. I didn't know you used one," she laughed.

"Not me . . ."

"Nor me. You won't be offended if I straddle a horse, will you?" Essie asked. "I promise to keep my skirt tucked down."

"You sound like Dacee June and Amber."

"Girl friends?"

"My aunt and my cousin. They love to ride in a man's saddle."

"Let's leave at four," she declared.

"Can you really get up and be ready that early?"

"I'm a sod farm girl from Nebraska, Frank Fortune. I can milk a cow at four a.m."

"I bet you can," Frank laughed.

He heard the door open across the yard at the big house.

She slipped her hands on his arm. "Here she comes. I'll slink over there in the dark and back to the big room. Now, be nice and pleasant and don't stay up too late. We have an early day tomorrow."

"Okay, Mama," he whispered back.

She laced her fingers in his and squeezed, then was gone.

CHAPTER SEVEN

F RANK DIDN'T SEE the flare of the match, but he smelled the sulphur. He opened his eyes to the flickering of a lamp on the table near the door. Barefoot, shirtless, wearing his ducking trousers, Sam Fortune shuffled over to where Frank lay on the over-stuffed brown leather couch.

"That's real cute." Sam pointed to the wraps around his nephew's ribs.

The wooden floor felt cold and dusty on his bare feet as Frank sat up and looked at his wrapped ribs. "Ain't that somethin'?" He laughed and shook his head. "She said it was a rose-colored cloth. But that's the brightest color I ever wore in my life. What time is it?"

"I can tell you one thing. It isn't rose, Little Frank. It's bright pink satin, that's what it is. I've never seen a man wear that color before. Well, maybe in New Orleans once. It's after 4:00. Won't break daylight for a half hour. I just heard you mumble somethin' about stirrin' around early."

Frank tugged the white cotton shirt over his head. It was wrinkled and smelled sweaty. "You know, it might be pink, but that's the first decent sleep I've had in a week. The señorita truly knows how to wrap a man's ribs."

"Seems to me she has someone wrapped around her

finger," Sam mumbled. "Are you and the schoolteacher headin' out before breakfast?"

Frank plucked a hand mirror off the end table and studied the swollen yellow bruise on his forehead. "We got to leave early if I want to get back here before Thomasville and Reid LeMay show up."

Sam massaged an old scar high on his left shoulder blade. The strength of his shoulders and arms belied his gray hair and drooping mustache. "I'll help the crew. Howdy's got the assigns, doesn't he?"

"Yep, but I changed my mind. Send them all over to Sweetwater Springs. I don't want anyone on that west line until I straighten things out with Thomasville. I'm not about to get a man shot at, especially Howdy Tompkins."

"I'll ride up and check the west line," Sam offered.

"I appreciate that Uncle Sammy, but don't go gettin' yourself shot at either."

"It wouldn't be the first time."

"Yeah, but you're an ol' man now."

"I ain't the one hobblin' around," Sam shot back.

Frank combed his matted hair with his fingers. "Dearyanna's going to supervise getting the place straightened up."

Sam stared over at the closed bedroom door. "She's a nice lady."

Frank glanced back at the divider in the great room that shielded Essie's couch. He tucked in his shirt and pulled his leather braces over his shoulders. "The señorita is amazing, isn't she? Beautiful, smart, and nice. Kind of a scary combination, Uncle Sammy."

"You mean, 'cause she doesn't have any flaws?" Sam roared.

Frank held his finger to his lips. "Shhhhh." He pointed back at the room divider.

Sam rubbed his two-day beard. "You worried about Miss Bowers listenin' in to you extollin' the virtues of another woman?"

Frank nodded and frowned, then sat on the arm of the couch and pulled on dirty gray socks.

"Miss Bowers left thirty minutes ago."

"What? Where did she go?"

Sam snatched up a tin coffee cup leftover from the night before. "The barn, I figure. I was still half asleep. I didn't talk to her." He took a gulp, then grimaced.

Frank pulled on his boots. "Why didn't you wake me?"

"I did, just now."

He jammed his boots down and stood. "Is that lady goin' to try to catch a horse in the dark?"

"You don't reckon she'll try to catch Cuddles before daylight, do you?" The next sip of cold coffee caused Sam to close his eyes and shake his head. "That's ugly coffee when it's hot. When it's cold, it could be lethal." He stared out the window at the black morning. "I surely hope Miss Bowers doesn't try to rope Cuddles," he mumbled again.

Frank slipped on his leather vest and crammed on his brown wide-brimmed hat. "She's got spunk. Essie's a hard-workin' gal, that's for sure."

"If you want a gal who's not afraid of dirt under her fingernails, find a homestead girl. They either turn out hardy or die tryin'. And there ain't nothin' wrong with a woman who's got callouses on her hands."

"I don't reckon the señorita had to milk too many cows before daylight." Frank opened the top drawer of the rolltop desk and grabbed a handful of fat .50 caliber bullets.

"No reason she should ever have to. You can hire a kid to milk cows," Sam laughed.

"I was thinkin' the same thing. My, oh my, she is a head-turner." Frank plucked up the Sharps carbine propped against the door. "I'll be back before supper."

"Just in case you're late, what did you intend to say to Thomasville and Reid?"

"If none of the three of us is stealin' cows, where are they going, and what can we do about it?"

"Are they bringin' posses with them?"

Frank paused in the doorway. "The invite was just for Thomasville and Reid LeMay. But that don't mean they'll do what I say. I'll see you this evenin'."

"Be careful. Don't get yourself in trouble. Could be a dangerous day for you."

"I know," Frank replied. "That anthrax is deadly stuff. I'll stay away."

"I wasn't talkin' about anthrax," Sam replied.

A light filtered out from the kitchen, but the sky was black and there was no wind. Frank listened to his boot heels crunch dirt as he hiked to the barn.

My feet feel gritty in cold boots. I should have worn clean socks, but my socks were in the señorita's room. There is no way I was goin' in there in the dark. Or in

daylight, for that matter. When we get back this after-
noon, I'll have Essie fetch me some clean socks. I hate
putting clean socks over dirty feet, but I don't reckon on
getting a bath for a while either, unless I drag the tub
out to the barn and lock the door.

I can't see stars, so there must be clouds. Maybe it will
rain. It doesn't smell like rain. The grass could sure use
some, but if it got too muddy, I couldn't move cows for a
few days. I need to get those cows down here before any
more walk off the ranch.

He took a deep breath.

It doesn't smell like rain, but it does have a nice
aroma. It smells like . . . rose water perfume.

He turned toward the light from the kitchen window.
A woman's silhouette approached.

She was packing something in both hands.

Her satin dress swished.

Even in the dark, Frank tipped his hat. "Mornin',
Señorita Rodriguez. I am surprised to see you up."

"Buenas dias, Francisco. I trust you slept some."

"It's the first night I didn't have pain in my ribs.
Thanks to you, Dearyanna. It really did help. I should
have done that the first day. Now, what are you doin' up
so early?"

Her wavy black hair tumbled down her back to her
waist. "I couldn't sleep."

"Sorry. That room probably isn't too comfortable for
the three of you."

"The feather bed is the most comfortable I've had
since I left Sonora. Just too many things to think about.
Latina and I came down to see Americus."

Frank glanced at the kitchen light. "Is he cookin' already?"

"Nothing but coffee so far. I brought you two cups."

Frank took one. The tin cup burned his fingers. "You plannin' on joinin' me for coffee?"

Although her brown face was still in the shadows, her white teeth revealed a slight smile. "No, that position is already taken. For this morning. The other cup is for Miss Bowers."

Frank took the other tin cup. "She's already down at the barn, I hear. A regular farm girl, I suppose."

"She's not a girl, Francisco, but a woman. She's wearing a simple but attractive yellow cotton dress with white lace at the bodice that accents her . . . well, her bodice."

How does she know what color dress Essie has on? It's pitch black. Frank took a sip and scalded the tip of his tongue. "Thank you for the coffee."

"There are some biscuits and ham in this sack. And a few apples."

Frank felt his heart race as she stepped closer. "Are you sending me off to school, mama?"

"I would imagine, Mr. Francisco Fortune, that you have been schooled long before now." Her words sang out in the dark morning like a song long memorized.

Not nearly as much as you think, Señorita. You would be surprised how little I know. He sipped the coffee from the tin cup. "I'd better get this coffee to Essie before it cools off."

Señorita Rodriguez shoved a flour sack of food under his arm. "Can you carry all that?"

"I reckon I'd better. Thanks, Dearyanna, but you didn't have to get up this early for me."

"Francisco, I must confess I don't sleep well. Ever since my brother was murdered, I have horrible nightmares. You did not wake me."

Frank's eyes adjusted to the predawn darkness enough to see her flawless cheeks, chin, and neck. "You have to tell me about losin' your brother when I get back."

"I will. Is Miss Bowers staying another night?"

"She mentioned only one night, but we will be getting back too late to make it to town. A person can get disoriented on this prairie at night."

"I will plan on her being here."

"Thanks, Dearyanna. You are very kind to me. And thanks again for the rib wrap."

"Oh, my, there's that flutter again. Something about the way you say my name," she cooed.

"Dearyanna is a beautiful name."

"Thank you. I didn't always like it. When I was young, some called me *Dreary*anna."

"Why didn't your mama stop them?"

"It was my mother who gave me the nickname."

"I say it is a beautiful name."

Her lips brushed against his unshaven cheek, then she swished away toward the kitchen.

Frank picked up a trail of lantern light and followed it into the barn. He glanced around. Carlos and Cuddles stood saddled, but he could see no one.

He set the coffee cups on top of a barrel. "Essie?"

"Good morning. I'm up here in the loft." Suddenly,

she appeared at the top of the stairs wearing a yellow calico dress with white lace at the bodice.

"What are you doin' up there?" he called out.

"Waiting for you and pondering how it would look to watch the sunrise from this loft."

"It's nice, Essie. Real peaceful."

"Did you sleep well, Frank? I didn't hear you toss and turn much."

"Wrapping my ribs really helped. I slept in longer than normal."

"Move away from the ladder, Frank."

"What?"

"Your heard me," Essie ordered. "I'm coming down. You move away from that ladder."

"Yes, ma'am." He retreated to the barrel. "Señorita Rodriguez fixed us some coffee and a lunch sack."

Essie reached the barn floor and marched over to him. "I like her, Frank. Just when I think I have her all figured out, she surprises me. I like that." She plucked up a tin cup of coffee and took a big sip. "Are we ready to ride?"

"I reckon we can finish our coffee first."

Essie sat on top of the barrel, holding her coffee cup. "Have you ever been to Nebraska, Frank?"

"I've been to Sidney a couple of times and once to Fort Robinson. I guess that's all."

"You've never see Chimney Rock or Scott's Bluff?"

"Nope."

"Someday you'll have to go down. When you do, let me know and I'll be there to give you a tour. I like sitting on top of Scott's Bluff to watch the sunrise. Even though there are hundreds of people living down below, from up on the bluff, it seems like I am the only person on the prairie. I wonder what it would have been like to hike up there when they were still coming over on the trail?"

"There's nothing more peaceful than a prairie sunrise when you're the only one around."

"Sharing a sunrise is nice too," she added. "Do you ever share sunrises or sunsets with anyone?"

Frank scooted over to the tethered horses. "Sure. Me and ol' Carlos have seen many a sunset and sunrise, haven't we, boy?"

She trailed behind him. "That doesn't count."

"It counts to Carlos." He patted the chestnut gelding's rump and strolled over to the other horse. "How did you get a saddle on Cuddles? He's kind of green."

Essie laughed as she threw her arm around the horse's neck and hugged him. "Is that his name?"

"Yep. That's Cuddles. He's a little hot-tempered and can be cantankerous. Don't worry, I'll ride him."

"Nonsense. He was a little naughty, that's all." Essie released the horse and stuck her eye within inches of the horse's. "But we had a very long talk, and he promised to behave."

"Oh, he promised, did he? And you believed him?"

"He's never lied to me before," Essie replied.

"Do you often have long talks with animals?"

"All the time. Don't you, Frank?"

"Me and Carlos do visit a lot." He grabbed the gelding's ear and gently twisted it. "But he doesn't pay much attention to me."

"Horses often pretend to ignore you, but they really listen. Much unlike cats. Cats actually do ignore you. They are quite scornful, in fact."

Frank downed the rest of his now lukewarm coffee. "Essie, I bet you are a very good teacher."

She combed Cuddles's mane with her fingers. "Because I talk to animals?"

"Because you are friendly and enthused about everything you do."

"When I was young, my daddy would say, 'You can't change your looks, Estelle Cinnia, but you can change your attitude.'"

Frank plucked a pair of medium rowel spurs from a peg on the barn post. "You wanted to change your looks?"

"You'd understand that if you knew my sister Jolie." Essie retrieved her straw hat from the top of a nail keg.

With his foot on a stall rail, Frank strapped on his spurs. "The pale-complexioned, browned-haired Dearyanna?"

"Yes. See, you remember my sister's description, don't you? Even though you've never seen her." She tied the yellow hat ribbon under her chin. "I'm the one everyone says, 'Oh, you know, the other Bowers girl . . . the plain one.'"

Frank studied her face. "You say that with a smile."

"That has taken years of practice. If you ever have a daughter, don't tell her she looks healthy."

"What do you mean?"

"I was the round one in the family. Jolie's perfect. Ask any man in Nebraska or Wyoming. Mama's a hundred-

and-nine-pound pixie. And then there's Essie. I was moaning about being too round one time, and Daddy, trying to cheer me up said, 'Darlin', you aren't chubby; you just look healthy.' I cried for a week."

"OK. I won't tell my daughter she looks healthy. But you do have a very nice smile, Essie Bowers."

"Thank you, Frank Fortune. Yours is rather fetching but used way too seldom. If it were not for the señorita, I would probably not see you smile at all." She wrinkled her nose, finished her coffee, and set her tin cup back on the barrel next to Frank's. "Are we ready to go?"

"As soon as I yank the cinches on these two." Frank tightened the latigos and tied the food sack behind the cantle on Carlos. "Are you sure you want to ride Cuddles?"

"I insist."

"If he's too hot for you, you'll trade with me, won't you?"

"Yes, and if Carlos is too hot for you, you'll trade with me," she shot back.

He stared at her.

"Frank, I was teasing you."

A smile broke across his face.

"There it is! See, Dearyanna isn't the only lady who can make you smile."

He led both horses out of the barn into the yard. In the east the dark sky faded to charcoal gray. Essie turned out the lantern in the barn and followed him, her silent yellow dress only inches above the dirt.

"Would you like a boost up?" he asked.

"OK."

Frank grabbed her by the waist with both hands and easily lifted her into the saddle.

She tugged her dress down and brushed out the wrinkles with her fingers.

"You are neither plain nor, eh, healthy, Estelle Cinnia," he mumbled, and he mounted the chestnut gelding.

"Thank you, Frank. You are indeed a gentleman. However, I have been wondering."

They rode the horses side by side across the yard. "What have you been wonderin'?"

"Did you assist me upon my horse because you didn't think I could make it on my own or because you wanted to put your hands around my waist?"

"Wha . . . I . . . I can't believe you said that!" he stammered.

"Oh, my. What a shame I can't see your blush. Race you to the top of the draw."

"Race?"

"Come on, Cuddles," she shouted. "Let's stretch our legs."

What superiority Cuddles had in leg power soon gave way to Carlos's confidence at running his own driveway. Frank Fortune made it to the top of the rim of Bear Butte Valley where the prairie levels off about two lengths ahead of Estelle Bowers. He reined up and waited. She sailed past him, then circled the black horse back, laughing as she rode up.

"You are a reckless woman, Essie!" Frank laughed. "You could have gotten yourself killed."

She leaned forward and patted Cuddles's neck. "It was worth it, Frank, just to witness that wide smile on your face."

"Yeah, it does feel good."

"The smile? Or the thunder of hooves? Or the cool mornin' wind in your face? Or the incredible power beneath you?"

Frank led the way to the northeast. "All of it. But it is dangerous."

"Mama says that's exactly why she races horses. Every run is victory over fear. For Mama, fear limits life, boxes us in. Robs us of all God made us to be."

"She sounds quite the philosopher."

"Oh, no. That's Daddy. He's the philosopher and politician. Everyone likes Daddy. He's president of the Farmer's Alliance that's getting irrigation canals for the upper North Platte Valley. He'll do it too."

"Does he race fast horses?"

She followed behind him as they wound their way through thick sagebrush. "No, that's just Mama and Jolie, at least before she started having children. You would have never beat either of them."

He leaned back on Carlos's rump and looked back at her. "You doubt my racin' ability?"

"No, I just know them." When Essie wrinkled her nose, her upper lip curled, revealing straight teeth. "Jolie would have kept racing 'till she reached Canada, pulled ahead of you, or the horse died. She doesn't accept defeat well."

"How about your mama? Does Mrs. Bowers accept defeat well?"

"In a horse race?" Essie laughed. "I wouldn't know. She's never lost."

He sat straight in the saddle. "You're teasin' me."

When they broke out of the sage, she rode up next to him. "Frank Fortune, why would I do that?"

"I told Uncle Sammy you are one spunky girl, Estelle Bowers."

"Thank you for both compliments."

"Both?"

"Calling me spunky . . . and girl. To the girls at the Indian school I'm an old unmarried lady."

"Do you like teaching, Essie?"

"I love it, Frank. I didn't think I would. My sis started teaching when she was seventeen. She was a natural. So I went over to Lincoln to college and decided to teach. But I wanted to do more than just teach a few farm kids to read and write. I wanted to do what others couldn't or at least didn't want to do."

"Teach at an Indian school?"

"No one wanted the job."

"Why is that?"

"It's remote. Primitive. Low paying. And worst of all, many of the kids don't want to be there."

Daylight streamed across the prairie. Frank tugged his felt hat low in front to block the sun. "Why not?"

"It's a boarding school, Frank. The kids are hundreds of miles from home. Most of them just want to go home and be themselves."

"Must be discouraging for you." To the north Frank watched a seven-month-old brindle calf frolic after its mother.

"Some days are rather disheartening. Like when the girls ran off. But most days, I love it. I love them. They are so smart. So inquisitive. So beautiful. Don't you think brown skin looks better out here on the prairie rather than this pathetic pale skin?"

An easy smile rolled across his face.

"Frank Fortune, you were not thinking of brown-skinned Indians but a certain brown-skinned señorita, weren't you?"

He leaned back as they continued northeast. "Essie, you disarm me before I speak. It's like you are crawling around in my mind and see everything from this side."

"I like that phrase, 'seeing everything from this side.' What does that mean?"

He sat up and spurred Carlos to a trot. Essie stayed with him. "It seems to me there's a line, a barrier, between a person and the entire rest of the world. Everyone and everything is 'out there' and I'm 'over here.' Most of life is spent by me peeking out at the world and observing. Every once in a while I allow others to peer over the line at me. But you, it feels like you are over here with me and we are both peeking out together. I don't reckon that makes a lot of sense . . . but from the minute I met you, it was like you were on this side of the line."

Essie clutched the saddle horn as she jostled along across the prairie. "Frank Fortune, that's about the nicest thing anyone ever said to me, and I'm going to change the subject or I'll start to cry."

"What? You want to cry? Why?"

She brushed her eyes with her fingertips. "I'm

changing the subject. Tell me about your ranch."

He scratched the back of his head. "Not too much to say. It's government land that nobody wanted 'cause it doesn't produce much grass. Too close to the Badlands, too alkaline, too desolate, too slick and gummy in the spring, and too far from decent water."

Essie burst out laughing. "Frank, you sound like all the old-timers in Nebraska. I used to listen to them talk at the feed store."

"This business is a disease. It don't make sense, but once bit, you never can quit."

The brown prairie grass thinned as they rode a long, gentle slope down to a waterless creek bed.

"So you took this ranch because you want to do something others couldn't?"

"I took it because it was the only land available to a nineteen-year-old kid."

"You had your own ranch when you were nineteen?"

"Yeah, but only if my Uncle Todd, Uncle Sammy, and Daddy would co-sign the lease."

They slowed the horses at the bottom of the draw. Essie wiped her neck with her embroidered handkerchief. "My brother Lawson is like you. When he turned twenty-one he bought a six-hundred-acre farm that three families had gone broke on."

"How's he doing?"

"He'll make it. He married a Nebraska homestead girl." A wide smile broke across Essie's round face. "April works the fields with Lawson from dawn until dark."

The trail up out of the draw wound between jagged

outcrops of limestone. They rode single file without talking.

At the top Frank took the canteen off the saddle horn and held it out to her. "Living near the Wind River Mountains in Wyoming is a long way from Scottsbluff, Nebraska. Do you miss your family, Essie?"

She took a head-tilting swig of water, wiped her mouth on the sleeve of her dress, and handed the canteen to Frank. "Some days I miss them terrible. But I'm on a quest."

Without wiping the canteen, he took a deep swig, wiped his mouth on his shirtsleeve, then stuck the cork back in the canteen. "What kind of quest?"

"To write stories that no one else has ever told."

"You want to be a writer?"

"Yes, although not many know it. I guess I'm letting you take a look on this side of the line."

Frank led the way to the northeast. "You ought to talk to my Aunt Dacee June. She's written some things."

Essie trotted Cuddles to catch up. "Has she actually gotten them published?"

"Yes. Most are short stories for the Eastern magazines." Frank rolled up his left sleeve.

"Is she in Deadwood?"

"Yep."

"I would love to meet her."

"You'd like my aunt. There is no one like her in the whole world."

"I like your Uncle Sammy. But yesterday after supper he sat on the porch chewing on a piece of straw; I noticed he has such sad eyes. Did you ever observe that?"

"Yeah. Uncle Sammy spent quite a few years runnin' from God and from Grandpa. He did some things he sorely regrets."

"But the Lord forgives him."

"Oh, yes. He'll be the first to sing of God's amazing grace. But the memories taunt him. He always tells me that the Lord's forgiveness heals the wounds of our heart but that sin leaves permanent scars. Some days the scars hurt worse than others."

"I wish I could teach my girls that lesson. They don't think there's much connection with what they do today and how they will feel about themselves tomorrow." She leaned back in the saddle and rubbed her shoulders.

"Are you feeling alright?"

"Yes, just a little stiff."

"Would you like us to get off and walk a while?"

"Oh, no, Frank Fortune. This homestead girl can take it." She pointed to his exposed arm. "What happened to your elbow?"

"The same as my ribs and forehead. I got drug behind a horse."

"It looks horrible."

"Thank you. Is that worse than lookin' healthy?"

"Frank Fortune, if you were closer, I'd slug you."

"I reckon you would, Estelle Cinnia." The sun was high enough for Frank to push his hat back and wipe his forehead.

"OK, I like teaching Indian girls and writing stories," she said. "Now, tell me about your future. What is Frank Fortune going to do with the rest of his life?"

"Kind of what I'm doin' today."

"You're going to ride across the prairie with a friendly homestead girl, while a beautiful princess waits for you at the big house?"

He laughed and shook his head. "You are somethin', Essie. No one in my life has ever teased me like you do."

"Aren't I horrible?"

"No, no . . . you are sort of like the first warm rain of spring. It just feels good no matter when it comes."

"I'll assume that's a compliment."

"It is. All I want to do is ranch, Essie. Just tend cows and put meat on the table of folks workin' in Chicago and St. Louis and Denver. I want to suck in a big old breath of cool prairie air and smell the sage. I want to watch long morning shadows creep across the plains like a cougar trailin' its prey. I want to work someplace where I can hear a hawk's cry when he swoops up his lunch. I want my face to be tan and my hands calloused."

"You are very poetic, Frank Fortune."

"My entire family would die laughin' to hear you say that. I am the most boring of all the Fortunes. Just ask them."

"Tell me about cows, Frank."

"What?"

"Why do you raise herefords? Don't they get the Texas fever?"

"But they calve hearty and winter well. They produce good solid meat. I think they might mama a little better."

"How many bulls do you own?" she pressed.

"Twenty-five. Five are young."

"What cattle yard do you drive them to?"

"Rapid City, although I've been offered more if I would drive them to Miles City. That's a long way, and the corridor is gettin' fenced more every year."

"Do you plan on buying this ranch?"

"If they would sell it, I suppose. I don't have an attachment to this place. There are others I would buy if I were a rich man. Mama thinks I should find a place near Minnesela."

"Tell me about your mother."

"You surely ask a lot of questions."

"I know. I just like to learn about people. You don't have to answer the question about your mother. Let's change the subject. What do you want to talk about?"

"Eh . . . well, it's just . . ." he stammered. "I really don't have any subject in mind. My mother's a saint, by the way."

"What's she like?"

"From the day I was born, and then the twins, Mama has been workin' for our best interest. She has it in her head that the Lord bestowed on her some great favor in granting us to be her children. Every day is a chance to prove herself worth his trust. She's amazin'."

"I like that. Are you lookin' for a gal like Mama?"

"Nope."

"That's good."

"Why did you say that?"

"No woman can live up to a perfect mother. Not even Dearyanna. Mothers like that are flawless and untouchable. Don't take that wrong. I mean it as a compliment."

Frank sat up and rubbed his sides.

"Do your ribs still hurt?"

"Only a little. This satin wrap really helps. Only La Dona Rodriguez would have extra satin material in her trunk."

"She tore up a dress, Frank."

"No, I think she just had . . ."

"I saw the rest of the dress. It was beautiful."

"She tore up a dress? For me?"

"Yes, but don't go getting proud on me."

"It's just that I don't reckon a girl ever tore up a dress for me."

"OK, now it's time to get personal."

"Are you going to embarrass me, Essie Bowers?"

"Oh, I certainly hope so!"

"Do you enjoy tormentin' me?"

"I enjoy bein' on this side of the line, Frank Fortune. No man has ever let me on this side before, and I like being over here looking out with you."

"No man? How about a boy? You had your share of boyfriends, no doubt."

"Did you ever hear of Leppy Verdue?"

"Is he one of those with Butch Cassidy?"

"No. Leppy was in the thick of that ruckus up in Cripple Creek."

"He's a gunman?"

"Used to be. He owns an orange grove in California now. Have you ever been to California?"

"Nope."

"Someday I want to swim in the Pacific Ocean," she said. "Do you want to swim in the Pacific?"

"Amber says it's cold," Frank replied.

"She's your very pretty cousin?"

"She's been an actress. She's been on the stage in San Francisco, Sacramento, Monterey . . . she's been all over. Do you know what she said? She said there's a guy who wants to take nickel picture shows and make them a whole half hour long. He asked her to do her actin' in one of them."

"Is she going to?"

"Nope. She's in a family way again. Wants to raise those babies of hers. Of course, Aunt Abby would pitch a fit if she acted in the picture shows. She says the theater is bad enough. Anyway, Amber said the Pacific Ocean around San Francisco is so cold it turned her blue all over."

"All over?"

"You have to know Amber. She went swimmin' in the . . . eh . . . well . . ."

Essie's hand went over her mouth. "She didn't!"

Frank shoved his hat off his head and let it dangle on his back. "She did."

"Oh, my."

"I'd like to dip my feet in, but don't know if I'd actually swim out there. I did swim in the Great Salt Lake one time."

"How was that?"

"Salty. But what does all of this have to do with Leppy Verdue, retired shootist and orange farmer?"

"I had a crush on him for a long time."

"I figured him for an old man."

"He's only ten years older than me."

"That ain't too bad. We had a family friend, Quiet Jim Trooper, whose wife was twenty-four years younger. They were very happy, but she's a widow now."

"When I was twelve and Leppy was twenty-two, it was a big difference. But he would tease me and say he'd wait. He always sent me letters and birthday presents. I think he really had his heart set on Jolie, like every other boy in the world, but Jolie had her Tanner by then."

"How did your mama and daddy take all that, you havin' an older fella?"

"They knew Leppy. They thought it was a game I'd grow out of. It didn't bother them until about the time I got to be seventeen and packed all my clothes in a trunk and said I was running away to Colorado to find him. I had heard he was in a Cripple Creek jail. He wasn't, but that's what I thought."

"What did your mama and daddy do?"

"Daddy said I couldn't go until I had an invitation in my hand from Leppy."

"And you didn't?"

"I hadn't heard from him in six months."

"So you waited?"

"Yes. Within days I had a telegram from Leppy."

"Quite a coincidence."

"That's what I thought. But later I found out my sister Jolie sent one to him and explained everything."

To the south, Frank watched a coyote slink through the sage. He resisted the urge to grab his carbine. "Did Leppy invite you to come to Colorado?"

"He told me to wait, that he was coming to Scottsbluff to see me."

"Did he?" Frank asked.

"Yes, but it took three weeks. I nearly died of worry. I was supposed to go back to college for my second year, and here I was all packed and waiting to go off with him to Colorado."

"But you didn't go?"

Essie tugged off her straw hat and fanned herself. "Leppy walked me down to the river and told me there was no way in his lifetime he would ever be worthy of as fine a lady as I turned out to be. Said he had too many mistakes in his past. But he would never forget me because I was the reminder of what he could have been in life."

"That's a nice way of putting it," Frank murmured. "What did you do?"

She draped her hat over the saddle horn. "I cried for three days, day and night. Then I got on the train and went back to college. Now, Frank Fortune, what was your girl's name?"

"My girl?"

Essie pulled her brown hair behind her ears and reset her combs. "I told you about Leppy. You have to tell me about your girl. There must have been one. What was her name?"

"Marla Jolene Austin."

They rode nearly a quarter of a mile without speaking.

Essie rode Cuddles in front of him and reined up. "Well? Frank Fortune, you have to tell me more than her name."

He rode around her and kept going. "She lived in

Rapid City. Her father was my dentist. She came out to watch me play baseball."

"You play baseball?"

"I used to."

"You were a pitcher, right?"

"How did you know that?" he asked.

She wrinkled her nose. "Because I'm on this side of the line."

"Anyway, me and Marla Jolene got chummy."

"Chummy? I like that. Yes, yes, yes! A chummy Frank Fortune."

"Now you are embarrassin' me."

The smile dropped off Essie's face. She faked a frown. "OK, why didn't you marry Marla Jolene?"

"She got married to someone else."

"That does tend to sink a relationship."

"I came out here to get the ranch started and figured once it was established, I'd marry her."

"How long were you out here before going back to see her?"

"Eighteen months the first time."

"Eighteen months? She had to go without seeing you for eighteen months?"

"I was busy."

"Even Leppy Verdue didn't make a teenage girl wait eighteen months between visits."

"It seemed shorter to me."

"And she waited for you?"

"As far as I know, she did. I was in town about a week, then had to get back out here. Things got balled up here, movin' the barn and big house from Fort Meade. It was another year before I got time to get away."

"She still waited?"

"I didn't get to Rapid City. Before I could get back, my mother and my Aunt Dacee June drove all the way out here to tell me that Marla had married some banker in Rapid City by the name of Cloquet. Not that I blame her."

"Oh, I'm sorry, Frank. Did you cry for three days?"

"Nope."

"Why not?" Essie asked.

"It was calvin' season."

"Oh, well, that explains it."

"I didn't have time to cry, Essie."

"I suppose there have been other ladies in your life."

"You are really pushin' it, aren't you?" he chided.

"I'm trying to see how much I can get out of you."

"There haven't been any serious ladies in my life other that Marla Jolene."

"None?"

"Not a one. How about you, Essie Bowers? Were there others besides your notorious gunman?"

"Yes, but they were all quite tedious and unmemorable."

Frank began to laugh.

"Why are you laughing?"

"How did we get to talkin' about such things? I don't talk personal to anyone. Not my mother. Not my father. Not my sisters."

"Not even to your Aunt Dacee June?"

"Especially not my Aunt Dacee June."

"You are easy to talk to, Frank Fortune."

"You are the only lady who thinks so."

She swept her hand across the prairie. "Perhaps they haven't known you as long as I have."

Three hours and two rest stops later they rode to the ridge of Devil's Wash and stared east at barren white clay. They dismounted and walked the horses to the edge of Hades Canyon.

"They went down into that?" Essie gasped.

Frank kicked some clods over the edge and watched them roll hundreds of yards down the steep embankment. "That's what Cron and Reynoso claimed."

"How does a horse go down something that precipitous?"

"Horses know what they're doin'." Frank shoved both shirt-sleeves above his elbows. "They will slide down on their rump. It's the riders that have a tough time stayin' on. Were your girls good riders?"

Essie folded her arms and studied the barren canyon below them. "Everyone at the Indian school is a good rider. But I don't know that they excelled above the others." She pointed at the distant eastern horizon. "What is out there?"

He shoved his hands in his back pockets. "Nothin', so they tell me. I've never been down there. I'm told there's no vegetation, not a blade of grass. Some say there's a water sink or two, but half of them are poisonous. That white clay crusts up on top and breaks through like thin ice when you ride across it. Underneath is gumbo so sticky it will pull your boots off, if you're lucky. They tell me there are skeletons of cows and horses that died standin' in the bog and had their bones picked clean by the birds. Hades Canyon gets its name honestly."

Essie shaded her eyes with her hand to survey the canyon. "You make it sound like no one could survive."

"On the other hand, some folks know their way through it, mainly the Indians and a few outlaws. They say if you pack in food and hay and know where the good water is, you could stay down there for weeks because no one would come lookin' for you. It's like a maze in places. A person could wander around and never find his way out. If your girls plunged off here into Hades Canyon, maybe they had some familiarity with the place."

"Two of them are thirteen. One's fourteen. They've been on the reservation since they were toddlers. I don't think they came over here much. But I just don't know." She eased closer to him. "Frank, look at my hands."

"They're shakin'." He reached over and held her hands.

"I'm so scared for them, Frank. What kind of system have we created if the best option for a young teenage girl is to ride a horse down into that?"

"I'm sure it wasn't you, Essie. They were just home-sick girls, like you said."

"I wish I could be sure."

"All of the Indians seem to be in a struggle for iden-tity and pride. Don't let it eat away at you. You can't take it personal."

"Why can't I?" She laced her fingers together and held them tight. "I give my life seven days a week to the girls. They not only walked away from school; they walked away from me."

He put his hand on her shoulder and patted her back. "I thought you said it was OK; you just wanted them home safe."

"I hadn't seen Hades Canyon." She reached up and patted the top of his hand. "For me to be rejected for home is quite understandable. To be rejected for this? Being with me was worse than riding off into this? I have got to try to find them."

"Down there?"

"I have to."

"Essie, before we came out here, I told you it was impossible to go down after them."

"But how can I live with myself? I would have been much better staying at Wind River and never knowing. But now . . ."

"I can't let you do that."

"What do you mean, you can't let me? You have no choice in the matter." She pushed his arm off her shoulder and stepped away.

Frank followed her. "Wait a minute, Estelle Cinnia Bowers. Don't I get the same consideration as you get?"

"They aren't your girls, Frank. You don't understand."

"Are they your girls, Essie? Or do they belong to the Lord?"

"What are you saying?"

"I'm saying if I let you go down there on your own, I will live with regrets the rest of my life."

"Then you do know how I feel."

"But you were not here when they chose to go down

there. You can mourn their decision to leave school but not the decision to go down into Hades Canyon. If you go down there, I'll have to look your mama and daddy in the eye some day and tell them I didn't stop you."

"What am I going to do, Frank?" There was panic in her voice.

"Pray."

"Oh, yes, but what else?"

"Is prayer ever enough, Essie?"

"What do you mean?"

"Are there some times in life where prayer is enough?"

"Are you getting theological on me, Frank Fortune?"

"I'm just wonderin'. Most times I pray and commit a matter to the Lord, then go out and try to solve it myself. Is prayer ever enough?"

"I can't return without looking for them. I can't make myself go back. I know it sounds illogical and bizarre, but the only way I could ride back with you is if you hog-tied me to the saddle and led the horse."

"I reckon I could do that."

A wide smile broke across Essie's face. "You could, couldn't you?"

"Yes, ma'am. If I set a mind to it."

She tried to smile. "Oh, Frank, what am I going to do? I know, I know . . . pray."

Cuddles shied away from the edge of the precipice and Essie stepped back with him. Carlos leaned his neck over the edge and twitched his ears back.

"Does he want to go down that?"

"He's never been known for bravery, but . . ." Frank

squinted his eyes. "Essie, come here."

"What is it?"

Frank pointed to the bottom of the canyon. "Carlos sees a horse down there."

Essie scooted to Frank's side. "Where?"

"Look behind that rollin' clay bank next to the dry creek bed. That's a horse's head peeking out. See it? If it's one of mine, maybe Carlos can sense that."

"Do you see any girls? Where? Oh yes, there's a horse! Do you think my girls are down there?"

"They've been in there two days. I would have thought they would be out the other side or . . ."

"How can we know if there is anyone down there?"

Frank pulled his Sharps out of the scabbard and handed her the reins to Carlos. "I'll fire a shot in the air for a signal."

"What if they are outlaws down there? They'll try to shoot you."

"I suppose, but it's a long way away."

"If it's the girls, they might think you are shooting at them," she cautioned. "In which case, they will hide even more."

"That's possible, but we'll at least get to see if the pony runs away by itself."

"Let me stand at the edge. If they see a woman, they might come out and wave or something."

Frank raised his thick dark eyebrows. "And if they are outlaws?"

Essie grinned. "They still might come out and wave."

"Are you serious?"

"We both know we have to try."

"OK, lead Carlos over there. He's not gun-shy. I don't know about Cuddles. And give it your best school-teacher silhouette."

"I'm afraid I don't have much of a silhouette at this distance."

"Essie Bowers, you have a very fine silhouette," he mumbled.

"Frank Fortune, my how you do blush! Thank you for the compliment. But if I looked like Dearyanna, I'd have more success."

If you looked like Dearyanna, you'd clean out all of Dakota and half of Wyoming. "Are you ready?"

"What do you want me to do?" she asked.

"Watch that horse down there and tell me what you see. If he bolts out in the open, see if anyone is with him."

The explosion from the .50 caliber Sharps rattled Frank's ears. The report echoed across the top of Hades Canyon.

"Yes!" Essie shouted. She yanked off her straw hat and waved it back and forth. "Yes! It's them! There's one . . . there's another . . . oh, no!" she gasped.

Frank led Cuddles to the edge. "What is it?"

"There are only two of them. Oh, no . . . oh, Lord Jesus, no!"

Frank used his hat to block the sun's glare. "There's one on the horse, Essie. Bareback, lyin' down across his neck, but she's there."

"Oh, thank you, Lord!" Essie threw her arms around Frank's neck and kissed his lips. "This is so exciting!"

"Finding the girls? Or kissing me?"

"Finding the girls, Frank Fortune. You kiss like a startled mule."

"Thank you, ma'am."

"How are we going to get them up here?"

"Let's ride the rim to the south. It's more gradual back there. If they hold on to their horses' tails, they would pull them up."

"But there is only one horse. What will we do?"

"I've got sixty foot of rope on my saddle. Cuddles has at least thirty. We'll pull them up one way or another."

They mounted the horses and rode south, keeping sight of the girls and horse far below in the canyon.

"I wonder why they are still here, and not halfway to the agency by now?" Essie asked.

"I wonder what happened to the other two horses?"

"I'll pay you for the horses."

"You will not. I'm just saying perhaps the horses ran away. Maybe that's why they didn't get too far."

"Are they coming south?" she asked.

"Yep."

"It still looks steep."

"It is."

"Do you really think we can get them up this way?"

"Do you really think anything called Devil's Wash can prevail against Frank Fortune and Essie Bowers?" he laughed.

She shook her head. "We are both too stubborn to fail."

CHAPTER EIGHT

ALL THREE GIRLS had long black hair. Raven eyes. Medium brown skin. Unadorned gray cotton dresses. Dirty faces. And ravenous appetites.

Two wore scuffed and torn high-top, lace-up boots. The other wore one moccasin.

It took thirty minutes to get the girls and one horse to the top of Hades Canyon. It took another half hour for them to empty one and a half canteens and all of the ham, biscuits, and apples. The wide-rumped, mouse-dun horse that came out of the canyon with the girls was one Frank had named Smokey. Saddleless, he sported a homemade rope halter.

Faith, who had the roundest face and roundest body, rode Smokey. Katie, with one moccasin because her other ankle was very swollen, rode behind Essie. Morgan, a few months older than the other two, sat on Frank's bedroll, his leather saddle strings wrapped around her wrists.

"Are we all ready?" Frank asked.

"Where are we going?" Katie pressed. Her waist-length black hair tumbled down the front of her dress.

"We will spend the night at Mr. Fortune's ranch head-quarters," Essie replied. "We need to hurry back there. He has other stops to make."

Faith rode Smokey next to Cuddles. "Who gets to go first?" she asked.

"Mr. Fortune and Morgan," Essie said.

"How come they go first?" Faith whined.

"Because Frank is the only one who knows his way back."

"Can we ride side by side?" Faith asked.

"For a while, but there are places we have to go single file," Essie reported.

Frank tipped his hat at Essie, then rode out on the rolling brown grass prairie.

"How come I can't put my arms around you?" Morgan asked him. "Don't you like Indian girls to touch you?"

Frank glanced over at Essie. "Darlin', Cheyenne girls are some of the prettiest ones in the world; just look at you three. I busted my ribs the other day. I'm all bandaged up. They hurt when I get hugged."

"It hurts when you get hugged?"

"Yep."

"How do you know? Has Miss Bowers been hugging you?"

"Morgan Denise!" Essie scolded.

Frank laughed. "No, Miss Bowers hasn't been huggin' me. But ever' time I rub my ribs against any-thin', it hurts."

Faith tugged the collar of her gray dress down and fanned herself. "What's going to happen to us, Miss Bowers? Are we going to get a whipping?"

"No, you aren't."

"Are we going to jail for stealing the horses?"

"No," Frank answered. "Those horses were mine."

"Were the mules yours too?" Katie asked.

"No. But I'm keepin' them safe for their owner to

come claim them."

"Girls," Essie added, "there will be some consequences for your running away. We'll talk about that later. I may have you write an extra report or two. And you'll get weekend chores for several weeks, or a month, I'm sure."

"You could just paddle me, if you want," Faith suggested.

"There will be no paddling," Essie insisted.

"Sometimes Mr. Clark doesn't do what you say," Morgan said.

"That's hard to believe," Frank replied.

"Girls, when we get back to Wind River, I will write your parents and tell them you would like to go home. If they ask for you to be sent home, we will do that. You can take a train most of the way."

"What if they want us to stay in school?" Katie asked.

"Then you shall stay in school. All three of you know that you need to obey your parents," Essie replied.

"My daddy's dead," Morgan announced.

Frank reached back and patted her knee. "I'm sorry about that, darlin'."

She grabbed onto his finger. "How come you call me darlin'?"

"Just a habit, Morgan. If you'd rather I stop, I'll surely try."

"Oh no, that's OK, I was just wondering." She latched onto his whole hand.

He squeezed her fingers, then tugged his hand back.

"I like your fella, Miss Bowers," Morgan called out.

"Thank you, Morgan, but Frank isn't my fella."

"Why not? Is there something wrong with him?" Faith asked.

Essie shook her head and laughed. "There are a few physical defects. Busted ribs, bruised elbow, and a yellow lump on his forehead."

"A girl should look for Christian commitment, courage, and inner strength of character," Katie blurted out.

All three girls giggled.

Frank spurred Carlos to a trot. "I take it you learned that lesson from Miss Bowers?"

Faith bounced along, keeping up with him. "She made us memorize it and make a list of all the boys we knew who were that way and not related to us."

"Did you have a long list?" he asked.

"I still can't think of anyone who fits the list and isn't a hundred years old," Faith moaned.

"There's one on my list," Katie giggled.

"He's too old for you," Morgan replied.

"Fifteen is not too old."

"You told us he was sixteen."

"He will be sixteen, soon. But he's only fifteen now."

"Miss Bowers, I want to know if he isn't your fella, who is he and what are you doing with him on the prairie alone?" Morgan asked.

"Essie and I have been good friends, well, it seems like forever," Frank explained.

"That's right, girls. This is Mr. Fortune's ranch, and like he said, those were his horses you stole."

"You weren't the one in the privy when we stole them, were you?" Faith snickered.

"No. That was a line shack you stole them from. We're headed for the big house."

"How big is it?" Morgan asked.

"The more company we have, the smaller it becomes," he murmured.

"I knew you'd come looking for us, Miss Bowers," Katie reported. "When I got bucked off and my horse ran away, I knew you'd come looking for us."

"You weren't too sure when we got lost and those men took our other two horses," Morgan challenged.

Frank glanced over his shoulder at the girl behind him. "You run across some men down in there?"

"Yes, but they didn't see us. They thought our horses were runaways. We wanted to steal them back, but there were six men," Katie reported.

Frank shuddered. "It's a good thing they didn't find you. There are desperate, dangerous men down in there."

"Did you decide to turn around and come back out after losing the horses?" Essie questioned.

"No, we thought we were headed out toward the agency, but we ended up right back where we started," Morgan explained.

"I wanted to come back," Katie reported.

"You did not," Morgan snapped.

"Yes I did."

"You didn't say anything to us."

"I kept it in my heart," Katie insisted.

"I was sort of wishing we were back at school a few times myself," Faith admitted.

"I can't believe this," Morgan huffed.

"Weren't you ever worried?" Frank asked Morgan.

"Of course not."

Frank rubbed his chin. "Not even when the wagon wrecked and the mules ran off?"

"Perhaps I was concerned, but not worried."

Frank kept his eyes on the horizon as he rode south. "Tell me about the men down in the canyon. Did they look like the type that would be hiding from the law?"

"They looked dirty and desperate. Is that what you mean?" Morgan replied.

"I reckon."

"Two of them were Mexicans," Faith blurted out.

"Maybe they were from Chile," Morgan declared. "There was a man at Fort Laramie from Chile."

"Did you hear them mention any names?" Frank asked.

"We didn't get that close!" Katie said. "Miss Bowers, can I rest my foot on your lap?"

Essie reached down and pulled the girl's swollen foot up.

"How about horse brands? Did you see any brands?" Frank asked.

"Not on the horses, but I saw some brands on the cattle," Faith declared. She slipped her dress off her shoulder and scratched her arm.

Frank reined up in front of the others. "Cattle? There were cows down in Devil's Wash?"

Faith straightened her dress and sat up on the unsaddled horse. "Yes, there were."

"But there isn't any food or water for cattle," he pointed out.

"There is plenty of water at Dead Owl Springs," Morgan explained. "And they had two freight wagons full of hay."

"I can't believe there were cows down there," Frank murmured. "Everyone said that no one can survive in that wilderness. What brand was on the cattle?"

Essie studied Katie's swollen foot. "I'm sure the girls didn't pay attention to details like brands."

"Some had Bar NP, some Rafter F, and some Axe-T," Morgan blurted out. "Some were mavericks with no brand at all."

"Those are mine, Thomasville's, and the railroad's," Frank said.

"If they had wagons, there must be some kind of road," Essie declared.

Frank took the lead as they descended into a brown grass-covered draw. "Perhaps there's a trail out of there to the northeast."

"Have you ever been down there?" Essie asked.

"No, I just believed ever'one's account. If there's a road, they can bunch up a few and drive 'em out the other side toward Pierre and no one would know about it. How many cows were down there, girls?"

"Forty-eight," Faith reported.

"Forty-nine," Morgan corrected.

"Somewhere between forty-eight and forty-nine," Katie added.

Fortune pushed back his black felt hat and rubbed his narrow, light-brown mustache.

"What are you thinking, Frank?" Essie asked.

"That gang's been pickin' off a few head of ever'

ranch and movin' them down to Devil's Wash, then makin' it look like we're stealin' from each other."

"But what about Toole and Meyers?" Essie asked. "You said they were stealing for Thomasville."

"That's what they claimed."

"You think they were a part of the Devil's Wash gang?"

"I believe they thought Thomasville or his henchmen would pay them five dollars a head. That doesn't fit the Devil's Wash gang."

"You mean your cattle are getting rustled from both sides?" Essie asked.

"Maybe, but it does solve part of the mystery. I don't know who they are down there, but we do know where the cattle are disappearin' to."

"What will you do about it?" Morgan asked.

"If we can throw together a big enough crew, we'll try to flush them out. It would be risky goin' in after them. Until then, I'll bring my cows down from that area. That will make it tougher for them to steal. They have to come out of Devil's Wash sooner or later, if just to buy supplies."

"Is this good news or bad, Frank?" Essie asked.

"It surely gives me and LeMay and Thomasville somethin' to talk about," he replied.

Morgan leaned forward and rested her cheek on the back of Frank's vest. "Do you think there is a reward for those men? And could we get some of it for finding them?"

"If they are captured, and if there's a reward, I reckon you should get some of it."

Faith sat up on Smokey and tried to straighten her oversized dress. "If I get money, I'm going to buy a new pair of shoes like Miss Bowers's. I've never had new store-bought shoes before."

Katie pulled a long strand of her hair across her mouth. "If I get money, I think I will send my mother a set of pans. She always wanted a complete set of pans just for herself that she doesn't have to share with others."

"Yeah, you would," Morgan sneered.

"I would what?" Katie replied.

"Send something to your mother. Some of us don't have mothers."

"But . . . but," Katie stammered, "you have a grand-mother."

Morgan sat up and tried to brush her gray dress down over her knees. "If I had money, I'd buy a red dress and take the train to Denver."

"Morgan Denise!" Essie scolded.

"Well, I would!"

Essie wiped her neck with her handkerchief. "We are all going back to Wind River, then we'll decide what to do next."

"Can we take the train?" Katie asked.

"Trains cost money," Essie insisted.

Faith rode over closer to Essie and Katie. "We could use the reward money."

Morgan tugged off Frank's hat and plopped it on her head. "Oh yes, let's do that!"

"If there is reward money, and if you girls get a part of it, yes, we could take the train."

Katie giggled. "Miss Bowers, that would be so wonderful!"

"Maybe we could stop by Denver on the way," Morgan said.

By mid-afternoon they came in sight of Sweetwater Springs draw and the crew that fenced the trail. A shirtless Howdy Tompkins greeted them. Morgan hid behind Frank.

"Boss, don't that beat all? You leave home with one purdy lady and come back with four. 'Course I can't see the face of that one behind you."

Morgan peeked her head around Frank and stuck out her tongue.

"And friendly too!" Howdy grinned.

Faith rode Smokey out on the prairie away from the men.

Jonas lumbered over next to Howdy. "And the boss has another at headquarters, too. He's a popular man these days."

"We haven't had a gal out here since Dacee June came out in July. Now, they arrive in swarms," Pete hooted.

"How many constitutes a swarm?" Essie called out. Katie pulled her foot off Essie's lap and remained hidden.

"When there's more women than men, it's a swarm," Howdy reported.

Katie peeked around Essie. "Do we get counted as women?"

"You aren't boys, are ya?" Howdy replied.

Morgan sat up straight and looked around Frank's

shoulder. "No, we are women," she insisted.

"Even then we aren't outnumbered yet," Frank said. "But it's gettin' closer."

"I wasn't countin' Cron and Reynoso, 'cause they're up at the rock house," Howdy explained.

Frank pointed to the split rails. "How's the fencin' comin'?"

"Sam said just to fence this trail across the draw. Is that right?" Jonas asked.

"That's the best we can do. Did you boys ride down there?"

Pete's sweat-drenched denim shirt plastered his chest and back. "We looked from a distance."

"What's that horrible smell?" Faith called out.

"Dead cows," Frank reported.

"Even the birds won't pick them clean. There's a couple dead coyotes down there too," Howdy said.

"It's a death trap, whatever it is," Frank said. "Don't get any closer, boys."

"We'll be done here soon. I reckon we'll trail in about an hour behind you," Howdy declared. "We don't want to be late for the party."

"Party? It's just supper," Frank said.

Jonas snatched up a canteen and pulled the cork out with his teeth. "That señorita is decoratin' the place. It's a regular party."

"What do you mean, decoratin'?" Frank asked.

"Mexican lanterns and ever'thin'," Jonas reported. "She must have had some goods in her wagon." He handed the canteen up to Essie.

Frank stared southwest across the prairie. "I didn't tell

her to decorate."

Essie took a swig of water, wiped her mouth on her dress sleeve, and handed the canteen back to Katie. "I don't believe any person tells Señorita Rodriguez anything."

Howdy tipped his hat. "I reckon you're right about that, Miss Essie."

"But I do have a question for you, Howdy."

"Yes, ma'am?"

"You said the ladies outnumber the men at the headquarters?" Essie pressed.

"Yep."

"I count seven men," Essie continued. "You three, Sam, Americus, Frank, and old Miguel. Is that correct?"

"Yep."

"And I count six women. Me and the girls, plus Dearyanna and Latina."

Howdy spit on the ground. "You forget them other two that pulled in about noon. I had to ride back in for another spade and they was there."

"Who was there?" Frank asked.

"Marla Jolene and that little red-headed toddler of hers, Lavada."

"At the ranch?" Frank gasped.

Howdy took the canteen from Katie and took a swig, then handed it to Frank. "I take it, you weren't expectin' them?"

"But . . . but . . . I haven't seen her in two years." He took a quick gulp of water and handed it back to Morgan.

"Two and a half years," Essie corrected.

Howdy grinned. "She surely does look different from last time I seen her."

"How different?" Frank asked.

"She's . . . you know," Howdy glanced up at Essie and the girls and held his hands in front of his stomach.

"My word, she's pregnant?" Essie replied.

Howdy blustered. "Yes ma'am . . ." He took the canteen from Morgan and passed it over to Faith.

"How far along is she?" Essie asked.

"She's ripe, Miss Essie. But I reckon it ain't polite to study her much."

Morgan giggled.

Frank wiped his face and neck with his red bandanna. "Why is she out here?"

"To see you. Why are any of 'em out here? She wants to talk to you, Boss. It's all Sam could do to keep her from mountin' up and ridin' after you."

"Oh my, that would be painful," Essie grimaced. "I can't imagine being pregnant and riding horseback."

"Have you ever been pregnant, Miss Bowers?" Morgan asked.

"No, I have not, young lady. And I have not fallen out of a barn on my head, but I can imagine the pain in both cases."

Howdy's mouth dropped open. "Boss, do you mind movin' these women along before I turn permanent bright red?"

Frank took a deep breath and shook his head. "This is crazy." He kicked Carlos's flanks and trotted to the southwest along a narrow dirt trail through the brown prairie grass. "It just keeps getting more complicated.

Marla Jolene Cloquet? At the ranch? This is like a night-mare that never ends."

"Did Mr. Fortune say we were like a nightmare?" Faith called out as she handed the canteen down to Jonas.

"I believe so. But the story isn't over, so maybe the dream turns out nice," Essie declared.

Frank continued to mutter. "I need to move my cows, sell some off, buy some fencing, stock up on winter feed, get that spring water tested . . . I just don't have time for this . . . Marla Jolene?"

"I had a nightmare last night," Morgan declared.

"You said you didn't sleep at all last night," Katie challenged.

Frank stared off to the southwest. "When does life ever get simpler? When is a crisis solved and gone so as not to torment my mind?"

Morgan shrugged. "It was a short nightmare."

"What did you dream about?" Faith asked.

"Maybe she was just in the neighborhood . . ." Frank babbled.

Morgan rested her hands on Frank's shoulders. "I dreamed that when we got home, my daddy said I could stay only if I married Blue Bishop."

"Ahhh, that is a nightmare," Faith moaned.

Frank ignored them all. "But my ranch isn't on the way to anywhere. What does Marla Jolene want to talk to me about? Is she sorry she married Cloquet?"

Katie raised her leg back into Essie's lap. "I've never heard you talk about Blue Bishop before."

"He's an old man," Morgan reported.

"It's a little late for thinkin' about being sorry," Frank mumbled.

"How old?" Katie asked.

"Twenty-five," Morgan said.

Frank tried rubbing the wrinkles out of his forehead with his fingertips. "Why did Marla come today? Why not last week? Or next week? Or next month? Or never?"

"He doesn't have any neck," Morgan blurted out.

Faith rode Smokey next to Carlos. "What do you mean?"

"Blue Bishop has so many muscles in his shoulders that you can't see his neck."

Frank glanced around. "Oh, Essie, I hope Marla's husband isn't mistreatin' her. There are some things I can't tolerate. If he's beatin' on her, I don't know what I'll do."

"Did you feel better when you woke up and found it was a dream?" Katie asked.

"Yes," Morgan smiled. "It felt like the most wonderful day in the world." She began to rub Frank's shoulders.

He felt his neck relax. "It has to be some kind of emergency. She wouldn't come out here to see me unless she was desperate. Would she?"

"Miss Bowers, why does God let us have bad dreams?" Katie asked.

Essie Bowers brushed the dirt off Katie's swollen foot. "Maybe Morgan already answered that. Maybe so we can wake up and realize how wonderful things really are."

Frank bounced in the saddle as Carlos broke into a

trot. "I just can't believe all of this dropped on me at once."

"He mumbles a lot, doesn't he?" Morgan declared.

"Yes, he does." Essie kicked Cuddles's flank to keep up with Frank. "Just relax, Frank. I'm sure it will all work out fine. Since there is no way of telling why Marla Jolene is here, you might as well expect the best."

"The best? I've got a beautiful Mexican señorita and two servants in one room," he fumed. "And a nice schoolteacher and three Cheyenne girls . . ."

Morgan continued to rub his shoulders and neck. "Three very pretty Cheyenne girls."

"And three very pretty Cheyenne girls in my other room. Now a woman I thought I was goin' to marry, who married someone else, shows up at my door with a toddler."

"A very ripe woman," Katie giggled.

"I can't believe this!" he moaned.

Essie kicked Cuddles and cantered past him. "Are you bragging or complaining, Frank Fortune?"

Bear Butte Valley was cast in shadows when the three horses dropped down the north grade toward headquarters. The dark western bluffs contrasted with the east-side ones, which still caught the setting sun. Two dozen horses and two mules grazed in the fenced pasture next to the corrals. Frank couldn't see any other movement around the big house or the barn or bunkhouse.

Morgan held on to his shoulders. "You have a nice house."

"Thank you, darlin'."

"Do any young boys work here?" Faith asked.

Frank reached back and patted her hand. "You mean maybe fourteen or fifteen?"

"Or even sixteen or seventeen?" she replied.

"Not a one. The youngest man left on the ranch is about twenty."

"Which one is he?" Morgan asked.

"He's the one livin' up in the stone house that you stole the horses from."

Morgan's shoulders slumped. "Oh."

"Are you really having a party?" Katie asked.

"I reckon," he said.

"Are we invited?" Faith asked.

"You most certainly are," he replied.

"Will there be dancing?" Morgan asked. "I don't have a dancing dress."

Frank laughed. "No, I don't surmise there will be dancing. Not too musical a crew out here until Abby and Dacee June or Amber comes out."

"Are they your sisters?" Faith asked him.

"Aunts and a cousin."

"Do you have any sisters?" Katie quizzed.

"Twin sisters, who will be getting married on Saturday."

"You have any younger brothers?" Morgan questioned.

"Morgan Denise!" Essie censured.

Morgan leaned forward and put her cheek on the back of Frank's vest again. "I'm just being friendly."

Red, green, and yellow lanterns were strung all along the long front porch that ran across the whole building.

"What's the table doin' out in the yard?" Frank said.

Essie rode up alongside him. "Looks like we're eating outside."

"I've got two men comin' over for some heated discussion about cattle rustlin'. It ain't a party atmosphere."

"You have seven women too."

"One's a baby," he corrected.

Essie brushed her bangs out of her eyes. "And one's . . ."

Frank held up his hand. "I know what she is."

Sam Fortune strolled out of the wide barn door and waited for them to ride up. "You found the girls!" he called out.

"We found each other," Essie declared.

"Are they OK?"

"Katie sprained an ankle," Essie said.

"Let me put up the horses," Sam offered. He took the reins from Essie and the lead rope from Faith. "I rode the west line but saw nothin'." He nodded toward the house. "You got extra company."

Frank stepped down out of the saddle. "Marla Jolene?"

"Yeah," Sam nodded, "it's quite a story."

Frank stared down the line at the front of the big house. "Looks like you've been busy." He reached up and helped Morgan to the ground.

"The señorita took charge and worked Latina, Miguel, and Americus solid all day. You'd think they were pitchin' a fandango," Sam reported. "I think it's her idea of a picnic. Maybe she wanted the dining room for a dance floor."

"Really?" Faith called out as she slipped off the saddleless horse.

Frank eased Katie off the back of Essie's horse.

"I heard that Miguel plays the fiddle and Latina strums the guitar," Sam reported.

"I get the first dance with Mr. Fortune," Faith called out.

"No, the dance was my idea. I get the first dance with Mr. Fortune," Morgan insisted.

"If there is a dance, you can both have your way," Essie smiled as she dismounted. "Both of these men are Mr. Fortune."

"I get the young one, you can have the old man," Morgan insisted.

Sam tipped his hat. "That's quite alright, ladies. I'll gladly yield to handsome Little Frank Fortune."

Katie limped over next to Essie. "Why is he called Little Frank?"

Sam led the horses toward the barn. "Because there used to be a Big Frank."

"There's another girl at school named Faith. I wanted to be called Little Faith. But the other girl said if they started calling her Big Faith, she would punch me in the nose, 'cause it would be all my fault. Anyway, Miss Bowers said Little Faith sounded too much like a sermon anyway."

Sam tipped his hat to Essie. "They are a talkative bunch, Miss Essie."

"And they are a dirty bunch. If they are going to a party, we must clean up. Frank, may the four of us appropriate your big room?"

"Essie, I reckon you know the answer to that. It's all yours."

She led the giggling girls to the house.

Frank helped Sam lead the horses into the barn. "What's this about Marla Jolene bein' here?"

"She drove a carriage in here around noon."

"Why did she come out here?" Frank asked.

"She'll tell you herself. She brought the baby with her," Sam said.

"So I heard."

Sam pulled the saddle off Cuddles. "And she's . . ."

"I heard that too," Frank said as he loosened the cinch on Carlos. "Where are they?"

"Señorita Rodriguez insisted she and Lavada take a nap in your room. In fact, Dearyanna moved all her belongings back to the wagon. She said they could stay there the night."

"She didn't have to do that." Frank pulled the sweaty saddle blanket off the chestnut gelding. "You mean, Marla Jolene is spending the night?"

Sam plucked up a brush and tossed a curry comb to Frank. "You aren't plannin' on kicking her out are you?"

Frank stood staring at the open barn door. "No. I just don't know why she is here."

"You will soon enough. Go on and see her," Sam insisted.

"Do you think she is still sleeping?"

"She said to wake her as soon as you got here. But I'll leave that up to you."

Frank tossed the curry comb down on a barrel and

meandered toward the door. "Where's Dearyanna?"

"In the kitchen, I expect. She has Americus, Latina, and Miguel hard at work cookin' some Spanish delights."

"I gave orders to cook chops."

"Little Frank, you do not give the orders when the señorita is here."

"I've been told that before, Uncle Sammy. It does look quite festive. I think I'll go see how things are in the kitchen," Frank mumbled.

"You are goin' to go over there and talk to Marla Jolene right now. That lady put herself in great physical peril to come see you."

Frank jammed his hands in his back pockets, then rocked back on his heels. "Yeah, I know. This is tough to do, after all these years."

"You think it was easy for her to drive up here?"

"Must be important."

"It is."

Frank left the barn and ambled along the front of the house toward the outside door to the bedroom. *Lord, I don't know what to say. I stayed at the ranch. I lost her. I've never blamed her. Still, to get married without saying anything. And never write to me at all, then suddenly show up. I don't need this. You know I don't need this. It's as if you are testing me to see how much I can take. I think I'm at the limit.*

Frank rapped three times on the heavy oak door.

"Yes, who's there?" The voice was deeper than he remembered, yet familiar.

"It's me, Marla Jolene. Frank."

The door swung open very slowly.

"Oh, my . . ." he stammered.

The round-faced woman with auburn hair licked her dry lips. "Hello, Frank."

"Oh, my . . ." he said again.

She patted the auburn hair of the little girl who stood beside her, clutching her fingers. "Frank, this is Lavada. She's thirteen months old and walks very well, doesn't she?"

Frank squatted down on his haunches in the doorway, then tipped his hat. "Evenin', Miss Lavada."

The toddler reached her hands up to him.

Lord, she looks just like Marla. I reckon, if I would have married her mama, our daughter might have looked just the same. "I'm covered with trail dirt, darlin'."

"Pick her up, Frank. Please. My back hurts too much to carry her. It was farther out here than I remembered. Perhaps we could sit down out on a bench," Marla suggested.

Frank stood with the happy toddler on his arm. "That would be fine."

"May I bring one of your pillows out to sit on?"

"Surely . . ." he murmured.

"Did you ever see a stomach this big?"

He stared across the corrals at the horses.

"Look at me, Frank. Look at this stomach. I'm a lot bigger than with Lavada."

"How long . . . eh . . . when . . ." Frank stammered.

"In two weeks." Marla positioned the pillow on the hard wooden bench.

He jostled the toddler up and down on his hip. "The baby's due in two weeks, and you rode a carriage this far? Marla, why in the world did you do that?"

She slumped down on the pillow. "Because it's that important, Frank."

He sat down on the bench in front of the bedroom window. "Lavada likes you," she commented.

Frank kissed the toddler's round cheek. "She's a cutie. An absolute cutie. Looks just like her mama."

He studied Marla's troubled green eyes.

An embarrassed smile broke across her face. "Why are you staring at me like that, Frank? Have I changed that much?"

"I was staring because I took a gamble four years ago. I lost you and gained a ranch, and for the life of me, I can't figure out whether I did the right thing or not."

"Thank you for sayin' that, Frank Fortune. You'll never know how much its means to me. But it was the best thing for both of us."

"Are you happy?"

"I am very happy with Alexander."

"Then, I'm happy, too. You still livin' in Rapid City?"

"Yes."

Lavada tugged at Frank's hat. He plopped it on her head. The hat drooped over the infant's eyes.

"He's a banker, I hear."

"One of the youngest bank presidents in South Dakota."

"How's your mama and daddy?"

"Daddy died, Frank."

"Oh no, darlin', I didn't know that." He reached over

and took Marla's hand. "I'm sorry. He was a very good and kind man. Did he ever make his peace with Jesus?"

"I don't think so, Frank." She clutched his fingers. "I already cried myself dry about that. But right now, I have bigger worries."

He lifted the hat off the grinning baby. "I surmised you didn't come out here just for a social call."

"Frank, I have to say some things before I get started. They have been eating at me for years. I know I didn't treat you right back then. I started seeing Alexander while you were out here, and I never told you because I kept hoping you'd show up at my door and sweep me off my feet again. But you didn't show up. Week after week, month after month. I know we said it would take time to establish the ranch, but I just couldn't wait. I'm weak, Frank. I never was strong like you. You know that. Alexander was so very sweet to me, and I grew to love him. I love him very much."

He took a long, deep sigh. "I am truly happy for you, Marla."

"I know I have no business being here, Frank." Marla laced her fingers together, rested them on her stomach, then stared at them. "But let me tell you the situation. When Daddy died last January, it left Mother in a bind. Daddy didn't save anything up. He liked his fancy house and fancy horse. You know how he was. Generous to a fault. Anyway, Mama went back to Rhode Island to live next to my aunt and uncle. She walked away from all the debts and told me to do what I could."

He sat Lavada astraddle his knee and began to bounce her. "That sounds rough, Marla."

"It gets much worse." Her voice was so soft he could barely hear it. "My husband, my dear Alexander . . . thought of a way to raise the money to pay off Daddy's debts. He would buy Nebraska cattle, drive them across South Dakota, and sell them at Rapid City."

"The cattle business is risky."

"Yes, I told him that. But he made a big deal with an Omaha meat packer last spring. They had money to spend, and they paid him in advance for a thousand head contracted to be delivered this fall."

"And he spent the money?" Frank asked.

"He had the cows all counted and contracted for down in the Beaver Mountains. So he paid off all of Daddy's debts with the profit he would make and had some left to build two bedrooms on to our one-bedroom house," Marla reported.

"What happened to the cows, darlin'?"

"Texas fever. They all died, Frank. Every one of them."

"Can he buy some more?"

"Not in the next two weeks. He asked the meat packer for an extension, but they refused. They said if he doesn't have the cows in the pens in two weeks, they want a full refund, or they'll have Alexander arrested."

"That's a bind. But sometimes that's the way business goes. He's got the buyin' cow money, right?"

"Half of it . . . he paid the rancher half the money . . . and now they have no way to deliver and he has no way to buy more."

"Then the rancher owes him the money."

"The man moved off to Texas and signed the deed

over to his creditors. Alexander figures his share will be four sections, if it ever gets settled."

"Twenty-four hundred acres?" Frank asked.

"Yes, but they say it will be tied up in courts for months."

Lavada reached forward and put her finger on Frank's chapped lips. He kissed the fingers. "So what does your Alexander want from me?"

"Nothing. He doesn't know I've come here, Frank. He went to Denver to see an uncle that he hasn't spoken to in twenty years to beg for a loan. I know he'll get turned down. Frank, Alexander isn't strong willed like Fortune men. This is going to crush him. I don't think he will live through it. I'm scared, Frank."

"Marla, I sympathize with your plight." Lavada leaned forward and planted a wet, slobbery kiss on Frank's lips. "I suppose you want me to supply the cattle. Why else would you be here? So what exactly did you have in mind?"

"If you could sell us one thousand head, delivered to Rapid City in two weeks . . ."

"Two weeks? I'd need a roundup crew the size of a small army." The toddler lay her head on Frank's shoulder.

"Let me finish, Frank. If you had a thousand head of cattle in Rapid City in two weeks, we would pay you one half the money now, and deed over Alexander's share of the Nebraska ranch."

"All twenty-four hundred acres?"

"Yes, it would all be yours."

"What if his share isn't that big?"

"Then you'd get part interest in the bank or the whole bank. Whatever is right," she said.

"The bank must be out of money."

"It's a nice two-story building in downtown Rapid City. It's the block building that was across from Daddy's old office. And you could have the mortgage on our home, Frank. Whatever is fair."

"But, Marla . . ."

"Think about it, Frank. Please tell me you'll think about it. And that you'll pray. Don't turn me down yet. Let me catch my breath, then I can take it."

"But you don't even know if Alexander would go for this deal," he said.

"No, and I don't even know if he'll come home from Denver."

"What do you mean? He'd desert you?"

"Never. But if he got melancholy enough, he'd put a revolver to his head rather than face the shame. Frank, he is scared to death of failure. Do you know what that's like?"

He studied her soft green eyes for a moment.

"Yes, I do know what it's like, Marla. I'll ponder it and let you know. It's not a matter of want to, Marla. I just have to figure if I can do that and still stay in the cattle business."

She reached out her hand.

He took it and squeezed. It was soft, warm, and sweaty.

"Lavada's asleep in your arms. She's been restless this whole long trip. I'm restless. Being way out here scares me. I'm afraid of the wilderness, Frank. I think we both knew that, didn't we?"

"I reckon we did."

"I'm not cut out for this, Frank. I need to be in town. You need someone different from me. I met Señorita Rodriguez. She's different from me. So beautiful . . . and thin."

"You have a mighty fine excuse for packin' extra weight."

"Frank, I know this must sound insane, but it sounded logical when we drove out of Rapid City."

"I'll give it serious thought, Marla."

"I knew you would. You were always so serious about everything."

"I do believe you complained about that a time or two."

"I was a foolish teenager then, Frank."

"No, neither one of us was foolish, Marla. We were both hopin' for somethin' the other one couldn't provide." He stood up with the toddler in his arms. "Where can I put this little darlin'?" He noticed a tear slide down Marla's cheek.

"On your bed would be nice," she said. "I need to wash her before supper. When will we eat?"

He looked up the valley to the north. "That's Howdy and the rest of my crew comin' in now. But I've got two men arrivin' later. We won't eat until they both show up."

"Frank, it feels good to talk to you again." She slipped her arm in his. "You always made me feel what I had to say was important."

"Marla, I'm indeed sorry for treatin' you the way I did.

Lookin' back, I surely should have done things different. I had no business desertin' you for months at a time. I was foolish. I thought about you a lot, Marla."

"I like that. Frank Fortune thinking of me. It makes me feel like a woman. Lately, all I've been feeling like is a mama." She held the small of her back and forced a smile.

After Frank left them in the bedroom, he moseyed back out to the barn. Sam had just finished brushing down the horses and turning them out.

"Looks like Howdy, Jonas, and Pete comin' in," Sam reported.

Frank pumped some fresh water at the stock tank and washed his face with his bandanna. "Did you hear all of Marla's story, Uncle Sammy?"

"Yep."

"What do you think?"

"It don't matter what I think. What does Frank Fortune think about it?" Sam declared.

"It puts me in a bind. How can I say no to a woman and a baby?"

"A very ripe woman and a baby."

"If I sell a thousand head for half price, I'll be broke by next summer."

"What if they can pay you? What about ownin' a bank? What about that Nebraska land?" Sam challenged.

"Yeah, that's what makes it tough."

"I don't know, Little Frank . . . list the good and the bad of the deal and pray over it."

"I don't think there's too much good about the deal."

"Holdin' five hundred head over the winter, with one polluted spring and potential for death, is easier than fifteen hundred," Sam suggested.

"Yeah, I could pull five hundred all back down here and not need a crew to ride north all winter."

"And if you got some Nebraska land . . . maybe it would be good winter ground. Just a thought."

"It's a gamble."

"You might go belly up on it, that's true. Guess it boils down to what you can live with," Sam said.

"You mean later on, lookin' back?" Frank asked.

"Yep."

"Are you in cahoots with the Lord on this?"

"I don't know," Sam replied. "What's he tellin' you?"

"It's not clear yet, but he's tuggin' on me. Essie didn't come out of the big room, did she?"

"I reckon she's scrubbin' Indian maidens."

Frank left the barn and strolled across the yard. Holding his hat, he rapped on the door to the great room.

"Go away," a young lady snapped.

"Morgan, this is Frank Fortune. I need to talk to Essie."

"How did you know it was me?"

" 'Cause you complain a lot. Tell Essie I need to talk to her."

"I do not!"

The door cracked open two inches. Morgan's nose, lips, and one eye appeared. "The Mexican lady gave us dresses to wear."

"Dearyanna?"

"Her name is Anna?" Morgan pressed.

"Señorita Rodriguez will be fine."

"I get the red one," she announced.

"May I speak to Essie?"

"Miss Bowers, it's your boyfriend."

Essie stepped outside with Frank. "The girls are so excited," she reported.

"I can see that. Did Dearyanna really give them dresses to wear?"

"Yes. They are beautiful and hang like big oversized sacks on the girls, but they want to wear them," Essie said.

"They seem to have recovered from their ordeal."

"Katie can hardly walk, but they are so relieved not to be captured by outlaws or beaten for running away."

"Essie, I need you to fetch a couple of things out of my rolltop desk for me."

"You can come on in."

"Are you sure?"

She stuck her head back inside the room. "Girls, hide behind that divider. Mr. Fortune needs to get some things out of his desk."

"We're back here under a blanket!" Katie shouted.

Frank walked in behind Essie.

"Modest things, aren't they?" he said.

"Only with men around. You should have seen them a minute ago running around here like . . ." Essie paused.

"Wild Indians?"

"Yes, that's their privilege, I suppose."

"I'll just be a minute. I need my ledger, a pencil, and some paper. A deal came up."

"With Marla Jolene? I heard."

He pulled open a desk drawer. "You heard?"

"She sat up by the front window and listened to you and that mama lady talkin'," Faith's voice filtered from the back of the room.

Essie's voice dropped low. "I need to apologize."

"No, I'm glad. Then I don't have to explain it all over."

"Where in Nebraska is the acreage? I didn't catch that part."

"Just west of the Beaver Mountains, I think. That's all I know. Do you know anything about land up there?"

"A good friend of mine lives up that way. Did she mention a rancher's name?"

Frank pulled a black ledger out of the desk. "No. I'll go ask her."

"Don't bother her and the baby now, Frank. They need to rest," Essie insisted.

He stared at the closed door between the great room and the bedroom. "Can you imagine a woman in that condition coming this far in a carriage?"

"Only if you were her last hope in the world."

"I know."

"Is he goin' to leave soon?" a voice called out.

"Morgan, I'm on my way out."

"How did you know it was me?"

"Darlin', it's always you."

Frank retrieved several other items from his desk and stepped to the door. "What do you think I ought to do, Essie?"

"In the twenty-four hours that I have known Frank

Fortune, I believe he could not live with himself if he didn't try to do something for Marla Jolene."

"It doesn't have to make good business sense, does it?"

"No, it just has to be the best option you have at the time."

"Pray for me, Essie."

"Frank, you know I will."

He closed the door behind him. "Yeah, I know," he murmured.

When Frank returned to the barn, Sam Fortune was chatting with Reid LeMay, who was brushing down his red roan gelding.

"Howdy, Reid," Frank nodded. "I didn't see you ride in."

"Your uncle and me been busy makin' up lies about how brave and handsome we used to be. 'Course with Sam, most of 'em aren't lies. That thievin' Thomasville isn't here yet, is he?"

Frank glanced out the barn to the north. "Nope, he's not here. You didn't see him comin' in?"

"Nope, we didn't see anyone," LeMay replied.

"We? I said just you were invited, Reid. I thought I made that clear."

LeMay plucked up a hay straw and picked at his teeth. "Just a couple of the boys came with me, to keep me company. But I made them camp out on the prairie. They ain't comin' in, Frank."

"That's not what I had in mind."

"We'll be ridin' north soon enough. You think this

meetin' is goin' to do any good?" LeMay said.

"I've got a couple or three items of news that might shed some light on the whole matter," Frank reported. "Thomasville will have to supply the rest."

"Don't expect much out of him. He only looks out for himself, no matter what the cost."

"I'm not going to have a row with you and Thomasville, am I?" Frank pressed.

"As long as he don't start it," LeMay replied as he rested his hand on his revolver.

"No one is goin' to start anything," Frank insisted. "If you can't go along with that, I'd prefer you ride out right now."

LeMay studied Frank for a moment. Then a smile broke across his face. "Sam, is ever' one of you Fortune men so rock-headed stubborn?"

"We're downright mellow compared to the Fortune women," Sam claimed.

LeMay pointed down the line toward the big house. "It truly looks festive around here. Sam said the ranch is teemin' with women, and he's not the blame for it."

Frank rubbed the back of his stiff neck. "It ain't the normal pattern, that's for sure. Just had a lot of company drop by."

"You got any coffee around?" LeMay asked.

"If you can get in the kitchen door, there should be some. Why don't you show him, Uncle Sammy? I've got some books to ponder."

Frank watched the two men stroll across the yard. *Lord, when I'm forty-eight, who will I have to talk to about the old days? I miss Quint Trooper, Lord. I don't know why he had to go to Cuba with Mr. Roosevelt. And I surely don't know why he had to die of malaria in some little tropic hut. And I don't know why I didn't go with him. Maybe his sister Fern was right. Maybe if I went we could have taken care of each other. But I didn't, Lord. I started a ranch and lost my friend. I lost a whole lot more. It wasn't a good trade.*

Frank climbed the ladder to the loft, toting his black leather ledger under his arm. He plopped down on the wood floor and leaned against the rough-cut post.

Twenty-four hours ago I sat up here with Essie Bowers. She's got to be the easiest gal to talk to I ever met. I don't feel any need to impress her. I don't know why. I've spent my life tryin' to live up to others' expectations. Maybe cause we're strangers I can be so relaxed. But I don't think so. I surely am not relaxed around Dearyanna. My, that señorita is one beautiful lady. My, oh my, Uncle Sammy is right. A beauty like that comes along once in a lifetime.

But, Lord, that's not the reason I'm here. It's Marla that needs me. Not Dearyanna. Not Essie. The way I figure it, Lord, there is no way I'll get any more cash than half price for the cows. Now, a bank that is tapped out of funds itself can't be worth too much more than the building. Even if it's a nice building, I don't know what I would do with it. Sell it, I reckon.

But the Nebraska property has potential. If I could run five hundred head. If I could fence it, I could take care of it with just one or two men. It's a long way from Deadwood and the Black Hills. Don't know what the family would say. It ain't your kind of ranch, Grandpa.

But maybe that's been the trouble. Maybe I've been tryin' to build a Brazos Fortune ranch. What I need is a Little Frank Fortune ranch.

But then, again, maybe I won't get anything. What if half pay is all I realize? I couldn't pay my bills. My five-year lease comes up next June. I won't ask the family for more money. I can't do that.

Lord, what am I talkin' about?

Essie's right.

She knows my heart.

I'd rather die than send Marla and the baby home with no hope.

I don't want to be here, Lord.

But I'm here.

Help me, Jesus.

Frank climbed down the ladder when he heard a horse trot up to the barn. He hiked out as George Washington Thomasville climbed off his overo paint with one blue eye and one brown eye.

"My word, Fortune, you didn't tell me you were havin' a party. Glad I wore a decent suit. I got lost tryin' to find this place."

"Welcome, Mr. Thomasville. Settin' down in this little valley against the cliff gives us some protection in the winter."

"We must have passed this place four times before we found it."

"We? Who did you bring with you?" Frank asked.

"A couple of the boys are camped up at the head of the valley. I told them to stay there."

"I've got a few extra visitors."

"I can see that." Thomasville nodded at the big house. "Did I see some ladies?"

"Ladies and girls. And a friend of yours."

"Who?" Thomasville pressed.

"Reid LeMay. He's reppin' for the railroad."

Thomasville reached for his revolver.

"You know, that's the same reaction that LeMay had when I mentioned your name."

"We've had run-ins before."

"We have a mutual problem. So let's set the past aside for a few hours and deal with missin' cattle."

"You got any idea what's goin' on?" Thomasville quizzed.

"Yep. Don't you?" Frank challenged.

"What does that mean?"

"That's what you and me and LeMay need to discuss."

Someone banged on the triangle in front of the dining room.

"Right now, it's time to go eat. Pull the saddle off, turn your pony in the corral. I'll meet you over at the tables."

By the time Frank reached the table, the other guests had gathered.

"Howdy, I ain't seen you and the boys this clean since the big dance in July," Frank teased.

"Now, Boss, it ain't ever' night that we have such a party at the ranch."

"Did you look at the table of food, Boss?" Jonas said. "I ain't seen this much to eat since Uncle Marvin's funeral."

"Was that Thomasville who rode in?" Reid LeMay asked.

"Yep, and I promised him you wouldn't shoot him on sight," Frank declared.

Latina and Americus toted out platters of steaming food.

"Sam says you got news of rustlers down in Devil's Wash," LeMay said.

"Yep. I got three witnesses who saw our cattle down there."

"You mean, your men went in there and came out alive?"

Frank pointed across the table. "The three girls in the bright-colored dresses were down there."

"Mexicans?" LeMay questioned.

"Cheyennes."

"You believe them?" he asked.

"Yep," Frank replied.

"What are we goin' to do about the rustlin'?"

"That's one of two things we will discuss with Thomasville."

"Was he in on it?"

"We worked all day cookin' this food. Are we goin' to eat it before it gets cold?" Americus shouted.

"I should introduce a couple of people, then say a blessing," Frank called out. "We don't normally need introductions at the ranch. But with all these guests, I reckon we do. This handsome old man is my Uncle Sammy. Next to him is Reid LeMay, who represents the railroad's ranch north of us. The man who just walked up in the tailor-made suit and tie is Mr. George Washington Thomasville, who ranches in Wyoming. Howdy, Pete, and Jonas work for me, as does the meanest cook in Dakota, Americus Ash. Standin' next to him is Miguel and Latina. Then you have a very good friend of mine, Mrs. Alexander Cloquet, and little Lavada. Next to Lavada is my Essie, I mean, my friend Estelle Bowers, and three of her purdiest students, Faith, Katie, and Morgan. Katie's the one with the bum ankle. Let's see . . . who did I miss . . . the Señorita? Where did she go?"

"She went to the wagon for something," Latina replied.

"Let's have a blessing and get started. A few of us have some mighty important business to take care of later on, but let's don't let that hamper our supper," Frank insisted.

He bowed his head. "Lord, give us strength from this food, and friendship from the visitin', and wisdom for the decisions that need to be made. In Jesus' name, amen."

When he looked up, Dearyanna stood next to Miguel, across the table from him.

"And here is the lady who made this whole evenin' a party, Señorita Rodriguez."

"What in blazes is she doing here?" Thomasville shouted.

"Why, I'm looking for you." Dearyanna pointed a small brass-frame revolver at George Washington Thomasville.

And pulled the trigger.

CHAPTER NINE

THOMASVILLE STAGGERED BACK and collapsed in the dirt yard.

Señorita Rodriguez tossed the revolver down on the table. It splattered into the bowl of enchiladas. Latina and Miguel hurried to her side.

Essie shoved Faith, Katie, and Morgan toward the front door of the great room, then hurried to Thomasville's side.

Marla Jolene and Lavada began a duet of tears.

Pete and Howdy dove under the table.

Jonas plucked up a tortilla and ate it.

Americus joined Essie to check out Thomasville's condition.

Sam and Reid drew their guns and scanned the shadowy perimeter of the headquarters.

And Frank Fortune just stared.

And stared.

"I can't believe you did that!" he finally croaked. "Why?"

Dearyanna's lip quivered. A strand of long black hair flopped down across her cheek. Her eyes flashed with rage. "Thomasville knows why," she charged.

"But, why vengeance? Why violence? Why here? Why now?" Frank stammered.

She plucked a bread knife off the table. "Because he killed my brother."

Frank stormed around the table toward her. "That was the whole reason you came, wasn't it? You aren't studying plants, you didn't want to visit me. You were stalkin' Major George Washington Thomasville."

She waved the knife toward the major. "He refused to talk to me in Cheyenne. He left town in the middle of the night. I was determined to find him somewhere."

"I can't believe you shot him," Frank muttered.

"You said that before. I shot him," she shrugged. "So now you can arrest me." She stabbed the knife into the stack of tortillas.

"Frank," Essie called, "let's get Mr. Thomasville to the porch where there's better light."

"Howdy, you, Jonas, and Pete grab him and move him around. Uncle Sammy, I need you to . . ."

"Reid and me are goin' to watch for Thomasville's men to come ridin' in. If they heard that gunfire, they may come barrelin' in, guns drawn. He said they were at the top of the rim. We'll be in the shadows." Sam dipped a rolled-up tortilla into a bowl of salsa and marched off into the darkness, Reid LeMay at his side.

"She works all day in the kitchen and then shoots the man before we eat?" Americus griped. "It ruins the whole supper."

"Where was he shot?" Frank asked.

"The left shoulder," Essie reported. "It missed his heart by maybe six inches. What are you going to do?"

"Try to get that bleeding stopped and get him to Dead-wood as soon as we can," Frank said.

Essie smashed the palm of her hand down on the wound. "I mean, what are you going to do about Señorita Rodriguez? Americus, find me some clean bandages."

Frank hovered at Essie's side. "I have no idea."

By the time they toted Thomasville to the bench, he had regained consciousness. Frank rolled up his vest and propped it under the man's head. Essie tugged off the wounded man's suit coat and raised his arm, so she could wrap his shoulder.

Thomasville's chin twitched as tried to form the words. "She actually shot me?"

Essie continued to bandage him. "The bullet went in and out of the shoulder, Mr. Thomasville. We'll get you into Deadwood as soon as possible, but now we'll get the bleeding stopped. As long as it doesn't fester, you'll survive. Why did she shoot you?"

Sweat beaded Thomasville's forehead. He closed his eyes. "She didn't explain?"

Frank glanced back at the señorita, her shoulders slumped, her head in her hands. "Not yet."

Thomasville started to speak, then coughed. "That was years ago."

"What was?" Frank asked.

"She can tell you."

"Mr. Thomasville, do you want me to haul her into jail?" Frank asked.

"No."

"Why not?"

Thomasville's voice was so soft as to be barely audible. "She had ever' reason to shoot me."

"What are we supposed to do?"

Thomasville opened his eyes. "Wrap up my shoulder and go eat supper."

"This is crazy," Frank moaned.

"We'll talk rustlin' after supper. I'm too tired to talk right now."

"You're shot."

"Let me catch my breath."

"I'll take care of him, Frank," Essie offered. "Gather everyone and eat."

It took thirty minutes for everyone to get settled down and back to the table. Thomasville was propped up on a bench on the porch with Essie. Reid LeMay and Sam Fortune, with plates of food, were somewhere in the shadows. The rest, including the señorita, sat at the table.

Frank glanced around in the lantern light. "Well folks, the food is blessed."

"And stone cold," Americus grumbled.

"Thanks to the señorita, it's not the party we thought it was goin' to be," Frank continued. "But all of us need to eat. No matter what the outcome of all of this, we have a lot of work to do around here."

He glanced at Marla Jolene and little Lavada who sat on her knee. He cleared his throat. "I've contracted to sell some beef to Mrs. Cloquet and her husband. Boys, we've got to get a thousand head to Rapid City in two weeks."

Marla Jolene began to cry.

"You're goin' to do what?" Thomasville puffed from the bench on the porch.

"It's a personal matter, Major," Frank replied. "I'm helpin' out a friend."

"We ain't got enough crew to get that done in two

274

weeks," Howdy added.

"We'll add some crew, but we're goin' to do it. Now, Señorita, I wonder if you would be considerate enough to explain why you ruined our supper by shooting Thomasville?"

Dearyanna sat at the huge table with her hands in her lap. Her plate was filled with untouched food. "I am glad he didn't die," she murmured. "I wanted him to, but I'm glad he didn't die."

"Excuse me, ma'am, would you pass them tortillas?" Jonas asked. "And that there spicy red stuff. Thank you, ma'am." The big man smacked his lips. "Did you say he killed your brother?"

"I didn't kill her brother!" Thomasville shouted.

Essie shoved a salsa-dipped piece of tortilla in his mouth. "Really, Mr. Thomasville, I must insist you refrain from such outbursts. We will never get this bleeding to stop if you don't lie still."

Thomasville choked and chewed. "Lie still?" he mumbled. "She tried to kill me!"

"You should try the carne verde. It is quite spicy." Essie shoved some in his mouth. "Please continue, Señorita. We really do want an explanation. A .25 cal-iber bullet fired from fifteen feet away is not an assassin's tool. You were lucky to hit him at all. It's a wonder you didn't hit me or Frank."

"How do you know all about guns, Miss Essie?" Howdy asked her.

"My brother's a U.S. marshal, and my brother-in-law is a gunsmith."

Dearyanna ran her fork across her plate. "Six years

ago Major Thomasville came to Sonora to buy Mexican cattle."

"Which is a mistake I will never repeat," Thomasville blustered. Essie shoved a bite of cold meat in his mouth.

"My brother delivered twelve hundred head to Nogales, where they crossed the border. Once they were in Arizona, the Major paid my brother a dollar a head, less than the agreed-upon price."

"It cost me a dollar a head to bribe the Federales into letting me bring them across," Thomasville mumbled between bites of tortilla. "He didn't bother telling me that ahead of time."

"So my brother called Thomasville out to the streets of Nogales," the Señorita declared.

"They had a gunfight?" Jonas asked.

"I'm not about to have a gunfight," Thomasville insisted. "I just rode off."

"My brother followed him to get the rest of the money."

"And Thomasville killed him?" Pete quizzed.

"I didn't kill him," the Major blurted out.

"My brother was ambushed as he snuck up on Thomasville and his men."

Thomasville tried to sit up. Essie pushed him back down with her hand on his forehead. "I didn't kill him," he insisted again.

"You had him killed," the Señorita accused.

"I didn't even know he was out there," Thomasville asserted.

"I don't believe you," she snapped.

"All I knew was that someone was sneaking up. I sent

the boys to go look, and there was a gunfight. The Mexican died. I'm sorry."

"Didn't the sheriff look into it?" Frank asked.

"There wasn't anything to investigate," Thomasville said. "Self-defense."

"You cheated us, then killed my brother when he came to collect. Nothing to investigate? That's absurd. I hadn't planned to shoot him tonight. Just confront him in public and demand the money he owes us. But I was angry."

"Yes, ma'am, I reckon you were," Howdy said.

"If I had thought about killing him, I would have used the Winchester 1886, .45-70," she declared.

"That surely would have done the job," Pete said. "Will someone pass that there plate of cheesy stuff? Not that one . . . that's it, that one."

Essie wiped sweat off Thomasville's forehead. "I made sure they sent the body back to Sonora with all his trappings," the Major reported.

"Yes, and his bullet belt was full, as were five chambers of his revolver. He never fired a shot."

"That there spicy gumbo is some of the best food I ever tasted since I left my mama's. Does anyone mind if I finish it up?" Jonas said.

"When a man points a gun at you, you have to assume he's going to pull the trigger. All of you know that," Thomasville explained. "If he didn't shoot, perhaps that's his fault. He never should have pulled the gun."

"Señor Ash," Latina spoke softly, "you were right. The pollo delicia is better with more garlic."

"See? Did ever'one hear that? I do know how to

cook!" Americus triumphed.

"I'm sorry about your brother," Thomasville continued. "I had no intention of that deal costing anyone his life."

"This is the only way I knew to find some justice," Dearyanna said. "The ambush was committed on American soil, and they were not going to take the side of a young Mexican man."

"Is the matter settled then?" Frank asked.

"I will not shoot him again on your ranch," Dearyanna assured him.

"I'm sure Major Thomasville wants to clear his conscience too. You will be paying Señorita Rodriguez the twelve hundred dollars you owe for the cattle, won't you?" Essie said.

"What?" he grumbled.

She shoved a hot pepper in his mouth.

"That was a yes, wasn't it?" Essie asked.

He shook his head. "No!" he coughed and choked.

Essie shoved another pepper in his swollen cheeks. "Now, Mr. Thomasville, you are just teasing. You do plan on paying your debts, don't you?" She held another pepper in front of his mouth. "You really don't want to spend the rest of your life wondering every day if the señorita will show up to shoot you."

"Yes . . . wait . . . perhaps you may be right."

"What a nice man you are." Essie dropped the pepper back down on her plate.

"I've been buffaloed," he mumbled.

"No, you've been peppered," Essie snickered. "But you know in your heart it's the right thing."

"I'll pay; just get those peppers away from me."

"Frank, we've got to get Major Thomasville to Deadwood," Essie announced. "The wound won't kill him, but the infection might. One time a neighbor in Nebraska died because he was too stubborn to get a wound doctored. Besides, he needs to withdraw some funds. Unless, of course, he carries that much with him. You don't, do you?"

"Well, hmmm, it . . . I . . ." the major stammered.

"Oh my, he does have the money. How convenient," Essie said.

"One of you will have to take him to town. We've got rustlers down in Devil's Wash to take care of," Frank announced.

"We do?" Howdy sprayed coffee across his plate.

"We've got to run them out of there before we round up our cattle. They have railroad, Axe-T, and Rafter F beef down there," Frank declared.

"My word," Thomasville sputtered, "you mean someone's stealing from all of us?"

"How are we goin' to recover them cows, Boss?" Howdy questioned. "We'll get lost down there."

"I can show you where they are," Morgan offered, then bit her lip.

Frank took a sip of cold, bitter coffee. "You are not goin' back down there."

"Why not? I know where the cattle are, and you don't," Morgan whined.

"If there's trouble, and there will be, I don't want to be responsible for baby-sittin'," Frank murmured.

"Baby-sitting? I am not a baby! I am fourteen years

old. Just for that, I won't go."

"What if I come along to look after Morgan?" Essie said.

"You don't want to ride down the wall of Hades Canyon, Miss Essie," Howdy insisted. "That's a no-man's-land. Eh, and surely a no-woman's-land too."

"Mr. Tompkins, of course I don't want to go down there. No one wants to go down there. But if that's what it takes, I will do it. There are many things in life we are called to do that we don't want to do."

Howdy scooped the .25 caliber pistol out of the enchiladas and scraped the cheese off of it into his plate. "Ain't that the truth."

"What about me?" Faith asked. "Do I get to go with you too?"

"Honey, I need you to stay here and take care of Katie," Essie replied.

"This is impossible." Frank pushed back from the table and ran his hands through his greasy, dirty hair.

"Now, Frank," Essie said as she dipped a red pepper in the salsa, then took a bite. "Think of it as a grand adventure."

"I don't want a grand adventure," he moaned.

She fanned her mouth with her hand. "Exactly what is your point, Frank Fortune?"

"There's no way humanly possible to deliver the cattle to Rapid City in two weeks, is there?" Marla Jolene asked.

"Then we'll simply have to call on divine help," Essie insisted. "The Lord will answer our prayers."

"We?" Frank said.

"You said you need a lot of help. The girls and I will stay and see it through," Essie replied.

"Oh, yes. We're in no hurry to get back to school," Katie added.

Sam Fortune and Reid LeMay hiked out of the shadows to the table.

"You got trouble up there?" Frank asked.

"Not now," Reid LeMay said. He loaded up his empty plate with more food.

Frank glanced at his uncle. "I didn't hear any gunfire."

"Two of Thomasville's men were sneakin' in, so me and Reid coldcocked them. They'll wake up with headaches, that's for sure." Sam poured himself a cup of cold coffee.

"Was one of them the big man in the gray hat?" Frank asked.

Sam grimaced at the taste of the coffee, then took another big gulp. "Yep."

Frank stared north into the darkness. "That's John Earl."

"My word, you decimated my crew," Thomasville said.

"They are alive," Sam murmured. "Pass me the tortillas."

Jonas handed him the plate. "Ain't none of them stuffed peppers left."

"Reid, you and Sam grab your plate and let's join Thomasville," Frank said. "We need to get some things hashed out."

"Do you want me to leave?" Essie asked.

Frank studied her face for a moment. *Lord, how does*

this lady always end up on my side of the line? "Eh, no . . . you stay. You stay!"

"You repeated yourself."

"I do that sometimes. I might never change." He never took his eyes off hers. "Can you get used to that?" Frank asked her.

Essie's smile was wide, soft. Her eyes danced. "I believe I can."

"Hmmmmpth," Sam Fortune cleared his throat. "If you too are through moonin', we have things to discuss."

Reid and Sam lounged on a bench, plates of food in their laps. Essie nursed a reclining Thomasville.

Frank paced the porch with an empty enameled tin coffee cup in his hand. "Thomasville, if the señorita hadn't shot you, I might have. I fired two of my men for rustlin' my own beef and puttin' your brand on them. They said you offered them five dollars a head delivered."

Thomasville tried to sit up. "That's preposterous."

"I heard 'em," Sam echoed. "It's true. They said they made a deal with John Earl."

"I don't know what you're talkin' about."

Frank looked back at the cowboys still at the table. "Howdy, you and the boys take a wagon and bring back those two lyin' along the road. We need to ask that big one a question or two." He turned back to Thomasville. "If you didn't give the order, someone did. Your boys are on the take."

"They wouldn't do that," Thomasville insisted. "I trust them."

"Yeah, and mine wouldn't rustle my own cattle. But they did," Frank said.

It was well after ten o'clock by the time supper was done, and most had retired to their quarters. Frank made the rounds. His first stop was the wagon of Señorita Rodriguez.

"We'll be pulling out at daylight," she told him. "Did you think about what I told you?"

"Yep."

"Did she agree?"

"I haven't spoken to her yet. Are you goin' home?"

"Yes," Dearyanna replied. "We will go straight back to Sonora. I have Thomasville's money in my purse, thanks to Miss Bowers. I'll feel some satisfaction. Daddy will need me at home."

"There wasn't ever any graduate study on prairie plants, was there?" he asked.

"No, but I did graduate from the University of California with a degree in botany," she insisted.

"And your whole purpose up here was just to find Major Thomasville and shoot him?"

She pulled her raven hair across her face like a veil. "And tease the mysterious Frank Fortune. I have thought about you from time to time since you let me out of the privy at Ft. Huachuca." She reached out and held his hand.

He noticed that his heart didn't skip a beat. "I haven't fallen off a horse in front of you in three days."

"Yes, it's getting dull. Time for me to leave."

"Are you going through Deadwood?"

"No, I think we should hurry back to Mexico before Major Thomasville decides to press charges after all."

"You are a fascinating lady, Dearyanna. I don't reckon I'll forget you too soon."

"I am a spoiled, stubborn, hot-headed Mexican," she countered.

He pulled off his hat. "And, perhaps, the most beautiful woman I've ever met in my life."

"Francisco Fortune, you will never know how much I value your words. I believe when I am old and fat and gray, I'll still hear those words you just spoke ringing in my ears."

"In my mind, you will never be old and fat and gray," he murmured.

"Not if I leave tomorrow. I like that. To know that there is a handsome rancher who always thinks of me as young and pretty. Do you know what I was thinking, Francisco? I wondered if your daddy had stayed in the army and you were still living in southern Arizona, what would our future have been? You know our parents would have remained close friends."

"I would not have allowed the twins to lock you in the privy ever' time you came over," he said.

"Thank you for that assurance. I live too much in the 'what if's'. I need to go home and find something to do with my life. And someone to do it with."

He stared for a moment, then shook his head.

"Are you thinking about Arizona too?"

"I suppose."

"I do have one regret about this trip north."

"That you shot Thomasville?"

"That I didn't get to kiss Frank Fortune." She stepped closer, slipped her arm around his neck, and pressed her wide, full lips into his. When she pulled back, he let out a deep sigh and shook his head. He started to speak, but she laid her fingers across his lips. "No, don't say it," she said. "We both know, don't we? I don't want to hear words of rejection. Not tonight."

He nodded and turned back to the dark of the night.

When Frank got to the house, the bedroom light was still on. He knocked softly.

Marla Jolene opened the door.

"Is the baby asleep?" he whispered.

"One of them." She patted her round stomach. "Junior here is kicking up a storm."

"Señorita Rodriguez, Latina, and Miguel are going south in the morning. They said they would go straight to Rapid City, and you could travel with them. Do you feel comfortable with that?"

"I would enjoy not being alone."

"Good. Marla, I'll have the cattle there in two weeks. I'm not sure how I will do it, but I will."

"I know you will, Frank. At supper, when you said you were going to drive the cattle to Rapid City, my spirit leaped. For weeks my entire future and my children's future has been up in the air. I didn't know what would happen to us. I have been praying for a month for the Lord's intervention. And he's answered my prayers. Now I know everything will be alright. Frank Fortune will see to that."

"All I can bring is a thousand head of cattle. That doesn't exactly take care of your entire life," he said.

"You have no idea what this means. Frank, this is all I will ever need from you." She paused and took a deep breath. "That's not entirely true. I do need one more thing."

Frank pulled off his hat. "What else do you need?"

She slipped her hand behind his neck and tugged him down to her lips. He could feel the soft warm lips on his. And a very round tummy pressed against him. Then she was gone, and the door softly shut.

A knock on the great room door brought Estelle Bowers out to the porch. "How's your patient?"

"He's asleep. I think he will be fine, as long as we get him to a doctor tomorrow."

"Sam is taking him in to Deadwood," Frank said.

"I thought you might want your uncle to ride with you down into Devil's Wash."

"I need him to hire a roundup crew in Deadwood and explain to Mama why I won't be there for all those prewedding suppers and rehearsals."

"Do you think he can do that?"

"If anyone can sweet-talk the ladies, it's my Uncle Sammy."

"No, I meant can he get a roundup crew?"

"That's a different matter. Mainly minin' men in Deadwood. But Uncle Sammy's a good judge of men. I reckon he can do as well as any."

"What's the plan for Devil's Wash?" she asked.

"Reid left already. He's goin' to ride all night and circle his crew out on the Ft. Pierre road. We'll drop down into the wash at Hades Canyon, just like the girls did, and see if we can get them to make a run."

"We will leave early, I presume?" Essie asked.

"Yep."

"And you are making the rounds?"

"Yep."

"Did you kiss all your ladies good night?" she teased.

His mouth dropped open. "Why did you say that?"

"You didn't answer me, Frank Fortune."

"Eh, no, I didn't kiss all my ladies goodnight." Frank slipped his arm around Essie's waist. Her hand encircled his neck. When their lips met, his shoulders and neck relaxed. He was surprised to hear himself sigh.

Essie pulled back and grinned.

He shook his head.

"It's true, Frank."

"I know it, Essie," he replied.

"We both know."

"You have any idea what you're gettin' into?"

"Yes, and you are not allowed to talk to my sister about what I'm really like until after we are married."

"Do you really think you could live out here in this isolated spot?" He leaned forward and kissed her cheek.

"Yes, I could. Do you think you could live on a smaller place in northwest Nebraska if that came up?" She laced her fingers into his.

"I reckon I could. Essie Bowers, can you tell me why our hands feel so good together?"

"That's because we've known each other for so long." She raised his hand to her lips and brushed a kiss across his fingers.

The door swung open behind her. "Are you two quite finished?" Morgan called out.

"Finished?" Frank grinned. "I surmise I won't be finished for a good fifty years."

"Well, in that case, I'm goin' to sleep," Morgan declared as she slammed the door behind them.

By daylight Frank led the crew northwest across the ranch. He, Essie, and Morgan led the way. Howdy and Jonas followed behind. They didn't stop until Lost Springs.

"Do you think Reid LeMay had enough time to make it clear around to the Ft. Pierre road?" Howdy asked as they filled their canteens.

"We'll find out this afternoon," Frank replied.

"If Thomasville wasn't rustlin' the cattle for the Axe-T, who was?"

"John Earl was tryin' to replace the ones this Devil's Wash gang was stealin'," Frank reported.

Howdy pulled his fixings out of his shirt pocket and started rolling a quirley. "So we are losin' them from both sides?"

"Yep."

"You think we have enough guns to force them out of Devil's Wash?" Jonas asked.

"Morgan said there were six men."

"Some more could have been out rustlin' at the time," Howdy called out.

"That's true," Frank said. "We can use every man. I wish Pete would have stuck."

"He had a chance to hitch a ride with Sam and them back to Deadwood. Said he didn't hire on for some fool suicide trip down into Hades Canyon,"

Howdy reported.

"We'll have Reynoso and Cron waitin' for us. That makes two more," Frank said, then unfastened the top two buttons of his canvas coat.

Jonas fingered the Winchester 1894 carbine that lay across his lap. "That only gives us five guns at best."

"I can shoot," Essie offered.

"I'm not goin' to get you ladies in a gunfight."

"But you will ride us all off into the dangerous canyon, possibly get yourself killed, and leave us stranded down there?" she challenged.

"I don't want anyone to get killed. Just want them to move out of the wash."

"And we have to ride off that ridge?" Howdy asked.

"The girls did it," Frank replied.

"Yeah, but they are Indians."

Frank pointed at Morgan. "You mean, they are tougher?"

Howdy studied the Cheyenne girl. "I reckon they are more limber."

Frank scratched the back of his neck. "Might be some truth in that. I'm about as limber as a dry stick with these ribs all wrapped up."

By noon they reached the cliff at Hades Canyon that led down into Devil's Wash. Reynoso sat with both legs off the right side of the saddle, waiting for them.

"Where's Cron?" Frank asked.

"He pulled his picket pin and took off after LeMay explained the deal," Reynoso reported.

"Afraid to go down there?" Howdy asked.

"No, embarrassed by the fact that three Indian girls

stole the ponies from under him. Is this one of the sneakin' thieves?"

"It didn't take much sneaking," Morgan replied.

"Yep, and she's the one that's goin' to lead us into the wash."

"Sounds crazy to me," Reynoso mumbled.

"Well, Reynoso . . . and it goes for Howdy and Jonas as well . . . this is the place to back out. If you want to ride off, you do it right now. I don't want anyone down there that isn't committed to seein' it through."

Reynoso frowned and stared at the ground. "It ain't that I'm afraid of a gunfight, but a man can die from a whole lot more than lead poisoning down there. That's La Casa Diablo down there. I thought we was goin' to have a big crew."

"Go on, Reynoso," Frank charged. "That's your horse and saddle. You can leave."

"It don't seem right to abandon you with women who need protectin'."

"These two ladies can take care of themselves, but I've got Howdy and Jonas."

"I can help you with the roundup," Reynoso added. "That's what I signed on to do."

"No, I need men who stick. Go on, Reynoso. I don't need you."

Reynoso slipped his feet in the stirrups. "You understand, don't ya?"

Frank waved his hand. "Go on."

"Howdy, you and Jonas want to go with me?" Reynoso called out as he saddled up.

"Nope. I'm kind of like a stray dog with no place to

go," Howdy added. "You feed me and give me a warm place at night, and you can't chase me off with a stick."

"Jonas?" Reynoso challenged.

"I would have left with Pete if I was goin'. I reckon I'll see it through. Sam Fortune saved my mama from injury, maybe her life. Ain't often a man gets to repay that debt. I couldn't look my mama in the eye if I didn't stick with the Fortunes."

"Send my back pay to the Piedmont in Deadwood."

"Go on, Reynoso."

Frank Fortune dismounted as Reynoso rode straight west along the ridge. He led Carlos over to the edge of the bluff. "Kind of feels like Gideon thinnin' down the troops," he remarked.

"They ended up victorious," Essie encouraged.

"That's true . . . I say we go in on that southern slope where we hauled the girls out. Stay on your horse at all costs. He'll make it down. Just don't fall off your horse."

"What order are we goin' in, Boss?" Howdy asked.

"I'll go first. If I don't make it alive, I expect the rest of you not to try it. If I do make it down, I don't want that gang waitin' for one of you. When you see me wave, send the next one down. Don't start down until the previous one signals. I don't want one of us runnin' over another one."

"I'll go second," Essie volunteered.

"Howdy, you come down last. As soon as you get there, get behind those boulders with your horse and hunker down. We don't know if they will spot us before we spot them. Don't holler and scream. Absolutely no noise. It's important that we sneak up on them. I reckon sound carries wild down there in that barren canyon."

Frank led them to the south end of the canyon. He jammed his Sharps carbine in the scabbard and looped the strap over the big hammer. He tied the canteen strap in a knot around the saddle horn.

"Ain't this fun?" Howdy blurted out.

"It will be OK, Frank," Essie encouraged.

"You sound very confident, darlin'."

"You promised me I get to have fifty years with you . . . and I'm holding you to your word, cowboy."

Frank jammed his felt hat down low on his head. He could feel his heartbeat through the lump on his forehead. He swung the stirrups toward Carlos's neck and leaned far back on his bedroll. The high cantle jammed his back. He wrapped the reins around his left hand and swatted Carlos's rump with his right.

The horse didn't budge.

"Maybe he's smarter than the rest of us," Frank mumbled.

Essie rode next to him. "Carlos, honey, you need to get Mr. Fortune down this mountain."

Carlos didn't move.

"I don't think he's in a visitin' mood," Jonas called out.

"Sure he is," Essie insisted. She untied her canteen from the saddle horn, held it by the strap, swung it around, and smacked it into Carlos's rump, just to the left of his black tail.

The chestnut gelding leaped straight over the edge of the canyon. Frank's head flopped back and crashed into

Carlos's rump when they hit the loose limestone. It was all he could do to hang on.

Those on top yelled something.

Frank hollered "whoaaaaaa" but couldn't release the word. They slid fifty feet, then Carlos stumbled. Frank was thrown forward. His belt buckle caught on the saddle horn and kept him from tumbling over the horse's head. Carlos threw his head back into Frank's ribs. He hollered in pain.

When he yanked himself back into the saddle, Frank caught his breath and could hear screams right behind him. Out of the corner of his eye he spotted Essie on her horse not more than thirty feet behind him. Her long brown hair tumbled down her back and flagged out even with the horse's tail. Her green dress was blown up to her knees, revealing ruffled white bloomers. She yelled "No!" over and over at the top of her voice.

Morgan looked no more that fifteen feet behind Essie. Her arms encircled her horse's neck. Her feet were out of the stirrups and were bouncing along the horse's rump. She screamed something in Cheyenne.

At least Frank assumed it was Cheyenne.

Howdy's horse went down to his knees, but when it righted itself, the lean cowboy was still in the saddle. Frank couldn't tell if Howdy's bellow was a praise or a curse.

Big Jonas's horse staggered, reared, leaped sideways, then slid on all fours. The black cowboy's baritone voice boomed "Oh Mama!" over and over.

No! That's not what I said. They are supposed to wait! We need to be quiet. We want to . . .

Frank's left foot caught in the stirrup when Carlos stumbled to the right. That kept him in the saddle, but the cantle pounded him in the kidneys with every step. He had just lost both stirrups and was bouncing like a kite without a tail when Carlos hit the more gradual slope and got all four hooves under him. They galloped to the boulders.

"Whoaaaaaaaa!" Frank screamed until the frightened gelding slowed. He grabbed his carbine and leaped off the horse.

He took two steps and his knees gave out.

Frank fell flat on his face just as Essie's horse galloped toward him. She shouted "Nooooo!" as her horse leaped over Frank and spun next to Carlos, tumbling Essie to the dirt.

Frank staggered to his feet in time to see Morgan's horse race toward them. "Stop him!" she screamed. He waved his hat and shouted at the buckskin horse, who slid to an immediate stop. Morgan flew over the horse's head and landed in Frank's arms, causing him to drop the carbine. He staggered back and collapsed on his rear next to Essie.

The pain in his ribs forced tears down his dirty cheeks.

Jonas got pitched off near the bottom of the descent. He limped along after the black horse, shouting a string of descriptive phrases and listing with precision the horse's parentage and graphic detail on the torments of equine eternity.

Howdy's horse hit the bottom of the canyon at a gallop and sprinted right past them all. The saddle had spun under the horse's stomach and Howdy hung on the cinch, now on the horse's back. The horse was fetlock deep in slimy white clay before he stopped. Howdy spurred the animal out of the bog.

Jonas and Howdy reached the others at about the same time. Howdy slid off the horse, fell on his back, and gasped for breath.

Jonas bent over with his hands on his knees, his breaths so deep they sounded like a deep rock-mine explosion.

Morgan crawled off Frank's lap and rolled over by Essie.

Only Jonas remained on his feet.

"Well, now . . ." Howdy drawled. "That wasn't so bad was it?"

"I thought I was dead six different times," Jonas moaned.

"That's the last time I'm ever going to do that," Morgan moaned. "If I could have remembered it, I would have sung my death chant."

"Did I scream 'NO!' all the way down?" Essie asked.

With his arms wrapped around his ribs, Frank struggled to his knees. "You were supposed to wait at the top until the others got down," he mumbled through clenched teeth.

"We all knew that, but we forgot to tell the horses. Once Carlos went over, the rest followed like lemmings," Essie reported.

"We made more noise than lower Main Street in Deadwood on the Fourth of July," Frank grumbled. "I can't believe they haven't found us and shot us already."

"What now, Boss?" Jonas asked.

Frank groaned to his feet. "Calm your horses. Reset your saddles." He retrieved his carbine. "I'll keep an eye out for the outlaws. They'll be lookin' for us now, that's for sure."

It took thirty minutes for riders and horses to be ready to proceed. Frank stood guard as the others brushed themselves off and tightened the saddles. After the canteen was passed around, they led the horses over to Frank.

"No sign of 'em?" Howdy asked.

"I can't figure why they haven't attacked yet. Unless they already left Devil's Wash."

"I do hope there is a different way than coming down the back slope of Hades Canyon," Jonas murmured. "For a while there I figured I'd never see my mama again."

Frank turned to Morgan. "You're the expert down here. Which way do we go?"

"I think maybe between those rock pillars and then east . . . which way is east?" she said.

"*Think, maybe?* We didn't come down here to *think, maybe*. You said you could lead us . . ."

"Frank!" Essie called out.

"I'm sorry, darlin'. Essie's right. Give us your best guess. The rest of you grab your guns. We'll walk the horses." He led Carlos up beside Morgan. "Are you worried, darlin'?"

Morgan brushed her long black hair off her ears. "A little bit. It doesn't look as familiar as I thought it would."

"That's OK. We'll make it because we have Miss

Bowers with us," Frank assured. "And she won't let anything bad happen."

"I know," Morgan replied. "That's the same thing that I was thinking."

The landscape at the bottom of Devil's Wash was the same in every direction . . . rounded, windblown white clay mountains and crags without any hint of vegetation.

No rocks. No pebbles. No sticks. No dead grass.

Just crusted white clay that stuck to their boots.

And fine white dust that lay like sugar frosting on top of the clay. Within fifty feet they looked as if they worked at a flour mill.

Several times they felt the crust break beneath their feet. They backed away to another route.

"Haven't we been this way before?" Howdy called.

"Do you see any tracks?"

"There ain't none in front of us . . . or behind us. That dust blows 'em clear as soon as they're set," Jonas replied. "Boss, do you reckon hell is worse than this?"

"Yep, cause there ain't no way out of it. Sooner or later, we'll get out of this, or get to Minnesota one," Frank said.

"It's up there," Morgan pointed east.

"What's up there, darlin'?" Frank asked.

"Dead Owl Springs and the cattle."

"How can you tell?"

"See how the shade on that cliff looks like two round owl eyes?" she pointed through the dusty haze.

"Where?" Frank asked.

"Right over there," Essie said.

"I don't see nothin'. Howdy, do you see anything?" Frank asked.

"Yep . . . two owl eyes." The thin cowboy waved his carbine to the east.

"Dadgumit, where?"

"Right up there, Boss!" Jonas pointed.

Frank searched the bleak white clay horizon. "I don't see anything that looks like an owl."

Essie stepped up in front of him. She backed up until her head touched his chin, her back against his chest. "Look right down my arm, Frank . . . closer . . . put your head closer . . . there . . . can you see them?"

"Maybe when you are through with the boss, you could point them out to me, Miss Essie," Howdy joshed.

"Those are owl eyes?" Frank questioned.

She leaned the back of her head against his shoulder. "What do they look like to you?"

"A couple of test holes where some fool was diggin' for gold."

Essie shook her head and looked at Morgan. "A total lack of imagination. I'm sure that's Dead Owl Springs."

With a bullet in the chamber and the big hammer cocked on the Sharps carbine, Frank guided the quintet around the last cliff and out into the tiny clearing at Dead Owl Springs.

"There's the cattle . . ." he mumbled. Frank left his horse with Essie and signaled for Howdy to come with him. They crawled in the white dusty clay until they could survey the whole area.

"Ain't no one here, Boss."

"Must be fifty or sixty head," Frank said. "And a half wagon of hay."

"There's a camp over there, but there ain't no one here."

"Do you reckon they have scouts up above?"

Howdy surveyed the white clay bluffs around them. "No way of knowin' that."

"You think this is so secure they can just ride off and leave it?"

"Could be. What are we goin' to do?"

"Find a way out and drive the cattle. Even if we don't get the rustlers, we can recover the cattle," Frank said. "Go get the others. Wait until I walk out in the middle. If no one shoots at me, then it's safe."

"Are you sure that's the only way to prove it?"

"No, it's not the only way. You can walk out there, and I'll stay back here and watch."

"No," Howdy said, "I like the first way best."

Within ten minutes they had all the cattle gathered and ready to move. Frank rode back to the others. "We're goin' to follow the wagon ruts out. It may be a dead end, but it's the best guess."

"The wagon tracks are goin' southeast, not northeast," Jonas offered.

Frank eyed the trail. "I trust they swing to the north or at least get us out on the prairie. I'll ride point 'cause I don't know what's up ahead. At any turn we could ride into this bunch and get pinned down in a hurry. But it will be white powder ridin' the drag back there. You'll have to cover your mouths with bandannas."

"I always wondered what it would be like to be sickly

white like you all," Jonas boomed.

Essie pulled her carbine from the scabbard and checked the lever. "I'll ride up front with Frank. I want to see what happens next. I might want to write about it some day."

"There could be trouble," he cautioned.

"Good, it will be an exciting chapter in my book."

"I'm staying with Miss Bowers," Morgan announced.

"There's nothing for them to graze on, so keep them movin' before their noses plug up," Frank told Howdy and Jonas.

"How many miles of wagon road do you surmise we'll face?" Howdy quizzed.

Frank smeared white dust across his forehead. "Maybe a couple."

The dust was so thick even at the head of the herd that Frank kept his mouth closed and eyes squinted.

No one spoke.

The Dakota sky paled light blue, and the sun sank yellow to the west. White dust hung like ground fog on a December morning. Essie followed Frank on the almost level trail a full length behind him on his right, Morgan a length behind him on his left. The sound of muted horse hooves and milling cattle was the only sound. No words were spoken. No coyote yipped. No hawk screeched.

Two miles turned to four.

Frank knew they had been on the trail an hour.

The wagon ruts turned north.

Four miles turned to six.

Then seven.

As if there had been a geological line drawn in the dirt, they rounded the barren white clay knoll and struck open prairie and clumps of brown buffalo grass.

Six men on horseback stormed straight at them.

"Race to the back. Get Howdy and Jonas up here." Frank choked out the words, spraying white dust with each one. "You two stay back there."

"We most certainly will not," Essie declared. She stood in the stirrups, stuck two fingers in her dusty mouth and whistled so loud that Carlos jumped to the left. Frank grabbed the saddle horn. Jonas and Howdy galloped around, bandannas down, faces streaked like two-tone war paint on Sioux warriors.

"Who is comin'?" Howdy shouted.

Frank kept his eyes on the approaching men. "We'll find out soon enough."

They lined up side by side across the wagon trail, each with carbines in their hands, and waited.

The riders drifted in a brown cloud of dust, and Frank strained to see the leader.

"I think it's Mr. LeMay," Essie called out.

"How can you tell?" Frank asked.

"Because all men look different."

"I can't recognize who it is," he murmured. "Keep your guns pointed at them."

"Can you distinguish one woman from another across a crowded train station?" she asked.

He tugged his hat down low. "That's different."

"It's Mr. LeMay," Morgan declared.

"I don't know how . . ."

"They are right, Boss," Howdy said.

Reid LeMay led six men straight at them.

"Frank! I'm mighty glad that's you. It is you, ain't it?"

"I'm glad it's you, LeMay. We got the herd out of there, but I don't know what happened to the rustlers."

"We already grabbed them," LeMay reported.

"They wandered out when you were all set up? That's lucky timin'," Frank said.

"More like divine providence, if you ask me. They were chased out of Devil's Wash."

"By whom?" Essie asked.

LeMay pulled off his flat straw hat and fanned himself. "A band of wild Indians, so they say."

"In Devil's Wash?" Morgan asked.

"They came flyin' out of the wash like a banker who just found an empty safe. We had no trouble capturin' the lot of them. We didn't even fire a shot," LeMay said. "We have 'em held back up the road a piece."

"They said Indians chased them?" Frank questioned.

"They said they heard wild war whoops and screaming and thunderin' hooves from the direction of Hades Canyon. They figured a bunch had broken off the reservation. They had spotted three Indian boys in the wash a few days ago."

"Boys?" Morgan whined. "They thought we were boys?"

"They were convinced they'd be slaughtered down in the wash and no one would know, so they made a dash for the open prairie. Did you see any wild Indians?"

Frank gawked at his white-dirt-covered companions. "Maybe next time we ride off Hades Canyon, we ought to make a ruckus," he grinned.

"There ain't never goin' to be a next time," Howdy replied.

They reached Two Rabbit Springs by sundown and washed off most of the dirt. It was dark when they reached the rock cabin at Buffalo Gap. Reynoso was gone, but the mules grazed nearby. After supper all five sat in front of the cabin and watched the stars.

"You ladies sleep in the cabin tonight," Frank offered.

"Stay in a smokey ol' stuffy room without windows, while you men enjoy the Lord's creation out here?" Essie replied. "I don't think so."

"She don't listen to you much, Boss," Howdy said.

Frank scratched his head. "You know, when I think about it, there has never been a woman in my life who ever listened to me. Not my mother, my sisters, nor my cousins, or my aunts."

"Marla Jolene listened to you last night," Essie said. "She hung on your every word."

"You're right about that. I stand corrected. You ladies are welcome to bunk anywhere you want."

"I want the fresh air," Jonas said. "It will take a month to get that Devil's Wash dust out of my lungs."

"You reckon LeMay is camped out on the prairie with those rustlers?" Howdy asked.

"He said he might keep movin' through the night, to get them to jail as fast as he could. But the others will be camped out with the cattle."

"Do we have to split the reward with all those men with LeMay?" Morgan asked.

"They are contracted by the railroad, so they can't

take railroad reward money," Frank reported. "If there is a reward, we'll split it among us all."

"I can't believe our disastrous descent got them running," Essie mused.

"Yeah, funny, isn't it?" Frank said. "Human plans go completely wrong, and the Lord uses the catastrophe to get the job done. Kind of the way he works."

"Frank, what things have gone according to your plans in the past week?" Essie pressed.

The wind cooled Frank's unshaven face. "I can't think of one thing."

Her voice softened, like a tender song. "Has it been a good week or a bad week?"

"It's been a misfortune," he admitted. "But things are lookin' up."

"Hmmm."

Frank studied Essie's silhouette. "What's that 'hmmm' mean?"

"I wondered if I am the disaster looking up?" Essie probed.

"Oh, brother," Morgan moaned. "Are we goin' to have to listen to this all night?"

"You aren't a disaster, Estelle Cinnia. But I can't rate this week until we get back to headquarters tomorrow. If Sam has a roundup crew waitin', then I suppose it's been a good week."

In the dark he reached toward Essie. Her fingers slipped into his.

At daybreak, Essie and Morgan cooked breakfast as Howdy and Jonas saddled the horses. Frank stood at the door.

"What did you decide about this rock house?" Essie asked as she fried biscuits in a big black skillet.

"We're goin' to need what hands we do have in the roundup. Howdy and Jonas will hang back this mornin' and board the place up. I told them to pack the mules with as much as they could. If we get the cattle moved south and only have to winter five hundred head, I won't need this cabin all winter."

"It's solid," she said. "You've never lived in a sod house, I suppose."

"No, I haven't, but it's bitter cold up here in the winter. No trees, no protection. Haul firewood about ten miles. It's a hassle to keep men up here. Nobody wants to be up here. I won't miss that. But that's only if we get the cattle moved to Rapid City in two weeks."

"Your sisters' wedding is the day after tomorrow," Essie reminded him. "Just how do you plan on attending?"

"I'll start the crew out tomorrow to start the roundup. Howdy can run things until I get back late Saturday."

"So big brother just runs in for the service, then back to the ranch?"

"I don't have any other option."

"The girls and I will help round up cows tomorrow," Essie offered.

"I wouldn't want you to do that. But I could put Americus on horseback if you all would take care of the cookin' chores," Frank proposed.

"Nonsense, Frank Fortune. The girls and I ride roundup or we don't stay," Essie declared.

"Are you threatenin' me?"

She flashed a wide grin. "Yes. Did it work?"

"Katie's a good cook," Morgan said. "She's at the head of Miss Bowers's class. She can cook and ride in the wagon. Faith and I can herd cattle. We've herded government beef before."

"I've never had women on the roundup crew."

"Why is that?" Essie asked.

" 'Cause . . . 'cause none ever wanted to."

"There you have it. We want to. You, Howdy, Americus, Jonas, Faith, Morgan, and me . . . that makes seven. Katie can drive the wagon and cook. How many would you like to have?"

"Twenty," he replied.

"Really?"

"If I had a month, ten would do. But we have two weeks. It takes time to scour every draw and gulch."

"You don't have to find every head. Couldn't you just round up the first thousand you can find, and drive them to Rapid City? Then you come back and take your time finding the others."

"That might work. But it means two roundups," he said.

"Do I get to wear a gun?" Morgan asked.

"A gun? What for?" Essie asked.

"In all the Penny Press novels, the cowboys wear guns when they push cattle."

"I don't want you to have a gun," Frank grinned. "I might be the one that gets shot."

"Oh, I wouldn't shoot you," Morgan said. "Unless you deserved it."

"That's comfortin', darlin'."

"Thank you," she giggled.

"I think this breakfast is as good as it's goin' to get," Essie declared. "Morgan, run out and tell Jonas and Howdy that breakfast is ready."

"I can do that," Frank offered.

"No, you can't," Essie insisted. "I, eh, need you here."

"Do you want me to take my time?" Morgan asked.

"Yes, thank you, honey." Essie sauntered over to the doorway and watched Morgan scamper toward the corral.

"OK, Miss Bowers, what is this about sending Morgan out the door?"

"Frank, yesterday, well actually the past couple of days are sort of like a blur. I can hardly remember what happened and what I just imagined. And since we won't have much time to talk in private for a while, I wanted to make sure . . ."

He put his finger to her lips.

"Estelle Cinnia Bowers, you walked into my world and parked yourself on my side of the line. I have no idea how you snuck in over here, but I found out I like havin' you here. And I'd like you to stay on this side of the line and help me look out at the world."

"Do you really want me to stay for fifty years?"

"That's only minimum."

"Oh, my . . . well, yes, I suppose that could be arranged. I do have some other obligations to take care of first."

"I understand." Frank glanced down at his boots. "Then we have that all worked out?"

"We have nothing worked out, Frank Fortune," she scolded. "But we have a good start."

"Nothin'? But I love you, Essie Bowers. I want you to be with me forever."

"OK. We do have some things worked out." Essie stood on her tiptoes and kissed his lips. "I love you too, Frank."

"Hmmmmmmth," Howdy cleared his throat. "I heard there was breakfast waitin'."

"Do you see what happens when I leave?" Morgan said. "Wait until I tell Mr. Clark about Miss Bowers."

Frank stepped aside and let the others into the room. "Mr. Clark is a mean fellow I take it?"

"Not too bad, but he does have a crush on Miss Bowers."

"He most certainly does not!" Essie protested.

"Yes, he does." Morgan walked over to the table with Frank. "You should see the way he watches Miss Bowers when she isn't looking."

"Oh? How is that?" Frank asked.

"Like a little boy at a candy counter."

Essie folded her arms across her chest. "Morgan Denise!"

"Well, it's true."

Frank grabbed up a tin plate and scooped up some scrambled eggs. "That's OK. I ain't worried about Mr. Clark."

Essie raised her eyebrows. "You sound mighty sure of yourself, Frank Fortune."

He plucked a hot biscuit from the pan. "It's the only thing I've been sure of in months, Miss Bowers."

. . .

Frank, Essie, and Morgan rode two hours south of Buffalo Gap before they pulled up at Hidden Gulch. Water still pooled at the bottom of the steep ravine.

"Shall we ride down and water the horses?" Essie asked.

"Why don't you and Morgan grab a canteen and take a break here on the rim. I'll lead the horses down."

"It's awfully steep," Essie warned.

"I've been down there a dozen times. At this time of the year, we have to take water where it is."

Essie and Morgan climbed down and handed him the reins.

Frank rode Carlos and threaded his way down the barranca. *OK, perhaps not dozens of times, but once or twice.*

When he got down to the base of the gulch, he slid off Carlos. All three horses drank from the pool in the middle of the narrow, sandy creek. He glanced up at the rim where Essie watched him.

Lord, she's the one. I reckon I knew it when Dearyanna walked in that night and Essie was rubbin' my temples. All my life I dreamed that I would marry someone who looked like Señorita Rodriguez. And then . . . well, in twenty-four hours you changed a lifetime of foolish dreams. When I get this roundup done, I'll ask her to come back to the Black Hills and introduce her to everyone. They will inspect her like a sheep goin' to market, I reckon. But it really doesn't matter. I like havin' her on my side of . . .

"Frank, watch out!" Essie hollered.

He spun around to see a short-horned hereford bull charge out of the brush straight at him.

"Windell?" he stammered. Frank dove back into the brush. The eighteen-hundred-pound bull charged at the horses. With Carlos leading, all three scampered up the south slope of the gulch.

"Catch the horses!" he screamed.

When he did, the bull spun around and faced him.

"Windell, I've had enough of you. You hid down here all summer, and I never could find you. So don't hassle me." Frank never took his eyes off the bull.

"Frank, be careful!" Essie shouted.

"Did you get the horses?"

"Morgan has them."

"Divert his attention. I'll come up the north slope."

"Divert his attention?" she yelled. "How can I do that?"

"Throw a stick at him."

"Really?"

"Quick!"

All of a sudden, a rock the size of an egg flew down into the gulch and hit the bull square on the nose.

"Sorry. I didn't mean to hit him," Essie called out.

Immediately, Windell charged at Frank.

Frank spun and ran north. His feet rubbed in his boots. His legs ached as he struggled hand over hand to climb the embankment.

Windell was now at his heels.

"Give me your hand!" Essie shouted from above.

Frank reached up. When he did, he felt his feet slip back down the soft clay embankment. The bull snorted.

He glanced over his shoulder to see the massive bull's head just inches away. Frank dove. Windell lunged.

Something ripped as Frank's hand slipped into Essie's.

"Pull me up," he shouted.

"Your shirt's caught on his horn."

"Pull harder!"

With her other hand now on his arm, Essie yanked. Frank tumbled over the top, landing on his side at her feet.

The bull slid back down the gulch.

"Where's my shirt?" Frank asked.

"Around Windell's horns."

Frank stood gasping for breath and glared at the big bull with the white cotton shirt on his horn.

"He looks quite pleased," she reported. "Are you goin' after your shirt?"

"There's not enough left to wear. My coat's in my bedroll."

"It should look nice with the bright pink satin rib wrap," she teased.

"It's rose, not bright pink," he insisted.

Morgan rode up with the other two horses in tow. "That is a very bright color. I don't think Mr. Fortune will ever get lost on the prairie."

He pulled the cold canvas coat on over his satin-wrapped ribs but didn't button it. He crawled back on Carlos. They had ridden about three miles south when Morgan hollered. "Look back there; that bull is following us."

Frank glanced over his shoulder.

"And he still has your shirt!" she giggled.

Around noon they reached the wagon road at the north end of Bear Butte Valley. Thick gray clouds covered the morning sun. An easterly wind whipped off the prairie, but there was no dust on the road.

The three rode side by side.

"Windell is still following us," Essie reported. "And he still has your shirt."

"That's nice of him." Frank unbuttoned his jacket when they dropped down into the valley.

"Do you name all your bulls?" Morgan asked.

"No, he's just about the only one with a name."

"Why Windell?"

"Howdy named him 'cause he acts up every time the wind blows."

"How often is that?" Essie asked.

"About three hundred days a year."

"How are your ribs feeling?"

"They will be much better once I pull a shirt on over this pink satin," he said.

"I think it's rose," Essie replied.

Frank gazed down at the headquarters. "There's smoke from the chimney in the kitchen, the big room, and the bedroom. Faith and Katie must be spread out."

"I believe there is a wagon or two down by the barn," Essie said.

Frank squinted his eyes. "I can't see any."

"When we are in Rapid City in two weeks, you are going to have your eyes examined. I think you need spectacles," Essie said.

"No, I'm too young to need . . ."

"Frank, when do you intend to let me look after you?"

He scratched his head. "I suppose I'll have to learn."

"I'll give you two weeks."

"There are wagons at the barn," Morgan insisted.

"That means Uncle Sammy is back."

"That's good!" Essie said.

"Or bad," Frank mumbled.

When they got within a half mile of the buildings, a horse galloped out of the barn toward them.

"Can you tell who that is?" Frank asked.

"Looks like a youngster," Essie said.

"Is it Faith?" he asked.

"It's a boy!" Morgan called.

Frank waited for the rider to approach. "It's Garrett!"

"Who's Garrett?" Essie asked.

"That's Uncle Sammy's son."

"How old is he?" Morgan asked.

"Eh, . . . I reckon about your age."

"Really? Oh, is he nice?" Morgan's voice died as the rider got closer.

"Hi, Little Frank!" Garrett shouted as he rode up. "Daddy said I could help you with the roundup."

"I'm glad he let you come. Did he get a crew?"

"Yep. Is that a dress you have wrapped around your waist?"

"It's just a wrap. I busted my ribs. How many did he bring?"

"Twenty or so. Did you get in a fight and bust your ribs?"

"No fight. He brought twenty?"

"I didn't count exact. Who's she?"

"Garrett, this is Miss Bowers, who is . . ."

"No, I meant her."

"This is Morgan. She's a student of Miss Bowers and . . ."

"Are you Sioux?" Garrett asked.

Morgan's chin was on her chest. Her gray dress hung straight down like a sack. "No, I'm Cheyenne."

"My best friend is half Sioux. His name is Chola. Do you like to ride fast horses?"

Morgan grinned and bit her lip. "I'll race you back to the barn," she offered.

"I don't race girls," he declared.

"You don't like to lose, huh?"

Garrett rode up next to Morgan. "I ain't never lost to a girl, that's for sure."

"That's only because you've never raced a girl. One . . . two . . . three . . . go!" Morgan shouted.

Both of them galloped toward the barn.

"That was a quick introduction," Essie said.

"Garrett's a natural on horseback, but his mama don't let him ride much."

They continued to ride toward the barn.

"I can't believe Sam got twenty hands," Frank murmured. "We are goin' to be able to do this. Some will have to sleep in the barn until we get out on the roundup."

"Garrett looks happy to be here. He doesn't look like your uncle at all."

"He looks just like his mother. I'm the only one who looks like Uncle Sammy."

As they got closer to the buildings, Essie pointed to the long porch. "Who's the tall woman with the straw hat in front of the kitchen door?"

"That's my Aunt Dacee June. What is she doin' here? She can't be here. The wedding is tomorrow . . ."

"Who are the three girls visiting with Faith and Katie down by the great room?" Essie asked.

"That's eh . . those are my cousins, Dacee June's girls. Elita, Jehane, and Ninete. But they are just . . ."

"They look about the same age as my girls."

"Yes, but they can't . . . it's . . ."

A teenage boy ran up to them as they dismounted in front of the corrals. "Hi, Little Frank!"

"Hi, Stuart."

"How come you got a dress around you waist?" Stuart asked.

"It's just a rag to hold my ribs."

"It's a bright pink rag." The young boy turned to Essie. "I'm Stuart Brannon Fortune. Who are you?"

"I'm Estelle Cinnia Bowers. Nice to meet you." She shook his hand.

"Are you goin' on the roundup too?" Stuart asked.

"Yes, I am," Essie replied.

"Are you a relative?" he asked.

Essie burst out laughing. "No, not yet."

"Do you want to be?"

"Yes, I do."

"I like you, Estelle Cinnia Bowers."

"Thank you, Stuart. You are a very precocious young man."

He sprinted back to the barn.

Sam Fortune hiked out and met Frank in the middle of the yard.

"Uncle Sammy, what's goin' on?"

"I got you a roundup crew."

"Family?"

"Todd and Rebekah, with Hank, Nettie, Stuart, and Casey. Abby and Garrett came with me. Wade and Amber are here. They left the baby with Camillia. Dacee June, Carty, and the girls. Your mama, daddy, and the twins."

"The twins?" Frank gasped. "What about the wedding tomorrow?"

"The wedding's been postponed two weeks."

"What happened?"

"You have to get the whole story from the girls. But the way I hear it, two nights ago there was a party for the girls and their fellas at the Merchant's Hotel. They turned the lights down for a midnight cotillion, and well, it seems that Patrick scooched up and kissed Patricia on the back of the neck."

"Oh, no!" Frank moaned.

"What's the matter with that?" Essie asked.

"Patrick is marrying Veronica . . . he got the twins mixed up. "

"So what happened?" Essie asked.

"Patricia got startled and clobbered him with her handbag."

"And?"

"Gave him a black eye. Now Veronica refuses to get married to Patrick while he has a black eye."

"They actually postponed the wedding because of a

black eye?" Essie asked.

"Yep. Everyone was sittin' around all depressed when I rode to town. Dacee June decided they should all ride out here and help Little Frank with the roundup. It would help the time pass until the rescheduled weddin'."

"I don't believe this," Frank said.

"Your mama and daddy are in the barn. They are happy for the diversion for a couple of weeks. They are callin' it Little Frank's Roundup. I don't reckon there's a Fortune left in Deadwood," Sam declared.

"We'll go see the folks," Frank said.

"Are you two . . ." Sam raised his thick gray eyebrows.

Frank glanced at Essie.

She bit her lip and nodded.

"That's what I figured. Well, go on. I'll go gather the rest of your crew, Boss." Sam traipsed toward the big house.

"We're going to meet your parents right now? I can't do that," Essie insisted. "I've been on horseback for two days. I need to comb my hair, wash my face, change my dress . . . I just can't . . ."

"You're a homestead girl. You can do it."

Essie slipped her hand in Frank's. "You're right. I can do it."

"Besides, you look really, really good," Frank murmured.

She took a deep breath and let it out slow. "Thanks, honey." She pulled her handkerchief from her sleeve, licked it, then wiped his cheek. "You had a smudge."

She straightened his hat, brushed his hair back over his ears, then pressed down his light brown mustache. "There."

When they entered the dark barn, Frank's father was pulling a McClellan saddle off the back of a brown gelding. A lady with gray and brown hair neatly tucked under a straw hat stood beside him.

They turned around at the sound of Frank's boots.

Frank tried to straighten his coat over the bright pink satin rib wrap. "Essie, this is my mother and father, Mr. and Mrs. Robert Fortune . . . and this, Mama and Daddy, is . . . is . . . my . . . fiancee, Miss Estelle Cinnia Bowers."

For a moment no one moved.

No one spoke.

No one breathed.

Then Jamie Sue Fortune clapped her hands. "Oh, this is so wonderful!" She stepped forward and threw her arms around Essie. "Oh, Estelle, darling, I have prayed for you since the day Little Frank was born."

Tears slid down Essie's cheeks. "You have?"

"I just didn't know your name until this very second."

Mrs. Fortune hugged Frank.

He winced and grabbed his ribs.

"Oh, dear . . . Sammy was right. He is hurt, Daddy."

A shout came from the middle of the yard. "Wait! Wait!"

With a thunder of shoes and boots, a dozen people appeared at the barn door, led by Dacee June. "Wait!" she hollered. "Don't make any plans yet. I have the whole wedding figured out."

"Whose wedding?" Frank said.

"Why, yours and Essie's, of course." Dacee June threw her arm around Essie's shoulder. "Hi, honey, I'm Aunt Dacee June. I just had a wonderful idea about your reception." She pulled a reluctant Essie to the side of the barn. "We'll decorate in peach and turquoise. You do like peach and turquoise, don't you? Then, we'll make sure . . ."

Frank watched as they disappeared into an empty stall. He pushed his hat back and rubbed his unshaven chin.

"You didn't really think you could run away from the Fortunes of the Black Hills, did you, son?" Robert Fortune asked.

"Little Frank," Casey called out, "how come there's a bull out by the corrals wearin' your shirt on his horns?"

"It's a long story, Case, but I promise to tell you ever'thin' around the dinner table."

"My mama is cookin' dinner, and she made Americus rewash all the dishes," Casey told him. "Aunt Abby is measurin' your windows for new curtains. Uncle Todd is sorting out your saddles."

Frank shook his head. "I'm glad to see you, Daddy. I am really glad to see all of you. This is turnin' out to be the first normal day I've had in a long, long time."

Center Point Publishing
600 Brooks Road ● PO Box 1
Thorndike ME 04986-0001 USA

(207) 568-3717

US & Canada:
1 800 929-9108